About the Author

A collector of records, stories, sins, whisky and words. A hopeless romantic who daydreams too much and writes not enough.

Closer

Jeffery Wiederkehr

Closer

Olympia Publishers
London

www.olympiapublishers.com
OLYMPIA PAPERBACK EDITION

A CIP catalogue record for this title is
available from the British Library.

ISBN: 978-1-80439-055-9

This is a work of fiction.
Names, characters, places and incidents originate from the writer's
imagination. Any resemblance to actual persons, living or dead, is
purely coincidental.

First Published in 2023

Olympia Publishers
Tallis House
2 Tallis Street
London
EC4Y 0AB
Printed in Great Britain

Dedication

This one is for the Harvest Moon.
And, for all of you heartbreakers, for without you, there just
might not be any art at all.

Acknowledgements

Lunk & Bug, I cannot put into words what your support has meant to me. B, who was pure internal critic, self-doubt, imposter syndrome, inoculum. Jennia Herold D'Lima, whose edits, guidance, and efforts kept me from burning it all.

Book I

I Am Afraid of What I've Become

Spoon in Mouth, Stake to Heart

This is a story about an affair. It is about not knowing how to let go of the partner I loved in a marriage that went bad long ago. Not just a marriage and an affair, it is about a cliché of an affair and an ending that hit with the sudden life-changing force of a fucking car crash. One moment it was a slow-motion dream on an open desert highway, warm and comforting with aged scenes running like it was shot in 8-millimeter: the windows are down, the AC is full blast, the stereo is pumping 'Don't Go,' by the Ramones. I take my hand off the wheel to touch her hand, to meet her smile and the next time we meet is on the other side of the windshield, bloodied and surrounded by bodies. It is a retelling, at best a conveniently cock-eyed version of an affair from the perspective of a hopeless romantic, who due to the blunt-force trauma of this ending has forgotten himself. So, for those not predisposed to the romantic perspective, it might be easy to think that I am writing solely to glorify or justify not just an affair, but the total destruction of two families, but I assure you, it isn't so. Consider this: it doesn't really do a good job of any of those things.

Let me tell you what this story is. It is pure acid and bile, a putrid rotting abscess of the gut, so full of death and rot and stench it is literally rotting me away from the insides. And this is what it wants to do – to rot, to change me. No, that isn't true, it wants more. It wants to end me, to see me opt out of this game, but it will settle for change. It will settle for grinding me away into the finest ash, for squeezing out the last bit of wonder and the last breath of romance from my broken, hollowed chest. If it can't take my life, it will settle for leaving me a lifeless shell. It wants me to give in. It wants to bask in the beautiful irony of breaking me down with my own acrid poison. It wants to peel away everything and leave a rabid, wild, and hungry animal. And I have been that animal too often these days. I am that animal now; drooling, panting, snarling at the keyboard, more wolf than man. Transformed by the words and the looming harvest moon, drunk on my own venom, crying out into the night, howling against all of humanity who says "This is it. The world is just this way." Fuck all of you who have ever uttered these words. You machines. You automatons. You fucking cogs. You reasonable ones and zeroes. Oh, you passionless pricks, you practical disciples of black and white, you lifeless ghosts, you empty shells of human fucking kind. You life-opportunists. Fuck off, all of you. This is for romance. This is for love. This is for that which lies beyond.

I am that animal fresh from standing in the middle of the street under a thundering sky, waiting for my silver bullet, a bus, a bolt of lightning, anything to shake me back to man-form, anything to shake me free from this earth. Standing there, I found what I had all along: nothing. Nothing but the will to write because through my words I will be able to live it all again. It *was* beautiful, after all. Even after all of the ugly that it made, it

14

was still beautiful. So, I will write and bathe in the beauty and the loss and I will feel it all again, I will let it build me up like a cresting wave to crush me once more into the concrete sand of reality. And after my fingers at the keys have ground my soul into mist, I hope to be reconstituted in the ether and reborn into someone who might bear this better, into someone who might be able to carry out the greatest revenge: to play this fucking game of life out to the very end. But first, there is this.

I must press this spoon of words hard against the back of my throat and wrench the gut until I vomit. I will vomit it here and pick through the soup of my rot. I will feel for the gifts my ulcers have formed over these last two years and I will keep only the beautiful pearls that my torment has lovingly shaped. And last, to ensure that all the devils have been released, I will press a wooden stake of words into my heart because this affair calls for bloodletting. I will fill a chalice, no three, and I will treat them with herbs; first Columbine for deceit, and Rue to abort the fetus of lies and half-truths; then rosemary for remembrance, basil for love, and thyme for courage; and last, marigold so that at least our souls can meet in our dreams and like Bathory, I will bathe in the blood and lick the chalice clean. I will do this, so that I might live. But first, I have to shape the spoon and stake of words. I have to write. This will be a violent purge of tangled emotions, an unleashing of everything that I held onto for far too long. This isn't done to explain away the horror of all of this, not to justify the love and the lust, not to make peace with the lack that drove me to become beast, but so that I might find myself somewhere in the end. These are my feelings, my words, my texts, my emails, her words through me, through us; and this is me trying to use those words to heal from all of the hurt: mine, theirs, ours. So, here I am in this one window post-modern concrete cell of an apartment behind a coffee shop. I am an animal in a concrete cage. Pacing. I don't sleep. I write. This is it, these words, this story, this is everything I've held in for two years, all of the ugly and the beautiful, all of it for a chance to be with her, for the chance to touch the divine. Spoon in mouth, stake to heart; let these words act as antidote for melancholy and as life-saving serum for the brokenhearted.

Of Drought and Desire

We Southern Californians exist in a state of perpetual drought. Like the trees, we breathe fire and ash, hunched and stunted from want. Crack their leaves and where one should hope to find mint and juniper, they gasp a faint but lingering acrid smoke. They should be full of pine and resin, dripping sap and life, wet and sticking to your fingers like the sex of those more northbound trees, but the fires here have been invited by a lack of rain. They have come and gone and will come again. They have dragged their cocks across this landscape leaving the earth bleeding, broken, and torn. It is always and forever this lack-drought-fire-death cycle. Shattered anew every season. Nothing here will ever be the same again. Always and forever shattered.

The trees remind me of how we learn to love in this desert. That love exists in this sea of lack is a testament to the hard-wired programming of the stubborn universal drive to be. Why trees grow here at all, crooked, hot, and broken, is a small protest, a "fuck you" to the gods. "We know who we are supposed to be," they cry, lurching out of the ground. "Our DNA screams at our deformities, cursing what we've allowed ourselves to become. We know how short we've fallen, how the gods have shaken their heads at our prayers for rain. We know how you've held back the rain to break us. To bend our backs away from the sun. Oh, how we have contorted our limbs, twisting them before us in this futile attempt to provide shade, our shadows burning around us like Pompei and Hiroshima."

Someone might say, "It's like they are reaching out to each other."

"Or trying to hide," another could respond while kicking at the cracked bark and roots that tumble out of the earth.

No shade, no fruit, home to nothing but the bites and stings of the ants and hornets who lend them purpose.

These crooked trees, with their crooked limbs, and their crooked-necked birds are the living totems for the love deprived. They are the markers we hold onto, the gods we try not to lose sight of in this dust-ridden forest of the broken crucifix, pregnant symbol for the masses wandering aimlessly through the desert. They crawl and drag their knees over the dunes, believing at least for a while that they've been offered the Kingdom of Heaven. Everything in exchange for submission to the salvation-promising lack.

What fools we are?

They say that with enough time the climate and the topography of a region will shape its inhabitants. Over time, the essence of a space leaches into and through our cell walls, penetrating and transforming. We are becoming Southern California. We inhabit this desert like the living dead, a true to life reflection of our surroundings, a wandering lost soul tribe, defined by false oases spaced by countless stretches of void, eyes full of mirage, hearts empty of all but the will to survive. Like the sand from the dunes, we drift on the wind, searching to fill that void, but the desert only gives us trees with thorns, stings and bites carried on wings, lizards and snakes with venom, mirage with nothing but more of the same, all capped with the burn of the sun. Our only respite from the desert is the moon, the mirage of the night, huge and full on the horizon, cooling the sting of the day's burn, dropping to earth every twenty-eight days to hold us in the black of night under the Milky Way. But it is never enough, so we cry for more and make offerings to the moon. We burn eucalyptus and the crack of exploding oils announces our presence, and we make oaths, promises, and prayers and we burn cedar to tempt her with its spice, and we offer pallets filled with nails so that we might build her a bridge, and oak fat and sick with beetles to carry her down from the sky, and we wait and hope that this time the ring shining around the moon foreshadows the answer to our prayers for rain.

We are Southern California.

Defined by the lack of… something. Defined by the loss of the whole that we knew at birth, the innate connection we were gifted at the moment of conception, before… before in the fields of stars where we played amongst the constellations, where Orion was home and we rode on the lion's head, where Alnilam, Mintaka, and Alnitak, and Betelgeuse and Bellatrix were our brothers and sisters.

From birth, from the moment we fell to earth, we have been searching to become whole again.

We are the wandering.
The lost souls of the desert.
A pitiful lost soul tribe.
Full of mirage.

Full of lack.

Marriage is this way.

Love is this way.

Need.

Desire.

Want.

Affairs.

Affairs are this way.

We have become too lonely, too burned and cracked, and too thirsty to be reasonable any longer.

I wander this desert waiting for the night to fall …

waiting for the harvest moon.

Waiting for it to drop its dew, to take the burn from my skin.

I am waiting…

for the harvest moon.

Fodder for the Thirst

Before Kat, I was dead, or dying; so far gone that I didn't recognize myself any longer. At best, I was an automaton mindlessly droning on through the fuck of the day – for my children, for my wife. Because duty and responsibility were how I was taught to love, I was willing to take my ration, the precise measured caloric need of a man of my weight and height and life experience measured precisely by my wife, just enough to tolerate another day, to allow me to pull the sheets over my head to try to find oblivion somewhere behind my insomnia, to live where life is livable – in dream. In the waking world, I felt as though I were living through an isolation experiment, testing just how long could I go without. I was atrophied, hope and heart dried and shriveled up from lack, desiccated and diseased, now covered in sand dunes, burning and dried by the white-hot sun. A soul left to wander, supported only by the cold reality of feeling comfort and connection in the performance of my duty from somewhere beneath life's hard grinding heel. I lived this way for years, a soulless shell of a man, pulverized and disintegrated, every ounce of life-sustaining moisture squeezed and drunk by those around him, becoming dried brush waiting to burn, becoming sand and ash, the desert, without hope or faith that the rains would come to restore what I once was, the vast fields of my heart left fallow. I was lost, starved, all bone, with deep set haunting heroin eyes; I had become unrecognizable even to myself.

***

Long ago, this moon came during the harvest, for reaping the fruit from the seeds we pushed into the earth with our hard-cracked fingers. The harvest moon still comes, but we have changed. Drowning in hubris, we try to shape the desert to suit our needs, but we no longer harvest the land for sustenance. We are here for show, for truth wrapped in lies, here to perform this planting ritual on our porches and ledges though we no longer know why. We try to fool the earth. We search for satisfaction by attempting to connect with something larger than ourselves; although, our methods belie the lesson. So, on our ledges we pot what should grow free, on our porches we build boxes to house the unruly and we think we have won, that we have fooled the desert with our store-bought mulch, that we have slowed the lack that bleeds into the seeds we planted, all the while knowing that plants contained in pots will never grow to their full height. And this is how I left the house on a Friday night, kissing the wife goodbye, feeling like a potted plant.

"Back home late, don't wait up."

Feeling stunted.

"Good night kids."

Caged.

"See ya in the morning."

Kept.

Compromiser, roommate, provider, father, symbol, ornament.

Sometimes husband, and yet somehow always married, always drained, withered, trying to be less than, wishing to be more than, feeling the lack eating from the inside, trying to settle into compromising myself away.

For the children.

That's why we do these things, right?

For the children.

Maybe I was a coward.

Maybe I just couldn't imagine how else to be in this world.

Godspeed! You Adulterer

September in Southern California is hot by most standards. It is marked by the Santa Ana winds that torch the highways during the day and the asphalt that pumps heat back into the ozone at night. Even at one a.m., it was too hot for the leather and denim jackets that filled the Casbah. Too hot for the leather belts and skinny jeans that swayed to the shoe-gaze drone of Godspeed! Fluids were replenished via tall cans and tiny red straws doubled up in well-Jack-and-Cokes, draped by loose fingers, held by loose tongues, and sucked by loose cherry-red lips.

I hung from a bar stool taking it all in, the lights, the music, Kat. She was lovely. Picture a bookish administrator who holds her own while teaching old white men how to reimagine education. She had an awkward frame: wiry, with rounded shoulders bent from sitting at a computer all day, and yet she carried herself with a confidence that I found alluring. It melted me. I found her peculiar, intriguing, and new every time I saw her. She said that she was an acquired taste, but all of the best things are, aren't they? Foreign movies, sushi, coffee, funky cheese, whisky, Kat.

She was of medium height, slender, small breasted, wearing Chuck Taylors, tight black high-waisted jeans with silver buttons, a gray plunging something barely covering her tiny breasts paired with a black cardigan, capped with a pair of glasses too big for her face. I loved how she was at ease with herself, how coolly, perhaps even unconsciously, she gained attention with her style of dress and the way she walked across a room. Her hips shook to the music, her black lace bra was peeking out. She didn't cover it up, and I didn't want her to. She danced in front of me, and I saw an awkward Debbie Harry with the soul of Patti Smith. An awkward punk-rock poet, complete with asthma, glasses, and an overbite. Anchored by the edge of the stool, I pulled her closer to feel her ass shake into my crotch. Kat faced the music with her back tucked into my chest. My left arm wound around her waist. Her hand covered mine, moving over the neck of our shared beer bottle. My free hand fell to her right hip to feel it move to the music. To gain purchase, I slid my thumb into her jeans and found the lace she wore for us. We were both mesmerized by the moment, the music moved her; it always did. It pulled her to that secret place where her mind would run free at night. I loved how easily she let go and surrendered to the feeling and how my thumb tucked in her jeans seemed to heighten everything. She pressed harder into my cock, shaking her ass to the beat.

There is something about a lover knowing there is lace hidden beneath an ordinary pair of jeans. It creates a mood. It evokes the aura of another time and place. That night, although I'd never been to France, it made me think of Paris and how one day Kat and I would be standing on a balcony overlooking the city at night. How I would press into her as she sighed. How my hand would move over her skirt, then under to find the lace. It made me think of how we would make that city disappear as we fucked, as I fucked her under that skirt, lace pulled to the side, breasts pointing to oblivion.

I thought of the wearer's intention and forethought that sets the mood. Even if the lace is never revealed, it awakens a certain essence in the wearer – one must dress for the fantasy they want, mustn't they? But when revealed, by chance, by a stolen glance, or by a probing thumb, it generates a series of questions and assumptions. Is it for the wearer, the observer, or both? How many times was *he* the observer, and how many times did Kat go ignored, or worse, how many times did he notice and try in his limited way? How many times did he peel her out of that lace without ceremony, without the pause that it suggested she would prefer, deserve, without the awe that it should inspire? In a flash, I wondered how I could actually be jealous of him. I wondered how I could criticize his shortcomings when they drove her to me.

Kat *was* sexy in her own way, but she'd argue that she didn't feel like a particularly sexy woman. The lace, however, helped bridge that gap in her mind between the daydreamer and the administrator. There is no doubt; initially Kat wore the lace hoping to be noticed by her husband, but he didn't see her that way, lace or not. As a consequence of being unseen, spending days and nights in her head, she had to learn to take care of herself and the lace made her feel things. She had been slowly cultivating this feeling for years, and it provided a bounty of fantasies that surrounded a guest speaker at a conference, a barista disappearing into the back room of the coffee shop, French movies, a good book, an artist in his gallery. She wanted to fuck. To be fucked. To have her hair pulled. To be spanked. To suck a cock. The lace was magical and with it, before the lace was for us, on the nights before we were loosed upon the world, as *he* put their children to bed, she'd find herself before her bathroom's full-length mirror. She'd see the lace, and find the memory of her latest missed connection, and then she'd be there, at the conference behind the curtain just beyond the podium, in the backroom of the coffee shop, in the art gallery ready-room, and she'd imagine the cock she'd be sucking, the lips he'd be kissing, and her hand would follow the line of her hips, to her breast, and then she'd pause at her naked tits to pull at her nipples before her hands sank to find the soft in the middle of the lace. Her hands would move over the lace, and she'd stroked it over and over until she had to pull it to the side to see just how wet she made herself. Yes, first, she wore it for him, then for herself... but now, she wore it for me.

Tonight, she knew I'd find the lace. I always found it.

When the music was over, we sat perfectly still, me on that stool and she tucked into me, her ass to my crotch as the stage hands moved through the faded red lights to break down the drums. We didn't stir until the house lights went on. We held on to that moment as the doors opened to the streets, satisfied to watch the exodus of the too tight jeans and red lips spilling into the streets with a hum of low chatter, framed by the light of a hundred mobile phones and the spark of a hundred cigarettes. Pulled by the flicker of those distant fleeting lights, we moved to the door as one. She took my arm and we slowly searched for her car, not wanting the night to end, not knowing how it would end.

Black asphalt, a white painted brick wall reaching up to smoldering apartments, a lamppost blinking a spotlight, the walk sign counting down "3... 2... 1..." A blinking neon sign from a lonely gas station that, like me, was sitting on top of a thousand gallons of explosive fuel. We found the car under the light of the harvest moon. She told me that she could feel us in the moon, that it was a moon of decisions and change. It was the moon for those with courage. For those who did not stand still. For those who had planted seeds and nourished them. She told me that she found herself under that moon eighteen years ago when she decided against the advice of friends and family to leave Minnesota for NYC. It was that night that she planted the seed to become the woman who stood before me in Converse, jeans, and black lace. She was the fruit of the harvest that night. I showed her my tattoo, a winged scarab carrying not the sun, but the moon. She called me her harvest moon and I leaned against the passenger door and pulled Kat into my chest, kissing her wildly. We still had work to do under that moon. I opened the door and said, "Sit on my lap." I turned Kat to face me as I queued the music on my phone. 'Leave It at That' by the Pist Idiots sang out just below the sound of her low moans. Singing about leaving home for happiness, all of the questions and answers, doing what's best… for all of us.

I pulled on the U-shaped neckline of her top to gain access to her neck and collarbone, and we lost time in the harvest.

"Fuck, I love you," Kat said with a sigh, shaking over me. The neck of her top stretched low inside her open cardigan, bra pulled down just below the pink. Jeans, black, high-waisted and still buttoned; the lace would have to wait.

My face was buried in one tiny breast, my mouth tight around her left nipple, tongue circling Vesuvius, my hand pulling the right mound of Herculaneum. Kat's head was buried in my shoulder, her forehead pressing down to balance her convulsing body, her hands everywhere, nowhere. They weren't hers any longer, her face twisted up beneath her hair, and she formed words for ritual fires.

"F f f f f f uck. Fuck. I fucking love you." The words tumbled out beneath a mass of hair.

"Did you cum already," I asked, laughing.

"Yeah," she said, returning the laugh with small sighs that escaped with each full-body contraction.

"Well, that was a new one for me. I've never orgasmed with my pants still on," she breathed, pulling her bra back to its usual position.

"Do you think they saw?" Kat asked, looking out at the couple twisted together, standing in contrast to the peeling white paint of the brick wall ten feet away.

"I don't think so, but I don't care if they did. Maybe we've given them something to talk about tonight."

Moving in closer so as not to break the mood, I whispered, "I love you too" into her ear.

"I said it first," she said with a laugh. "Fuck, I didn't want to say it out loud. God, I hate you. How'd you do that?"

"Do what? Wait, wait, which is it? Love or hate?"

"I love you, and I hate that I do." She laughed again.

"Yeah, same."

"How did you do that anyway? That was incredible."

The Smith Street Band played us out to 'Young Drunk' as we both fought tears at the idea of parting. That night, we became the luckiest of the wandering desert scavengers, feeding off the sweetest part of the kill, the parts our others inexplicably left behind.

As the song faded, we talked about love, what we did for each other, what we would do for each other, and all the "onlys" we had together.

The following morning, I found this email from Kat:

Here are Les Seulements. The "Onlys."

You see me and the feelings, the thoughts I try to hide.

Because you see me, I feel stronger.

You match my silliness and seem to find it contagious. I have rarely found someone who can laugh as freely.

Your love of music and the way you are taken over by the scene and sounds.

Unabashed, you reach for connection in a way that I have only wished for and imagined.

You don't laugh at my desires, and you greet each one with an air of seriousness.

And your ability to anticipate… listen… infer… remember…

How do you do it?

You're not scared of me when I talk of books, poetry, or my latest ponderings

You don't make me feel ridiculous or absurd.

Those are some of my seulements…

I have other Onlys with you, for you, but my tears are preventing me from writing more

It has been one of those days

How do we move forward from here?

I am so in love with you.

~ k

p.s. Please tell me again why you love me.

When she asked me again why I loved her, I responded:
I call you ocean, mountain, paradox.
Ocean because you are too deep to know.
Powerful because you possess the most beautiful and deepest depths, yet are violent if the winds push you too hard.
~ If you are at sea, never take your eyes off her ~
I call you mountain because you are too big to be seen in a single view. Grounded, but born with a passion that can shake the trees that try to cling to you. You forge rivers, give shape to lakes, and wring the tears from the clouds as you hurl them to new heights.
You are paradox.
The sun and the moon.
You are mine.
I am yours.

The next day, we met for a beer. Kat recounted our evening as if I wasn't the one sitting beneath her. She told me how it felt silly and exciting. Leaning against a car making out. She sipped her beer and smiled. "Then you suggested we get in the car. I was confused. Were we leaving? Then you got into the passenger side and said, 'Sit on my lap.' I was laughing. Ridiculous, I thought. This was high school shit. But I learned that night, again, how no matter how hard my proper mind ... would you say 'proper,'" she asked and continued without waiting for my response. "I cannot say no to your suggestions. And I never regret it. I straddled you. I let myself go. I never do that. Or should I say, I've never gotten to do that. And so, as you said, I let myself go just one more time before we ended things for the night. I don't even remember your hands on me at all. Just your face and your mouth on my tits. And I came. Came to the connection and release. God, it was incredible."

The Twilight Spaces

The sun was falling outside the window, over the interstate, over the airport, out to sea. Kat and I sat in a high-backed fake leather booth surrounded by the quiet comfort of the fading light in a dive bar, and we stared into the face of love. She was smiling and a little awkward, and I was madly in love. As the light in the room shifted with the setting sun, the eternal Christmas lights that lit a wall of whisky became apparent. Were they always on, but, like us, needing a shift in the lighting to be seen?

My hand slid beneath the table to touch her knee and to tug at the hem of her sun dress. My free hand took hers and I said the words again. She laughed and said, "It doesn't count, I said it first."

"But I felt it first."

"Yeah right, when?"

"Islay."

"Hmmm, I was too busy feeding a new baby to notice anything."

"When did you know?"

"Edinburgh. Remember when I was texting you?"

"Yeah."

"I knew then that you were the only person that could ever understand me."

The twilight was pouring in, and the Aero Club was full into its transformation, becoming its true Tuesday at five p.m. self, a dark dive-bar time machine hidden from the world where people with secrets and broken dreams came to small talk a bartender who didn't know enough about them to hurt them, or to hide in a high-backed booth to touch a new love beneath the table. To touch knees, pull at hems, test the fading material of bulging jeans by tugging on the inseams. We sat in the empty bar save for one tiki-style couple who played pool in the back. It was as if they were planted there to complete the dream-like dive bar fantasy. He had greased-back black hair and classic Americana style tattoos – a dagger and a gypsy peeked out from under the sleeves of his Hawaiian shirt. She wore her hair pin-up style with a dyed blue twist, and she twirled in a dress patterned with toucans. They put a few dollars in the jukebox and Iggy's 'The Passenger' jangled out of the speakers, completing the transformation.

The song took Kat from me for a moment. She loved Iggy and normally the song threw her into motion, but this time it held her still and stole her voice. The effect of the dusk surprised us both by pressing hard into our post-work date, making her eyes fall to her glass of Talisker, and the hand on my thigh dropped to the imitation leather cushion. We were there to sit with the words that we let escape only a few days before and we were both haunted by the lyrics Iggy rattled off about driving through a city high on life with his lover. On this night, the song that usually empowered us to dance tortured us to silence. We wanted to run, but it was too soon, we knew that tonight we'd have to go home to our others.

"Singin' la la la la la-la-la la."

  * Funny, just like the song, she'd often text me her la-la-la's in the form of "I la la la love you!" Only now did I put it together that the passenger was her inspiration.

That night I sent this poem to Kat:

  We belong to the Twilight Spaces

  We belong to the twilight spaces
  where the light swings in low under the eaves
  and spills into the room more like water than light
  It casts its shadows in the in-between-spaces of time and
  light
  where our magic is strongest
  I tuck the loose hair back behind your ear
  to see the eyes that the shadows have hidden
  and I can sense a distance growing.
  The water-light of twilight has swept you away for a
  moment—I can feel it tugging at you like the tide and I worry for
  just a moment, because I know that tides will take what they can.
  But we are here now, together in the twilight
  and I am not afraid.

Kat responded:

  I woke slowly this morning with thoughts of you laughing with me in bed. Your eyes crinkled with joy. I kissed the tattoos on your right arm. One hand over the written prose on your left.

  I held my eyes shut to try and make the scene last longer, but it faded with the morning sounds that surrounded me. How do we hold on to the twilight spaces?

How do we hold back the dawn?

My desire, yearning, need, whatever this is, for you is beyond my control. The moments we share are pure joy. I want to know the potential for love and sex and life with you. I miss you more than ever. I need to hold your face in my hands and kiss you.

Faith, Loopholes, and Driveway Soliloquies

Kat and I had lost ourselves entirely. We met almost every weekend. It didn't take us long to find our groove, to learn how to be whatever we had become, to learn how to slip away from our families in the night. We adapted well. Tonight, she planned to meet a friend at Hamilton's Tavern. A true date with a friend from work, set up to cloak our meeting. Kat had found that it was much easier to wrap our lie in a truth. Mike thought her meeting would run all night. "Nikki is having man problems. You know how that goes; we could be at it all night. I wouldn't wait up," she might say, letting him imagine whatever it is that ladies talk about. Elle knew I would be out all night. My Fridays had been pretty consistent. Friends, drinks, shenanigans, home when clock strikes single digit something. Elle used to go with me on these nights, but she faded away because that was who we were now, shadows, an outline, no soul. I used to ask her to join me, but I stopped long before Kat and I became what we were; and, now that we were what we were, I didn't even hint at Elle joining me any longer.

Kat's friend Nikki thought she only had an hour. "I have just enough time for a quick drink. Gotta get home to help put the kids to bed," she would tell her. That was when I arrived at

Hamilton's, just as Kat pretended to head to her car, just as she was about to circle back to have a beer with me. I waited for her by the door. We kissed dangerously on the sidewalk, in front of whoever, and moved inside to sit in a booth to find each other's knees, feet, and eyes. We talked about our perfect alibis and all the time we'd have on this night to fog the windows in her car again, but as time passed, the space in the booth became melancholic. The booth was stained with our ponderings on the ludicrous reality we occupied, the one where we were the couple, but we had to tell lies to be together. Beers finished and long sighs expired, Kat said, "Let's go to my car. My sister gave me some flower."

In a moment, we were at the door. We walked, and bumped, and laughed through the market-like feel of Beech and 30th into the dark and quiet just half a block away. Somewhere just past the last street light we had emerged on the other side of the veil, the place left behind by the twilight, the place where we belonged.

"Are we really being unfaithful if this is what we need to live?" she asked, passing the joint.

"Our others will think so," I replied, pulling her into my chest.

"I mean, to be unfaithful... that word. What *is* faithful? Them. Mike and Elle. Faithful – that word is a mindfuck. Like, we are supposed to have this supreme confidence in something, despite not ever bearing witness to the something? What the fuck is that anyway?" I was starting to feel my mind lifting with the fog we inhaled. I had said enough. We had other things to keep us occupied. We were still high from touching each other beneath the booth at Hamilton's, still high from our walk to her car, and buzzing from the shaking we did beneath her skirt in that car's front seat just moments ago. We didn't speak the name of that 'un' word again that night. We were all hands and mouths and sighs. I leaned back against the hood of her car, and she fell into me to warm her hands under my shirt. We laughed as we wondered at the lives going on in the houses on Dale and Beech Street.

In between the fog and the hands, the mouths, sighs, and the wondering, I was lost in thought, but didn't say enough, or had I already said too much? I often felt I did. Thinking, *"Don't speak. Be where you are. Be where. Be where? Beware!"* Laughing.

"What's so funny," she said with a laugh while punching me softly in the gut.

"Nothing, Bunny" – mouth to neck – *"Nothing."*

"Come on... What are you thinking?"

A wry smile emerged while beneath her hair; I was thankful for my burrow. I wouldn't have to explain the imagery pounding my skull. I blamed the fog. I was chasing California and adultery. I was here in California, in this desert, in this false oasis, lost *in my wasteland marriage,* neck deep (Neck! *Laughing*), neck deep in Kat. Wondering, just how long were we supposed to be faithful, just how long were we to exist without bearing witness? Drowning in this thought, just how long was I supposed to be faithful? Fuck. I never should have been unfaithful, this wasn't me. It wasn't who I wanted to be. I should have left Elle long ago. That was what we were supposed to do, right? Acknowledge, declare, and move on; then find true love. That is what adults do. Wait, is it what adults do? Do they really? Not that I knew of. No one knew how to do this. Where were we supposed to learn this? I wasn't ready for what Kat and I had become. I wasn't ready for Kat, for what I felt with her on the hood of her car. I wasn't ready for our love, nor our looming endings. I wasn't ready for heartbreak; even if our hearts didn't belong to our others any longer, I wasn't ready for any of this. I stayed in my burrow beneath Kat's ear thinking somehow, oddly, ironically, conveniently, honestly, I didn't feel like I was being unfaithful to Elle. I gave her the space she wanted. I was gone. I felt like we found the true-love loophole.

Another playful punch to the gut. "Oh, yeah, right. What am I thinking? Just thinking I love you. You know how much I love you, don't you?"

"I do." She kissed me. "And I love you so much I can't even explain it."

As we kissed, I imagined our throats dry and burning with need and desire, our eyes bleeding sand, our ears full of the banshee cries of hot swirling wind. We existed without faith because we knew what it meant when there wasn't even the slightest cloud upon the horizon suggesting that the rains we needed might find their way to us just this once. "*Faithful?*" The tension in the gray folds of my mind were tightening up, winding, then losing the spinning top of this theme. I wanted to let it go, but it wouldn't let go of me. I was bound centrifugally against the wall of my skull. I was spinning, swimming in the fog, and in a split second, in my head, I soliloquized a fog-inspired rant, an entire act under the stars framed by the light of someone's driveway motion detector.

"Alas, poor Yorick!" We were the ass and faith was the carrot

40

eternally beyond the nose. It was just a grand and cruel manipulation: *holds the skull thusly*. And each day that passed, we were left kicking against the pricks that drove us in pursuit of that which we would never reach. It took on fecund religious meaning, sir, which trickled down into the family structure that your Church of the Status Quo shaped for us. *Faith sir?* The rub dear Yorick, as I understand you, is that *faithfully,* blindly, we are to hold on chasing that foul carrot until we fall down dead in our shackles... and if we bore those shackles and this cruel game patiently, quietly; if we bore this well (*holding imaginary shackles*), in our death, we may be satisfied. Maybe. Faithful? I... We reject this flawed design. We outright reject this life-charade. We seek to live free of the anxiety that seeks to trap us into believing blindly what we would never choose on our own. Kat and I would never choose this. We are true Libertines, dear Yorick. We want more than your tiny world has to offer.

The Soda Bar Gave Me the Quakes

Before the melancholy booth, before we sat on the hood of her car amongst the fog beneath the stars on Dale and Beech Street, before the cracked and sweating Aero Club vinyl clung to our skin, before the blinking Christmas lights reflected a wall of whisky, before the falling sun sank below the sea and transformed the Aero Club into a dive bar sanctuary, before the cherry-red lips found the twin straws, before the black eyes swayed at the Casbah, before I found the lace, before we found the front seat of her car, before we knew that we were both of the desert, of the drought, of the harvest moon, of the Lost Soul Tribe, there was an awakening at the Soda Bar. But, before that night at the Soda Bar, Mike, Kat, Elle, and I had dinner. Dinner like we'd had together for years, but this dinner, followed by this night, would change everything.

The four of us on these nights would slide into each other happy and relieved, the way one might imagine a lover coming home from a long day. Eyes were wide and smiles came easy. There was bustle; not too much, just enough to feel the excitement from the change of air in the room. There'd be food on the stove, a cheese plate, someone would bring more beer and more cheese; there would be whisky and chocolate. We existed in a heightened state of platonic intimacy that few couples achieve with another couple. We were intertwined and in balance, allowing us a certain amount of trust. Elle and I were evenly matched by Mike and Kat. We were all college educated; three of us worked in education at one time or another, the other as an editor. We were politically and socially aligned, we each had two kids. In fact, we had just returned from a group trip to Ireland a month before Kat and I ever kissed. For the record, we had plenty of opportunities before Ireland, and many in Ireland, but never once did we touch romantically.

Mike and Elle vibed every bit as well as Kat and I did. Their connection may have been more of a reciprocal support for a friend who had to suffer through a similar sort of 'partner management,' the sorrows associated with having an unruly other. Considering our objectionable ways, Kat and I gave them plenty to bond over: our tendency to stray too far from respectable dinner table conversation; our shared love of unabashed nudity while at home; pushing our ideas of love, romance, and sex too far; our shared desire to blow off steam in a controlled sort of 'Fuck it All;' our love of provocative art and a belief that we should not censor nor shield these things from our children. It was a lot for Mike and Elle, I think maybe because it all hinted at what lay beneath... the words they couldn't keep in any longer, that we were indeed too much and maybe too similar. That was often the phrase they threw about. "You are too much. You are both too much." Whatever the case, we four had a great, at least interesting balance that created space for us to weave about as we might not have with another couple.

Kat and I had a powerful yet playful electricity in our banter that sometimes sounded like we were arguing to the others, when really, we were just having fun. I think the others thought we didn't like each other. In reality, Kat and I were great friends with a lot in common. We played it down in front of Mike because he was jealous to his core. Elle, on the other hand, didn't seem to care that Kat and I were friends. I don't think that any of us ever doubted the intentions of any one else in the group. We all knew that we had a lot to lose: kids, friends, ties to our work, each other. Not to mention, I was a little afraid of Kat. She had very loyal, always watching female friends. She was a forward-thinking woman, a proud feminist (I'd say I was as well, although she'd argue with me about men being feminists). Whatever the case, add this all together and it clearly read *"We are just friends."*

It all seemed pretty unshakable. We had known their kids since they were born, they'd known mine and Elle's over half their lives, and Kat took no shit. There was no way I was going to fuck with that. We were too tangled up to think any one at the dinner table was a threat to the balance of our friendships and our lives, but what we never spoke of at the dinner table, what Kat told me that night, what I shared with Kat, was that we were both drifting, and we were both too thirsty to be reasonable any longer.

That night I cast my usual line announcing my post-dinner plans. On occasion Mike or Kat would join me, Kat more often than Mike. He didn't like to leave the house if he could help it, whereas she often had an itch to get out. It was a small town, and even on her ladies' nights, we'd often see each other out at the same places. Nothing weird going on, we just had common interests and I loved having a partner in crime. So, with all of us balanced evenly on the surface, and with zero intention of fucking things up, I planted my announcement sowing the seed

44

for changing the course of our lives forever.

I said, "Later tonight I'm meeting some friends to see a psychobilly band called The Quakes; who's in?" No one said anything. At ten p.m. outing in a dark, beer-soaked bar was not Elle's scene, not to mention, we didn't have a babysitter. Mike paused, didn't say anything, and looked at Kat. He was waiting for her to say "yes," but wanting her to say "no." I could sense that Kat was waiting for him to say some version of, "You can't," hoping he would say, "You should." It had been quiet for too long. I said, "No worries, just throwing it out there. I won't be lonely; I'm meeting Tyler and Dan and I think a few other friends might show up. Besides, none of you cats are into psychobilly anyway."

Kat protested, "Uh, I am, but we have to get the girls ready for bed..." I shrugged. "The bands start at ten." She paused and cast a look to Mike. He yielded. "You should go." It was settled. "Cool. I'm planning on being there at nine-thirty p.m. Text me when you leave or if you change your mind."

The Soda Bar was a dark hallway of a dive bar, its one door manned with an ink pad and a stamp, its one window painted black. It was the kind of place where my eyes needed a minute to adjust on either side of my stay, blacked out and seeing spots on my way in or blinded by the combination of my buzz and the street lamps on my way out. Hand stamped, I walked into darkness, led only by the neon beer lights behind the bar and the faint smell of stale beer lying just beneath the hint of ammonia. A few trucker caps, sleeveless flannels, and leather jackets floated near the bar; their female counterparts quietly held down the too few and precious booths. All bathed in cell-phone light, their phones cast large round shadows on the wall behind them, the moving stage lights flickering on their loose peasant tops hanging just above their tight retro pencil skirts. They were the gate keepers, the booth-guardians who awaited their tribute: the hats and the flannels and the leathers lined up to bring back the kill: PBR's, Miller High Life's, Hamm's. Seven-year-old me was a little jealous and thought silly thoughts—I don't want those booths anyway, I pouted as I searched for a table.

K: parking

Me: cool.

Me: stage right. Belly-up by the stage.

She showed up in old Converse, a pair of torn blue-jeans, and a floral print top under a black cardigan.

"Let me grab a beer," she said, handing me her cardigan. I threw it on the table as Tyler and Dan found their way over. The opening band was a three piece from Mexico. The singer-guitarist wore ladies' lingerie and howled into the mic. At times he'd scream in unison with the Siouxsie Sioux look-alike on standup bass while the drummer whaled like Keith Moon. I had no idea who they were, but they were wild. They rolled through their set and Tyler and Dan rotated in and out to buy the next two rounds of lager.

"Did any one catch their name?" I asked. No one had, but Tyler and Dan drifted off to check out the merch stand to look for clues.

Kat reached for her beer on the belly-up and I said, "It looked like you had a good time in Edinburgh." She left for Edinburgh shortly after we returned from Ireland, and had just come back this week. She was there for a work conference. Instagram tells all.

"Yeah, it was pretty incredible." She told me a bit about the conference and then about the whisky she found.

"That photo of the whisky you sent me looked pretty incredible."

"It was great. Have you had the Talisker 25?"

"No, it is waaaayy too expensive at the Aero Club."

We rambled on like this, in an awkward sort of small talk, until Dan and The Quakes interrupted. Dan's hands, dripping with foam, stretched with three glasses of lager. He mouthed something that was buried under the singer's countdown: "2, 3, 4." He smiled and shrugged and put his hands out to offload the beers. I set them down on the belly-up as Kat moved just in front of the table where it lined the floor's edge. She was in a trance, fixed on the stage, and I settled in lazily just behind and to her left, leaning against the table to protect the almighty beers.

The Quakes tore through their set like a dream with blinding energy. The crowd was moving and pulsing like a dust-devil twisting and building with the heat from their songs. The crowd bumped and turned and pushed just in front of us, all hands, trucker hats, and blurry faces. Kat moved to the music. Occasionally she was sent back into the table by the crowd splashing our beers about. I adjusted my arm to the front edge of the table, hoping to soften Kat's next blow. The crowd lunged again, and Kat slid back, hitting my arm instead of the table. If she noticed it was me, she bumped into, I couldn't tell. She went right back to pulsing with the beat and the crowd, paying no mind to me, nor the table. Things happened on the edge of the pit. We knew the drill. We all chose to make ourselves vulnerable, to

47

forget ourselves and the space we'd normally give other people: elbows found ribs, feet got tangled, bodies collided, and crotches ground into a stranger's ass; she knew that and stood there just on the edge, seemingly daring the crowd to touch her. The dust-devil came again, *lunge*, and she was pushed back into my arm, only this time she didn't return to the edge of the pit. She stayed there, dancing against my arm that was locked between her waist and the table. I didn't know what to do, but I could feel all of the tumblers in my brain engaging. Turning, opening, unlocking, creating pathways, creating meaning, literally reforming memories and coloring them with *this*, with this sort of possibility. Every time we touched over the years, every time she sent me a message separate from the group text, every time we both swayed to the records I played at her house while Mike and Elle talked about the kids and work, every time we bonded over a book or a record, every time we knew we were being judged harshly over some provocative theory, every time we stared into each other's eyes before we drank, when we took the ferry to Islay, just the two of us, and we laughed and drank whisky sipped from each other's glasses and ate cheese and Victoria sponge cake, and we walked together over the small hills between distilleries, and we met strangers, and ran, and laughed, and thought we were best secret friends. And I thought of how I loved when she wore dresses too short for her age, her job, her husband, and blouses buttoned too low to drop her kids off at the YMCA, too low for business meetings, too low for my wife, and bikinis too small for her kids' playdates at the beach, how she danced as she flipped a record, cooked, stared into my eyes. And I loved how, when Elle and I would visit for dinner, she'd tease by

48

leaning in low, unbuttoned and braless, and how she paid no mind to how her tits might show as she talked of politics, how I'd see Mike attempt to slyly gesture to her to button up as she went on some rant about moving out of the country. How in the presence of our others she'd suggest driving to the desert "with whoever would go" to see Idles at Pappy and Harriet's. The tumblers lined up; it was for me every time.

And now, with Kat dancing into me, the small of her back pressed tight against my arm and my arm growing tired, but not wanting to move, and me justifying moving my thumb into her belt loop to try to hold on, then just inside the top, then just over, then just inside, and then feeling how, in that moment, we were becoming something else altogether.

As the band's set wound down, I found Kat full in my arm, my first finger hooked in her belt loop and my thumb wandering on the waistline of her jeans. She pushed back tight into my arm, removing any doubt that I was still protecting the drinks. She was leaning into me, and my arm was touching her in ways it shouldn't, in ways she wanted, I wanted. If Elle or Mike walked in right now, I could laugh it off and tell them I put my arm there to protect the beer from the lunging pit, and Kat needed to be steadied, hence the finger in the belt loop. Plausible, maybe, but our faces would have given it all away. We knew what we were doing.

*Feedback. *Thump thump thump* *

A finger taps the mic

"Yo. San Diego, is this fucking thing on?"

Beer cans lifted along with a chorus of catcalls

"This is our last song; I want to see you all *go crazy*."

49

I had already gone too far. I pulled back and Kat repositioned herself just in front of me. I needed to find Tyler and Dan. They knew us and our families too well to see us acting like this. Kat must have thought the same; she was surveying the crowd. I pointed just over her left ear. They were lost in the crowd, spinning with the dust-devil. She moved back and settled once again into my arm, only now I bypassed the belt loop and tucked my thumb inside her jeans, stroking back and forth with the beat.

As the last song faded, Tyler and Dan said they had to hurry out ahead of the crowd to flag down a ride-share. I was in no hurry; I was walking home. I told Kat I was going to hang for one last beer. "When do you have to get back?" I asked, motioning toward the bar. I knew she hated thinking she *had* to do anything. So, she joined me at the empty bar to drink one last beer and to watch the band tear down their equipment.

Sitting on the edge of the bar, we each slowly sipped a beer, barely even buzzed from the alcohol. Fighting the crowds for a beer didn't leave us time for more than two or three during the show, but we were both high on our connection.

Kat asked, "Do you remember when I was texting you from Edinburgh?"

"I do. I remember doing the math on the time difference; you were out all night."

"I was and it was amazing. I hope you didn't mind. If Mike knew I was out that late he'd be furious."

"Weird. Why?"

"He gets mad about that stuff. He doesn't want me out gallivanting around town. He's super protective. Is that weird? It is pretty weird, right? I mean, I'm a grown woman, I shouldn't feel guilty for wanting to enjoy the city."

"That is a little weird."

"Yeah, I don't know... Is it controlling? I feel like it is..." She trailed off.

"I guess, but what do I know?"

"I don't know, I've been thinking..." Kat paused and took a long, slow sip of beer. She was on the verge of tears. "I shouldn't be married. Marriage just isn't for me. I want to be and be free, but it's hard because everyone thinks Mike is so amazing, and he is, but... look, I know people envy my life, they tell me how lucky I am, but if I'm so lucky, why do I want to run? I don't know, I don't see myself married to him in the next five years."

"Wow, I had no idea."

Drunk on the proximity to another married soul in torment, I told her that I too had been going through some stuff with Elle, that we'd been failing at connecting, even with years of marriage counseling, that we were on our last thread, that I could feel the end approaching, but I didn't know how to end it.

We finished our beers and just as we were about to get up, she asked me, "Can you keep a secret?"

I smiled, saying, "Not really, but I'll try."

"After the conference, a friend and I ran into a few tourists from Germany. They started flirting a little, told us they were going to dinner and asked if we'd like to join. We were actually on our way to eat, so we saw no harm in joining them. After we ate, we sat around talking and drinking. Around midnight or so my friend was too tired to stay out any longer. I was about to join her, but a band started playing. I told her that I wanted to hear a song or two, so I stayed behind. Then this guy, one of the tourists, asked me to dance."

"Did this mysterious dancing tourist have a name?" I asked.

"Johannes."

"So fancy," I joked.

"Johannes and I danced for an hour before we noticed that the bar was beginning to empty. I told him I had to get going because the conference started early in the morning. I went to call a cab, but my phone was dead. So, he offered to walk me to my hotel. I said, 'Sure' and as we crossed the street he reached out for my hand."

I didn't say a thing, but my eyes must have gotten bigger.

"I know," she said. "It was crazy. We held hands the whole way. When we reached the alley by my hotel I said, 'This is it,' and we just stood there holding hands, not saying anything. Then all of a sudden, he kissed me, and I kissed him back and the next thing I knew I was pressed up against the alley wall and we made out like we were in a movie or something. It was so immature, but also amazing. We were kissing, necking with our hands under each other's sweaters. We were ridiculous. It was so clichéd, but also so invigorating. The sun was coming up and we both had places to be that morning. He asked if he could come up. I said that I saw his wedding ring, he said that he saw mine and we kissed again, and then…"

All I could do was say, "Wow."

"I know, I know," Kat said. "I cried all the next day. I always thought I was different from my family. They're all cheaters. All of them. And now…" The words trailed off as we both lifted our glasses. "But it was incredible, everything. I haven't felt like that in years…" she said as she stared into her glass.

We sat motionless watching the light move with the beads of sweat on our pint glasses. The tumblers in my brain were still wide-open, thinking of Kat nestling into my arm. The Edinburgh story was ringing in my head. We were the same. We wanted to dance and love and be loved. We wanted romance. We wanted to be asked, to be seen. We wanted to make out in an alley, fuck wildly until the sun came up. We wanted romance, life, electricity. And with the courage of a few beers in my veins, the energy of the Quakes in my ears, and the Edinburgh confession in my head, I laughed and said, "You want to kiss me, don't you? Will you kiss me? I feel like you want to."

She laughed, eyes bright, and said, "What! No… no way," with a turned-up finish, implying a question.

I was frozen for a few beats and then I said, "Yeah, that's crazy. What the hell am I saying?" and I pulled at the last of my beer. "All righty, I better get to walking home. Call your ride, I'll wait out front with you."

"No, it's OK. It's a beautiful night, I'll walk with you for a bit. I can call a ride from anywhere."

Just then, the house lights went on, telling us it was time to slide. I glanced around the bar and watched Kat slinking out the door. I stood there thinking about how I'd never seen this place with the lights on, everything in the dark until it wasn't. So much that I had never seen: the graffiti carved into the table of the booth by the door telling all the dirty secrets rolling around in my mind: for a good time call… if you want some cock… to have your cocked sucked… tears rolling out of cocks carved into tables just next to pussies drawn with 1970's-style bush; cocks and balls and tits and pussies and Kat smiling, pausing by the door. And this time, as I exited the Soda Bar, I wasn't blinded by the street lights, I was blinded by Kat. Not ten feet past the door, we were walking, bumping shoulders and laughing, and somehow, we were holding hands just like she and Johannes were in Edinburgh, and around the corner, by the bridge on Central and Meade, by an old Winnebago, I found out I was right ... she did want to kiss me.

A Ménage-à-Trois for Christmas

For the next few months, we tried hard to ignore our natural connection. We tried not to seem excited when we saw the other walk into the room, we tried not to look at each other as lovers might, we tried not to think of each other while we hovered over our others in the dark, we tried to imagine that what we had at home was what we wanted. It wasn't until we were separated by divergent family plans for Christmas that we gave into the idea that we were indeed made of the same stardust. That Christmas she and the family were visiting her mom in Mendocino. Each morning, she'd go for a run on the edge of the Headlands and each morning she'd send me a photo with a few spontaneous lines about what the sea, the waves, the mist and I were doing to her. She would write to say that we were like the moon and the tide, that she could feel my pull. She would say that our connection was written in the stars, that there was nothing that could be done about it but to give in to the pull. She would say that she could feel the power of the waves pounding the shore and it made her think of how I would take her right there on that spot in the dark of the morning, or under the moon at night. She would say that the fog and the mist left her wet like I did, like she found herself that morning after reading the lines I sent her. She would say that this spot, like no other, contained our essence: it was haunting and beautiful, and it suggested what we were and what we could be together.

Each day we exchanged emails and poems on how we belonged together, how our distance was ridiculous, how I should be there with her. She'd add a line or two about a quiet place she found beneath the trees, where she and I would need to lay when I'd join her on some future visit north. "You would come with me, wouldn't you?" she'd write. "Of course, I would." And when she'd return from her run, I'd find a video taken during the shower she used to work out her forest fantasy. In the evening we'd text and send poems and at night, she'd read and tell me about how she found us in *Henry and June* and *The Delta of Venus*. We'd tease, both claiming to be the Nin of our relationship. And then when the family went to bed, she'd settle in alone to read by the fireplace.

Christmas Eve exemplified our early twisted existence. On that night with everyone asleep, we stayed up texting each other. Kat reclined beneath a blanket on a couch before Nin and flames while I sat alone in the perfect dark. She texted that she was reading *Delta*, imagining me lying next to her.

"When we are together, I want you to read to me while I masturbate and then I want you to take me," she wrote as Nin worked her into frenzy. She texted me that she was touching herself under the blanket.

*photo

The top of her white bodysuit unbuttoned to reveal her breast.

*photo

Bottoms below her knees.

Bodysuit snaps unsnapped.

Fingers in folds.

*photo

"Fuck I need you so badly," she wrote.

"I need you."

"This book reminds me of us. I love you. This is stupid. We should be together."

"It is stupid. How do we do this?"

"I don't know, but it's too much. I can't stand being apart any longer."

"Where is everyone?" I asked.

"Sleeping... I hope. If any one walks in, I'm in trouble."

"Seriously! What are you going to do with the rest of your night?"

"I'm going to send you one more photo and then masturbate while imagining you fucking me in front of this fire."

*photo

"Fuck, you are amazing. Tell me something..." I begged.

Tell me something. I loved what this line came to mean for us. It meant we weren't finished yet, that we needed one more line of poetry, a poetic allusion, a lusty thought, just a bit more before we signed off; it was a request for connection that was never denied.

At my request, my phone teased with the three dots to show that she was writing, but nothing...

I waited with my cock still hard from her previous photos.

Three dots.

57

Five minutes.

"Hello? No sign off? No goodnight? No xoxoxo? What happened?"

Five more minutes…

"I'm sorry about that."

"What happened?"

"M walked in as I was taking your last photo."

"Holy shit. What did you do?"

"I panicked and told him that I was sending it to him…"

*** (those dots again) plenty of time for me to fill the silence with meaning. I knew what happened.

"I'm so sorry."

Three dots.

No message.

Three dots.

Another minute.

… "I'm sorry. I couldn't think of anything else to say. I was naked on the living room couch, and he walked in when the flash went off."

"It's OK. We know where we are, but I don't think I can take much more of this."

"Me neither. And I am really sorry. It didn't mean anything. Really. Ugh. This is hard. Too hard."

"It's just the way it is. I get it. I should get to bed. We can talk more tomorrow, yes? Good night, my love. Merry Christmas."

"Yes, of course. Merry Christmas. I am sorry to end the night this way. I will see you in my dreams. I love you."

"I love you."

"Goodnight."

"xoxo"

"xoxo"

While I readied myself for bed with the already long-sleeping Elle, I shaped the details of this long-distance ménage-à-trois in my mind. I pieced the scene together from the little details she'd told me about their lovemaking and the layout of her mother's house. I was positioned inside her head, she was positioned over him (their usual way as Kat informed me), and she came quickly to the idea of pleasuring two men; albeit one man six hundred and forty-seven miles away. In that awkward moment, I attempted to soothe all of the savage beasts that rattled their cages in the forefront of my mind with the bits and scraps of our pre-and-post-fuck text exchange. I fed them with the knowledge that in those ten minutes she was gone leaving me with a hard-on and those cock-softening blinking dots, he spent a quiet five minutes under her in the pitchest of blacks trying not to wake the girls, while I'd be with her the rest of the night as she read by the fire and slipped into dream on that couch. I told the beasts that she would beg for bruises when she returned, and they were satisfied.

***

Before Christmas, we existed in an odd state of balance. We were satisfied leaning into each other, holding the other together just enough so that we didn't completely disintegrate in the ever-widening black hole at the center of our mirrored marriages. Together, we had given ourselves permission to be seen, understood, appreciated, validated by each other without forcing anything. In those first few months, we dared to dream that there was a way to navigate this married, best friend, sexual partner existence without having to suffer the lack we had grown accustomed to in our marriages. We had resolved to be the balm that smoothed the cracks from the life-crippling heat of a desert-marriage-mirage. But after Christmas break, everything changed. The distance showed us just how overcome with lack we were. We couldn't take it, we both knew that we were too much to lose, so we gave in to the affair. No, the affair? That isn't quite right. It wasn't an affair any longer. It was us. We weren't there for the high of the affair, we weren't into the thrill of sneaking around, we weren't just fucking, *or* patching holes in our shattered marriages, we were a rogue wave whose purpose was to elevate life, we were true reciprocal and secure partners. Once Christmas break ended, we met whenever we could find time. "I'm going to pick up some coffee, meet me at Café Virtuoso," she would text. "I have to pick up some papers in Point Loma; do you have time to meet at Eppig?" she would call. "M just left to pick up the girls, come over to the house now!" she would write. And I'd say yes, every time. I said yes to everything.

Not long after she returned to San Diego, we found ourselves in a sleeping bag in the back of my SUV. Kat wanted me to know that while she was gone, she had done a lot of thinking. She told me, "I think I frighten people. When I start to talk, I can see it in their eyes. But you, you aren't frightened of me. Do you remember when we all went to that brewery anniversary party? When you took my hand and dragged me around to try all the beers?"

"I do," I said.

"At one station, you wouldn't let go of my hand and you looked me in the eyes and said, 'I wish you didn't hate me so much. We'd be best friends if you would let your guard down.' I said that we *were* best friends. But you shook your head. Then I wandered back to Mike and Elle, laughing to myself about how emo and drunk you were. But I didn't tell them what you said. For months, I thought about that night. Often. I'd just lie there and think about what you meant and why I hold back with you. I thought about how you held my hand. I thought about you way too often. It is because of all of this, the connection we've always had, that I knew, even before coming home from Edinburgh, that you understood me. Sitting at the Soda Bar, you nodded and listened and told me that I shouldn't feel so crazy. And the music that night. The dancing. I love how you touch me when we dance."

She must have spent the twelve-hour drive back from Mendocino thinking about how settling down with Mike had changed her. In that sleeping bag, she told me that she married because that's what she thought she was supposed to do. He was great, she'd say, but he was for settling, and what's worse, it was clear that he wanted her to settle. It made me think of a verse I heard: if you *like* a flower you pluck it, but when you *love* a flower, you water it daily. She had been plucked. Any sign of the person that Kat loved in herself, the person she was before she moved from New York to San Diego, was shunned and shut down. He became the father over-watcher she never had, the anchor she never really wanted, but who she thought she was supposed to need, or was supposed to have. Had she only known that she'd have to give up all the pieces of herself that truly made her special. Had she only known that she had signed up to have all her interesting edges sanded down by a woodworker husband in San Diego. Had she only known that she had signed up to settle.

"I wrote this for you on my drive back. Can I read it to you?"

"Of course," I said, sliding over to tuck up tighter beside her.

"I need to find my rhythm," she read. "I've lost it. I used to wander into art galleries. I'd go to bars alone and just sit and read. I'd come home and read or write until all hours of the night, I'd frantically scribble lines working on some grandiose piece. I even played guitar; can you believe that? Mostly, I was creative and alive. I need to find that person again. I want you to know, you feel like home, like equal parts home and adventure. A new kind of home. You don't shame or judge. I am whole in your presence. I don't have to hide anything. I never feel shame with you. With you, I just get to be who I always thought I was. I need to figure out how to end this with him. I need to figure this out for me, for my girls, for you. I want to be who I am when I'm with you. I want to be with you. We will figure this out. Thank you for being my partner these last few months. You have been the electricity that has kept me awake and alive and feeling loved. This is so hard, but it is worth it, you will see. I love how you trust, how you let me trust myself. I just need to do that for myself.

I want you to know that I see you, hear you, feel you.

I want you to know that my bruises have faded." She smiled, as if wondering when they might come out again.

Even in the Stars We are Famous

Not long after the Soda Bar confessions and our Christmas
ménage-à-trois, and not long after Kat and I decided we weren't
just an emotional support unit literally and figuratively filling the
holes in our perforated marriages, we began to build our own
mythology. We fell hard for each other, and everything became a
sign that we were meant to be together. We truly believed that we
met in the stars long before we were born. Our cosmic connection
permeated all. It was evidenced in our metaphysical reality and
was so undeniable that it was even reflected in the paranormal.
This connection and inevitability was a theme that we extended
to the ghosts we knew: Kat's grandmother and Mike's sister
Maya.

Over beers, Kat would repeat the bedtime stories her mother
told her. She beamed as she told me that nonconformity and
restlessness ran in her blood. I noted that there was a striking
similarity between these stories and her current home life. Her
grandmother was not happy with her marriage, and she did the
only thing a woman could do in the early 20th century - she ran
away to live her own life. She risked it all and lived a second life
freely as a burlesque dancer in New York City bars. She was bold
and brave and took action when she was backed into a corner.
She wasn't from a time of no-fault, 50/50 custody. She was from

a time where she had to give up her family to break free from the world's expectations. She left everything behind and, as hard as that had to be, it was progress. Kat and I would discuss her in relation to some of our favorite literature characters trying to justify what *we* were doing. I'd make an allusion to *The Awakening* and say, "leaving for freedom sure beat wading out to sea to the hum of bees and the musky odor of pinks" and she'd pick up my probably too forced reference with ease and cap it with, "in protest of a world that wasn't ready for a woman who would not be shackled." We'd froth over how she was not Chopin's Edna who melted beneath the waves, but the living embodiment of Ibsen's Nora as she slammed the door. We'd rant and preach, recognizing that we were actually talking about Kat when we reasoned that her grandmother had decided that she was not just a pretty doll, a figurine in a doll's house paired with someone who didn't really know her. No longer a stunted pseudo-human. No longer a kept woman who found that as expectations would have it, care for herself was far, far down her list of duties. I added to the fervor, and waxed poetically reading a line I had written about her, "and she slammed that door because her duty was not to the roles thrust upon her, but to that which came with the responsibility of being made of stardust, of braving the violent passage through the wet and bloody birth canal, to that which came with the first raspy breaths of life, spitting pink-tinged mucus, to that which came with the first view of the harvest moon and the desire to run naked beneath it."

Being in the throes of romance and true love as we were, one ghost wasn't enough for us. Our second, perhaps most important ghost was Mike's sister Maya. Her passing was the matchmaking event that literally brought us together. Without Maya, there would be no story to tell. She moved the four of us from casual acquaintances to an intimate foursome. Maya and I knew each other apart from everyone else. She and I were good friends who would loiter at parties and drink and have the most amazing and random conversations. We talked bourbon and music and Dostoevsky: *the worst sin is that you have betrayed yourself for nothing;* Kafka; *don't edit your soul.* We laughed at Cecelia Giménez's *Ecce Homo / Monkey Christ,* talked border politics and Ana Teresa Fernández's *Borrando la Frontera,* and Cally Spooner's *And You Were Wonderful;* she loved this one and it was made all the more poignant at her passing. She had great depth and interests that weren't like those of her peers. Her aura radiated confidence and contentment and she had the loveliest way of making everyone feel special. She made *me* feel special.

On the night of her memorial, after everyone went home, I decided to pop over to Mike and Kat's to drop off a bottle of Devil's Share whiskey I'd been holding onto for a special occasion. Mike invited me in and we three just about finished that bottle sitting in their living room crying and telling stories about Maya. We cursed death for taking someone so full of life and we thanked her for bringing all of us together. Our connection grew quickly and deep that night, sparking an eight-year run of family dinners that began the very next week.

***

Years later, when Kat and I were at sea with romance, when we realized everything was connected, when we knew that we were no longer filling holes in the monotony of marriage, when we realized that we didn't have holes to fill, but rather that we were open to finding a partner in the crime of life, someone to help sharpen our interesting edges, not dull them, when we realized we were for watering not plucking, we became a pair of lampposts, the brightest spotlights, the fullest dual-moon on this new horizon, on this new planet, and our paired light illuminated the smallest and deepest crevices of our minds, reminding us of things that were dear to us, but that for reasons we didn't understand, we had to hide away. Our union didn't just illuminate life, it gave life deeper meaning by restoring access to that which we hid away. I remember standing on the eighth floor of the Sheraton on Harbor Island overlooking the anchored ships. We stood in the window naked looking out onto the sea, tucked into each other the same way we stood when we went to an art gallery or a club. She before me, me melting into her curved spine. My arms draped over her shoulders; one found her belly, the other made a V over her breasts and held her opposite shoulder.

"We'd be out there," I said, pointing out over the horizon. I whispered, "We aren't like those anchored ships," as I moved her hair to kiss her neck.

"Today is Maya's anniversary," she said.

"Yeah, I know."

"I think she knows?" she said, turning to kiss me

"She does. I really think she does."

"I know it's crazy," she said, "but I think that her death was meant to bring us together."

"I know what you mean. I know she loved us both," I said, moving to the bed.

"I know that it's messed up," she said as she lay by my side, her head on my chest, "but what if, what if she just wanted everyone to be happy?" She reasoned that loyalty to true love and soulmates was of the highest order. I did not disagree. Kat told me that it wasn't just for us, it was also for them. "I think she wants Mike and Elle to get together too," she said. "Do you think we four could still hang out if they did?"

"Hmm, that would be nice, I could do it."

"Me too," she said.

"But it's unlikely," I whispered. "Mike and Elle aren't the type. They don't look to the stars. They don't listen for the whispers of ghosts."

"We'll need to help them find each other, so that we can all be happy," she said. "Maya did this for all of us," she said as she crawled on top of me.

"Even in the stars we are famous," I said.

"Yes, we are." She kissed into my chest.

In full view of the boats on the horizon, she took me in. We fucked slowly, moving like the ships out on the horizon. We rolled and pulled and pushed with imagined winds. Today we weren't the rabid beasts we'd normally find under the sheets. We were the soft rolling sea, we were poets, lovers who were always there lying just behind the beasts who snarled to be fed. We were weighted, held, supported, not by a bed, but by the sea. And as we found each other's eyes, we held on and rolled like the ships until we came together with the blue sky and the sea beating in from the open window.

In moments like those, it was easy to see how Maya wanted this for us. As I lay there thinking about Maya, Mike, and Elle, still full inside Kat, still holding her on my chest as the aftershocks of her orgasm worked through her body, she started to giggle. Her giggle turned into a laugh.

"I'm sorry," she said.

"For what?"

"For laughing."

"You don't have to apologize."

"OK … I won't. It's just that … never mind."

"What?"

"It's just that … well … others … have gotten mad when I laugh."

"Why? I just thought you were laughing because you were happy. Sort of from experiencing pure joy." I shrugged. "Is that not it?"

She began to cry. "What's going on," I asked.

"Nothing. It's that … that *is* why. Sometimes I just want to laugh. No one has ever understood that before. Even when I'd tell them why, they'd just get mad."

"I'm sorry, baby. If those people couldn't understand that you were just happy, they don't deserve you. I know you know this, but men by nature are just insecure. That's all that is."

"Thank you … I love you so much."

"I know," I said with a smile. "I love you more."

"No. No, you don't."

***

When Kat was quietly drifting off at the dinner table, lying still in the bath, when she read and slipped away, forgetting that she was reading at all, when she watched Casablanca and imagined us in that Paris flashback, she could hear Maya whispering her approval, and she could feel her grandmother tugging at her insides, telling her to say, "Fuck it. Run. Dance. Cry. Laugh. Be." In those small moments, Kat could see Edna swimming out to sea, she could hear Nora slamming that door, she could feel the stardust tingle in her veins, she could see the harvest moon in her eyes when she stared into the mirror after waking up naked and alone in the morning, wondering what to do about her life as she listened to the Charles Ives-like soundtrack of her family eating breakfast downstairs. She hadn't quite slammed the door, but she was standing there with me, preparing for a new world that was just on the other side. That energy, those ghosts, paired with a lazy sort of settling that our others had adopted, thrust us together in a rogue wave of connection, romance, and gravity defying sex. We found it impossible to escape the mythology that we had created.

Too Much Moon Dust

Even before Kat and I routinely fucked in my car down the street from her house, before we broke her sister's bed and defiled her kitchen, before we bloodied hotel sheets, the others said that we wanted too much, that we were insatiable, that we were in fact too much.

Is wanting what one needs unreasonable?

In truth, after years of wandering, surviving on muddy puddles posing as one lush oasis after another, we were now both too thirsty to be reasonable any longer. And that was how it started. We were left to twist in the sweltering heat of a good enough life, when it wasn't. We were left on our own to fill our lack. With enough time and opportunity, it was inevitable, either together or apart, we would have our thirst quenched. Add in our undeniable connection, and we were indeed inevitable. The slow disconnect from our others, which created the space we needed to see each other, played out like most improv bits driven by the prime-directive 'yes and,' because this is how one wrings the most out of a bit, out of a lover, a lie, a promise, and not surprisingly, this is how one wrings the most out of an affair. Kat and I were students of 'yes and' the theater bill promised a romantic and sexual farce centered around the unlikeliest of candidates because this heightens the tension, the comedy, and the tragedy, right?

Fuck, did it ever.

***

Someone: Mike, Elle, Kat, me suggests, "Let's hang out this weekend."

Someone else: Dinner? A bonfire? Beer? Whisky?

Me: I'll be record shopping before dinner, who wants to go?

Kat: Well, I was planning to pick up a book. Who wants to meet me at Verbatim? We could meet there and pick up some beer and cheese at Bottle Craft.

Me: Oh, and later tonight there's an art show, a Robert Burns reading, an event at the Hamilton's, a few friends wanted to meet late at BLAH, an Irish band playing at the Ould Sod, I have an extra ticket for a show at the Casbah, a tasting at the Aero Club, a band at the Soda Bar... who's in?

Dinner...?

Of course. And of course, "Yes, and."

After years of playing this game around the platonic dinner table, we four came to be unconsciously paired with our improv-style counterparts. The 'Yes, Ands:' Kat and me, and the 'No, Buts:' Mike and Elle.

As I pondered this dynamic, I thought about how people who have affairs are perceived. I thought about how those that play outside the boundaries of socially accepted behavior rarely are seen as heroes triumphing over stasis, lack, the status quo. Adulterers don't get to win. And as labels and opinions go, those that do win write the history, so then, find the ledger of the well-adjusted in their therapists' notes where the winners bend and stretch the truth to fit the story that best comforts them. If you were to ask Elle and Mike, they tried, they tried *hard*. Not to mention, they were indeed good people and yet, somehow, someone they loved felt unsatisfied. Couldn't be them, right? So, in this scene fitted with two mix-matched lack-defined couples coming together for dinner paired with (against?) those that slid comfortably into their roles as martyr-keepers of the classically defined social expectations, as shepherds for their children, preferring to stay seated lest they rock the boat … in most tellings of this affair, the 'No, Buts' applied the brand to the hides of the wandering herd and we were nothing more than takers who hadn't quite learned to quell our more animal nature, but there was more to it.

This.

Us.

Kat and me.

It wasn't about taking.

It was about reciprocity and the second sight that a pure unhindered connection provides.

I was not a fan of this taker/ leaver, keeper/ guardian model. It was an oversimplification, a conveniently binary take on a multidimensional issue. They weren't choosing to stay behind because that was what they should do. They chose to stay behind because that was what they wanted to do. Sure, it was easy for them to say, "Don't you think I'd rather run all over town? Don't you think I'd like a night out? A night free from the kids?" But that's just it, they didn't. And no matter how much it would have made our lives easier to want what they wanted, Kat and I just couldn't. As I pondered this, I asked her, "Do you wish it was him? It would make life easier, wouldn't it?" Kat thought for a moment and replied, "I don't want to be misunderstood. Of course, I wish M would see me the way you do, feel me the way you feel me. And I wish I could see him the way I see you. Feel him the way I feel you. It would be easier for all of us. But I recognize that it isn't possible. You and I are something else altogether. We are made from the same piece of moon rock that turned to dust and created life on earth. We merge life and lust brilliantly and soulfully. For the girls, I often wish it could be him. But for me, for us, it can only be you."

I didn't blame her for wishing that he could have seen her. We'd said this to each other before. Elle and I played this same game at home. I knew it would be easier if Elle could see me the way that Kat did. Shit, early on with Elle I would have settled for a quarter of something resembling being seen, but not any more. Not now when I knew what it felt like to be satisfied, not after being fooled into thinking that it wasn't possible to be satisfied, not after being tricked into believing that I was the reason I wasn't satisfied.

We both knew it would be easier, but it was too late for easy, we were drying up in front of Mike and Elle. So, while Kat and I were negotiating how to make a life together, in the background, all they could hope for was that the fragile balance of family and friends was enough to keep beasts at bay. Meanwhile, we had given in to the idea that it shouldn't be this hard, that we'd found our true other who understood that it shouldn't cost us our soul, or our humanity, just to have a roof over our head, to be with our children and simultaneously find freedom, ecstasy, and joy in between the business of life. The door that they left open for us was decorated with lack, we were abandoned, unseen, unheard, unappreciated, and felt unwanted. It was about wondering, "Is this it?" Kids, work, dinner, conversation at the dinner table illustrating the growing distance, illustrating just how large that distance had grown, feeling the slow-trickle of disconnect over a string of years that went by in a flash (too fucking fast), "Where did it go? ... Where did I go?," read to the kids, slink to the bedroom, drop your clothes at the foot of the bed, let them see you naked, cast another line – make a comment about something provocative, lay in bed half-naked, or entirely naked with a book, turn to tell the other about the "interesting" sex scene you just read, discover that they are already asleep, or worse, they aren't asleep and they clumsily and awkwardly reach out and within minutes, without ceremony, have performed their obligations and left you still wanting, needing to finish on your own, quietly in the dark, being sure to pick up that book again to let them drift to sleep before you do.

Was this it?

Could this really be it?

No. We refused the bridle, the boredom, the cage, and we walked the streets punching holes in the tired expectations that bound us. Kat and I would meet at Vinyl Junkies and hold hands as we flipped through the records looking for music that moved us like we moved each other: The Cramps, Iggy Pop, Warsaw Pakt, Idles, Patti Smith, Talking Heads; or we would meet at Verbatim where we'd wander the aisles touching hips and hanging on to belt loops, looking for literature that told a version of our own story: Miller, Woolf, Nin. We'd part to shower, to show our faces to our others long enough to avoid suspicion, and between it all we'd text.

K: God, I love you.

K: I miss you terribly.

Me: I miss you.

Kat: We need to write this story, no one would believe it.

Me: They would, this is the cliche.

Me: We are both fucking each other's friends.

Kat: Uh, you know there is much more to this. We aren't fucking to fuck.

Kat: We are in love, and we still want them to be happy.

Me: We do, and we are. It is beautiful and complicated.

Me: We should write this story. I'll start.

K: Promise?

Me: Of course.

K: I know that we are meant to be.

Me: We are, but when will we be?

K: I am having the conversations.

Me: Promise?

K: I know it doesn't look like it, but I am.

K: We will be together.

Me: I know, baby.

Me: You can't fuck with the stars.

K: That's why no one will believe this story.

K: We are choosing true love.

Me: Who does that?

K: Truth

K: Gotta get dressed.

K: (Photo)

Me: Ugh! I miss you.

Me: More please!

K: I love you

K: (photo)

K: (photo)

Me: Fuck!

K: I love you

Me: I love you

And we'd find each other that night touching feet beneath their dinner table, kissing in their hallway, hiding in the bathroom to text a line of poetry. "Tell me something …"

A Swan Will Not Linger Long at Any Pond

Like every night that first summer, we ate dinner at Kat's sister's place. Mary had been hosting the family so Mike could tear down and rebuild their house. To build Kat the dream house she never wanted. Later at a cheap hotel, Kat would fill in all the awkward gaps in that night's conversation. I hadn't put it together on my own, but the evening, the summer, Kat, everything, was dripping with overripe Ibsen-like *A Doll's House* imagery: *"Before all else, you are a wife and mother."* Her husband, a quiet man who kept to himself, recognized that a beautiful swan may not linger long on any pond. She must have a fitting cage, a cage so beautiful she might not think it a cage at all.

We four sat around the dinner table on Kat's 39th birthday, getting high on her sister's new pen. We ate garlic olives and roasted rosemary almonds and drank the hoppiest of beer and the smokiest of whiskies as we danced around the topic of the destruction of a perfectly good, but tiny, home to build their forever house.

"What's the latest on the house?" Elle asked, genuinely interested as Kat opened our joint birthday gift (that I picked out for her).

Mike: "More delays, we have to redo the plans."

Kat: "Patti Smith, Radio Ethiopia! Iggy, Party! The Mamas and the Papas... How'd you know?"

I took special pride in observing her wants and needs.

"I know things," I said with a smile intended to hide my sadness. I got up and walked away to wet my face in the bathroom to hide my tears. It was hard for me to hold back. We should have kissed; we should have been fucking on the living room floor. I should have had my face between her legs as Patti sang *Ask the Angels*. All of Side A with my face between her legs, only lifting my head to flip the record.

Returning, Kat checked my face. I'd said, "Redoing the plans, again?" As if I never left the table. "Didn't you just redo them? That's gotta be expensive."

"It is, and the real expensive part is paying the mortgage while I'm remodeling and paying rent to stay here in PB," Mike responded with pregnant glances both sent to and then returned from Kat. It seemed that in the ultimate act of irony, Kat had to borrow thousands from her family to make up for the delays, further funding her own discomfort.

Kat: "Well, ya know, if we had kept the house the way it was, we could've been retiring in Scotland in five years."

I watched her face, and she avoided my eyes. She was feeling guilty for letting that comment slip. She knew that the dream of leaving the country wasn't theirs any longer; it was ours. But I didn't mind, it was just another sign that he didn't listen to her, that he didn't see her, that he ignored her, that he had plans to carry out, and the implication was that she needed to fall in line. I knew she wouldn't.

That dig that Kat aimed at Mike, laced with the hint that she wished things were different (better) for them, hit me; it did sting a little, but who was I to criticize? Elle and I danced this same dance, the only difference was that I never did it in front of Kat. But Kat had something else going on. I got the sense from the way many of these dinner party conversations went that these digs and probes weren't new, that they were extensions of failed private conversations. They were signs of cracks in the façade, and here in full view of the guests Kat was pushing her side, hoping for a sympathetic audience.

Pattern Recognition

Mother, is that You?

The morning after dinner at Mary's, Kat completed her weekly phone call to her mother. It was a weekly ritual made famous by providing all of us at the dinner table with plenty to discuss. If Kat was feeling enthusiastic about something, this phone call would fix that; if Kat dared feel good about herself, this call was the cure; if Kat was uncertain about anything in her life, this phone call would double her uncertainty. Why Kat continued to make these calls was a problem to set before the dinner-party arm-chair-therapist committee. Imagine Kat, a restless but insecure wife to a subtle controller and mild manipulator, a mother of two young girls. She was fatherless for much of her youth; hers preferred getting high to traditional fatherly responsibilities. She was raised by a ghost of a mother, more story than substance, more friend than caregiver, more idea than matter. The house swirled with the spirit of her mother. She wasn't dead, she just wasn't really there. She was a liberated, but oddly judgmental, bohemian-artist. She was revered by friends and neighbors. But during Kat's adolescent years, she often took better care of herself, her art, those friends and neighbors, than she did her own children.

She raised Kat and Mary on the ideal of self-sufficiency and the meat of art gallery opening leftovers, saltines, and Oreos. She'd make up for the long hours away with stories about her famous run-ins, her near misses, and her adventurous (very self-sufficient) burlesque loving mom, 'god rest her soul,' she'd say. These stories were the meat of Kat's adolescence and this loose insecure bohemian lifestyle taught her how to love. Insecurely. In constant survival mode. It taught her to live in her head where it was safe, where dreams could fill the gaps her life generated. As a child, she was administered a life wound. She would never admit this, but she was essentially abandoned as a child, pushed away, and then drawn back by the one a.m. bedtime stories, the art, the friends. It cut deep. Perhaps worse was how all of this spun in her head. It was the time spent with and the regard her mother had for her bohemian friends that made Kat envious and created a cacophony of confusing internal dialogue. They weren't just rivals; they were mirrors reflecting the value of her mother. They taught her that her mother was important. So, despite the lack Kat felt, with the help of those friends, those validating adult eyes, she came to idolize her mother as she was pushed away and broken down. She was taught to love, to seek out that which pushed her away; worse, she was taught that the hole in her chest was a defect attributable to herself alone. She was taught that she made the lack.

She was victim to the "build-up, then beat-down" approach to love. As any good narcissist knows, this is how you strike: applied properly, it won't take much to save her, to make her think it was her, that she caused whatever, that she did it (whatever it was), to guide her into thinking, 'boy, you sure are lucky to have me.' Applied to save, to stabilize, to control (hello Mike). And this mother, who now in her adult life, through passive-aggressive, and sometimes less passive ways, if Kat happened to call after seven p.m. (too far into happy-hour), would attempt to instruct, guide, or guilt Kat into being the mother that *she* never was, wanting things that she could never provide. The phone sessions with her mother would feed on all the insecurities that she had planted in Kat's head during her fragile adolescence.

Mother would sing a line, and Kat would *almost respond* with the words she saved for her journal.

"New hair cut? I liked your hair before."

I knew you'd hate it.

"Did you choose that color? Aren't you a little old to be dying your hair like that?"

Project much?

"You know, your kids should really be reading more."

How would you know how often they read? They read all day and before bedtime.

"The girls, is their vocabulary on track for their age? I feel like it isn't. Remember what I said about the reading."

I am doing the best I can. If I said this to her, she'd tell me, 'Not good enough.'

Ibsen, Chopin, mother, grandmother, husband: It is a hard thing to be tugged at like this. It is hard to know who to please. It is harder to know who to be. It is hardest to trust yourself. The tug of war between the ghost grandmother and the living ghost of a mother paired with the all-too-ready to conform, catch-for-any one Ibsen-manufactured savior-husband was enough to send quakes through any mountain.

Why didn't Kat just say those words to her mother? We spent plenty of time sitting around the dinner table discussing that very question. Kat would respond, "That's just Mom. It won't do any good to tell her how I feel. She just needs to say what she has to say. If I let her without interrupting, it makes my life easier." Beneath it all Kat wanted to please everyone, to make everyone happy. She learned how to become a 'people-pleaser' waiting for her mom to come home with her face pressed up against that cold Minnesota bedroom window. Father gone, mother out all night, it became about survival, holding on to whatever she had, and she didn't have much. Even as she waited for hours at that window looking out to see if her mom was coming home, all it took was for her to come home at all. That was enough. In the waiting, Kat would spiral: if she could only please her, she might come home earlier tomorrow. It was a damaging cycle that came to feel all too natural. To be pushed away, forgotten, ignored, and then showered with Saltines, Oreos, and fantastic grandmother fairy tales and art-show revelries, it was medicine for monsters.

Kat found the same cycle in her marrying years, although, in different packaging. In her adult life, her adolescent psychological soup subconsciously pulled Kat toward anything that looked like stability. She did not vibe well with other women, so this manifested solely in relationships with non-threating older men she met at work, married men she met on playdates for her kids, or gay men she befriended in college, further evidenced by a fling or two with an Irish professor at Trinity College. These men were everything she never had: consistent, calm, encouraging, genuinely interested in who she was, aroused by her lust for life (not threatened by it as other women appeared to be), and most importantly, they were non-threatening because none of them were available (gay, married, old, very old, or living in another country). It was everything Mike appeared to be when they met until time revealed that his jealousy and insecurities created a marriage-relationship cocktail eerily similar to the way in which her mother raised her.

At home, Mike appeared to be unlike the mother. He was always there appearing quiet and calm, but his manipulations were just less obvious to others. It started with mild jealousy. Old friends crowded too much. Old boyfriends lingered too often (the gay friends were allowed). The jealousy was compounded by a quiet and cold distance. He rarely touched Kat. There was no romance to speak of. He wasn't outwardly cruel in public, but according to Kat, psychologically he was bordering on abusive and privately he was not above breaking a few of her things to show her his rage. Like Kat's mother, Mike was loved by all, but failed to connect with Kat deeply. Fortunately for Mike, her mother taught her well. Kat learned that she was the problem. She learned that being ignored and abused by those you love and depend on was normal. In response, Kat relied on her adolescent-learned people-pleaser skills and tried hard to be seen at home. Her attempts were subtle at first – the aforementioned lace, the mention of a provocative book, an artsy movie with a few well-timed sex scenes – all artfully ignored by Mike, feeding Kat's lack-driven anxiety. If only she were better at pleasing him, he would see her. He didn't. So, she worked up the courage to be bolder. She would take a lady's night out and she'd drink and come home and report all the outlandish things that the ladies discussed with wonder and enthusiasm, hoping to spark the connection she wanted. She would tell him about how they danced, she would tell him about a guy that bought them drinks, hoping the jealousy would turn into satisfying action in bed, but without fail, she was ignored. "Tut-tut child. Tut-tut wife." In the end, raised on the crush of narcissism, she went where she always went, where it was supposed to go: it was her, she caused the awkwardness, the unsettling feelings, the pain, the lack. "Tut-tut child-wife. Settle. I've got you."

Ironically, here under the weight of her looming doll's house, she would tell me that she'd feel guilty for never saying the words. But she did say them, I was there. The reality was that no one listened, not her mom, not her sister, and certainly not Mike. She was so used to feeling low and unseen that she internalized her rejection as silence when in reality she was unintentionally gas-lit. She said the words, but the others weren't capable of hearing what was contrary to what they would have wanted for themselves.

So, on her birthday when she should have been hovering above me to Side B of Radio Ethiopia, I saw her face drop during the discussion, I saw her desire to say more, and I saw her struggle with her internal dialog that told her that she was supposed to be silent and want what everyone else would want. I saw her struggle with the story that her mother told her: that most would count themselves lucky to be where she was. I mean, fuck, she had repeated it to me several times and what did it mean? It meant, "Kat, we know who you are. You know who you are. You have all of *this*, but you do know that it is too good for you, right? Stay in your lane and keep your head down and you might just manage to have a good enough life. Don't mess this up!"

Kat was complex and host to a wide range of moods that affected her deeply. She was proud of her two young girls. She was almost as proud of her four-year itch and the story of how the harvest moon taught her to live. I told her that the itch was her ghost grandmother trying to help her shake free from the rivers, lakes, and clouds that had attempted to define her. She told me that I was her moon. She wanted to run, dance, travel, sometimes all at once. The itch was the eruption that said, "I have held still too long. I will not any longer." While odd, confusing, and scary for Mike and Elle, the itch never concerned me. I understood it. I told her that we didn't have to worry about it because we'd shake the world every day and because this was so, there would be no need to run. But her mother would continue...

"You know, you're lucky. Your husband is building you the house of your dreams"

His *dream house.*

"You want too much!"

No. Not true. You just don't understand me.

"You can't have everything, you know."

Why not?

"That just isn't how life works."

Why not?

"Do you know how many people would be happy to have what you have?"

Yes. Everyone. Everyone but me.

As soon as she hung up, she sent me our hotel reservations, thinking something like, "I don't want too much, I want less. I don't want a huge house or money. I want to be seen, to have fun, dance, laugh, be silly, and dance some more. I want to have my simple needs met, anticipated." But wasn't that the crux of all this? To have one's needs met implies that we have selected someone that wants to meet those needs. Actually, it isn't about *want* at all. If it was just that, Kat and I wouldn't be counting how many more hotel stays until we'd earned a free night. Our others imagined that they wanted to be the people to satisfy our needs … if only we'd be less of ourselves, not be so much, not be too much all the time, never be reckless and wild, not be provocative when we teased, not be silly in front of the children ("what are you teaching them?"), not be silly at all, certainly not a lot of things in order for it to work.

This *wanting* to be the other that satisfied was a simple thing. It wasn't a matter of anything as slippery as transubstantiation. It didn't require any one's god, their holy spirit, any one's mother of anything, it didn't have to be mystical although it was, it didn't have to be spiritual, though it couldn't be anything less, for we were all made up of the same putrid space dust, we were composed of the same insignificant universal effluvia, and yet because we couldn't all connect in ways that took care of our most basic needs, I believed there was no better argument for the soulmate. Despite the fact that we were molded from the same shit and clay, the fact that we couldn't all connect the same way, even when we should, even when we wanted nothing more, even when we signed the papers with the papal witnesses packed full of the fear of god, even when we made complicated lives and babies, we still fell short. For me, it said something about an unconscious cosmic code. Don't get me wrong, I was not imagining nine billion space ghosts hovering beyond the stars ready to enlist in an earthbound love-themed scavenger hunt. It was more of an energy with a secret code carved into the essence of an accidental clump of DNA that just happened to resonate with another. From birth we shriek out our signal to the world and in return the world works hard to quiet us, to muffle our signal lest we outshine those who have chosen less. A thousand hands reaching out throughout the day, every day, gripping around our necks, down our throats. "One mustn't want too much," they squeeze. Our trick in this cacophony of squeezing hands, of loss, of love, misery, lust, and children, is in the finding. And fuck it all if I hadn't found someone. Who, when she felt lonely, when she wore lace, or when she was bent over a pool table showing the crescent moon of her ass beneath her skirt, when she danced in front of a jukebox, when she felt like Holly Golightly in *Breakfast at Tiffany's*, a fickle cat belonging to nobody, when she knew most days she was Fran Kubelik from *The Apartment*, she sent her energy out into the universe, and that was what her true love would find.

That was what I found.

Another Cheap Hotel and a Journal Left to be Found

We always found a way. Kat was working on campus. She told her partner Nadia that she had to leave early to pick up the girls. There was always a way to get out of working late: she had to go shopping, get a haircut, a massage, family visiting, family leaving, the kids, the neighbors. I was every one of these excuses. She had told Mike that she'd likely be late, and he'd need to pick up the girls.

I had told Elle that I had a late meeting. "I'll be home by six-thirty p.m."

Days Inn had early check in. We'd meet at two p.m.

She waited inside, bra on the chair, T-shirt formed by small breasts, lace wet and ready. She'd hide at the edge of the curtain; she liked to watch me approach the room. Apparently, the nerves brought on by the possibility of being followed made me walk with a certain gait. Ready to spring, maybe? Whatever the case, it turned her on.

She saw me coming, but she made me knock every time.

"Hi baby."

"Hi." She smiled, stretching up to throw her arms around me as we kissed.

I moved her hair to find her neck and I teased there for just a moment, lightly biting and sucking, then I dropped my backpack and kicked off my shoes.

"How much time do you have?"

"Till six," she said.

Sitting at the small table by the window, I emptied my backpack. I cracked a beer and opened some chocolate. As we passed the beer can between us, I watched how she leaned back to take a sip, how her T-shirt tightened around her breasts and pushed her nipples through the thin material.

Our hotel history was long and varied. Most often we were savage lovers having gone too long without, too long between oases. Normally, we'd tear our clothes off upon entry and I'd be left standing naked where I walked in the door, cock full hard in her mouth before I could fasten the lock, but today, Kat said we needed to talk "before we *did anything*." I was prepared to talk, but as Kat reached to open the chocolate, I flashed to the dream-like reality of our last night together:

Just the week before, we stood together in front of the bureau mirror marveling at how we melted into each other. She wanted to take a photo. (I can't remember if we did). I pulled her hair back, she sighed as I kissed her neck and moved to her shoulders. She turned to kiss my neck and whispered, "I want your cock in my mouth." The kisses moved down my neck to my chest. She dropped to her knees and took me in as her body bent and convulsed; another *Only*, another *Les Seulements* for Kat: she orgasmed as she filled her mouth with my cock. She smiled as her right hand dropped to find the space between her legs. Her left hand took over so that she could mouth the words, "God, I love your cock." Her lips touched the edge of the tip and dove in deeper, as deep as she could go, one hand to steady my cock, one hand on my ass to steady my frame. Her hands took my cock as her body twisted to her orgasm. Her right hand disappeared between her thighs as she laughed through her quakes.

She stood giggling to show me her wet and sticky fingers and I picked her up (she loved this) and tossed her onto the bed.

Last week it was like that, a pure hair on fire, climbing out of our skins fuck session, but today, we had things to talk about. Kat handed me a piece of chocolate and smiled. We knew that we'd end up together, but we had no idea how to make it happen without completely destroying our families in the undoing. I assumed the ending of something would be the topic of today's conversation.

In between sips of beer, her hand found mine and she said, "M found my journal yesterday." I smiled a nervous smile; this was not how I wanted us to tell the others, named in some modern Victorian journal. Still smiling, I remembered an article I read somewhere, stating that no one who writes a journal doesn't want it to be found. "M found it and read everything." We never said their full names out of respect (maybe?), or fear that they might feel our connection in their gut and accuse us at the dinner table, or probably closer to the truth, for fear of breaking the spell.

"Holy shit! Your journal? Read everything? Of course, he did. Where did you leave it? What exactly is written in that thing?"

"He was cleaning out my car. It was under the driver's seat. There isn't anything pointing to you, or anything about our affair. It's mostly themes and ideas."

"Who leaves their journal in their car? Themes like …?" Hands moving, suggesting she should fill in the blanks.

"It must have fallen out of my bag while I was driving. Anyways, [she was thirty-nine and still said anyways. I thought it was cute, but I couldn't tell if she was saying it that way on purpose] well, you know Ibsen's A Doll's House," she said.

"Uh huh," I answered, wondering where this was going.

"I, uh … it's about being trapped like Nora. It says…"

I thought, peculiar choice of words, *"It says?"* I noticed she was distancing herself. *"It says?"* I might have said, "I wrote, I said, I felt." I reasoned that this distancing was a defense mechanism, but I had a flash that it could have been a window into how she played it down for Mike, hiding her true feelings to buy more time at home with her girls.

"*It says* that I feel like I am trapped in a marriage with someone who doesn't know me. That I am trapped in the house. His house. It says that I never wanted *this*. It says that I know I won't be married to him much longer."

"Yikes, how'd he take it?"

"Not well, he's really mad. He pouts and doesn't eat when he's mad. I'm worried."

"It seems like a good opportunity to get that all out. We can finally get started, right?"

"It's hard. I have meetings finishing up this week. And next week I'm taking the girls to visit my mom, so my plan is to write it all out when I'm up there and have the conversation with him when I get back."

"I just wanted you to know because he'll be watching me extra closely tonight."

"Noted. No sex while M and E do the dishes. Got it."

I sipped the last sip of beer and she smiled and said, "Do we get to fuck now?"

I was lost in how we had flipped gender roles: I wanted to talk everything out to find a solution. She wanted to fuck it out and hoped that a solution would find us. She always preferred working through our issues physically, naked, grinding, panting, drooling, joined as one, as opposed to actually working on them. I didn't fault her. It was hard.

I returned the smile. "Let's fuck."

The Magic of Bones and Bruises

She stood up next to the table, already shaking from anticipation. Seeing her this way, I thought about how over those early months she had undergone such a transformation. She didn't hold back any more. I kissed her neck and said, "Think of how you have changed." *Shoulder,* "How, because you were a proper, educated feminist," *collar bone,* "you would only say vagina," *lips,* "breasts," *neck* "and penis," *ear lobe* and I whispered into it, "but now it's all pussy, tits and cock."

Shirt off

In those months, the echoes of restraint that kept her hidden at home vanished,

Panties on the floor

they had been silenced.

Crawling on the bed

She, there with me,

Pillows thrown to the floor

bent over on all fours, she trusted that she wouldn't be ridiculed or laughed at for exposing her desire.

Hair covering face

She had gone mad.

Ass pulsing in air

She was ready.

Her right hand finds the warmth between her legs and lingers

"God, I'm so wet," she whispered.

She was pure muscle, wet, and lust.

Rocking ever so slightly on her hands and knees

She was breathing through her yoga poses, Cat then Cow; Earth-heart, trying to find herself in her breath before I took her away.

***

Kat, do you remember? It was like this ... earth-heart, we start there.

When you wait, your torso bends and twists searching for my hands

They find your ass and move with your body.

I am growing, vibrating with the knowledge that I will be spanking you soon.

You know it is coming, because this is what you asked for. Bruises, marks, broken blood-vessel reminders. Something to find in the mirror tomorrow.

I make you wait.

I love to make you wait; I love how I can sense your frustration building as your rocking intensifies.

My hands move, sliding toward the center. My thumbs find your crease and I spread you open so that I can see all of you.

Not too close, just the edge.

I pull apart and release.

I remind myself not to touch between too soon.

I move with you. Your breath guides my hands as it builds.
You force your breath through pursed lips.
You are trying to control it. To hold it.
Trying to use your breath to keep your soul grounded.

She was used to her partners letting her drift. Before all others, she was like a balloon. She'd float away alone, those other men somewhere far away beneath her, further away until she expired; a learned behavior from less passionate couplings.

I held her with my eyes. I called her back when she began to float.

You don't want to drift away too soon.
You want to feel, to remember, all of it.
I move closer, still trying to hold back.
I want to stay here where I can smell the musk of your wet.

My hands trace your lines … slowly. First your edges, from the side of your breast down to the side of your ass. Then from your neck to your spine. Down, to spread your ass: you begin to move faster. I press my hand into the small script tattoo at the base of your spine to center your body. To slow the quakes, my free hand gives you the rhythm. I massage and shake your ass slowly. I take my time spreading and grinding each half, slowly slapping it before I massage and shake it again. I pause to watch you breathe, arms outstretched as if to dive into the headboard, head down, face to the side half-buried in the sheets, performing the Earth-Heart-Fuck pose. I watch you settle into your Anahataasana with a large inhale, and I slap your ass hard to see you smile, to hear the gasp as you exhale. I paw and release. I work here long enough to be sure to leave the bruises you begged for, designed to hold you until our next visit. Your ass pumps with want. My tattoo-covering hand is losing its purchase.

You whisper, "Please, please, I need you in my pussy," and I can see the wet building, hanging from your center, begging to be touched.

With my fingers, I press into your pussy. Circle it, spread it, penetrate it. One, two, three fingers and when my fingers are wet enough, I let one finger stray, tapping against your other entry point. I tap and circle slowly and push in and pull out as I fuck your pussy with my other fingers. Making you wet, wetter, readying your ass for my cock. I relish in how my fingers have disappeared deep in you. Both holes full of me. I hear your breath telling me that you are struggling on the edge of the precipice, and again you say, "Please … I need your cock inside."

You reach back and spread your ass to give access to the tip of my cock. I let it touch slightly, testing again with my fingers, pushing in all the way, fucking you hard and fast with my hand to bring you to the brink. Just then, I slide the tip of my cock inside your waiting ass. I hold it there and check in with you, "Are you OK?" You gasp, "Yes, fuck me, god I love how you fuck me," and I push deeper and deeper. I reach around to pull at your breasts, move to your shoulder, the back of your neck, your hair. I pull your hair and as I pull harder, you turn toward me, and I see your slightly crooked smile pulling to the right. I hold on to the smile for a moment. It is a smile of pure ecstasy that turns to surprise as my cock presses further inside you.

And when I've kissed your neck and pulled your hair enough, I pull out slowly so that I can press the tip inside once again. This act defines us crossing the threshold. I let the tip of my cock cross beyond, then pull it out again, over and over as you twist on your side, waiting to turn over. I make you wait until you cum again and you gasp, "OK, OK," seemingly on the verge of panic, "Please ... I need you in my pussy."

I throw the condom on the floor, and you mount me with tight lips and eyes ablaze. You are on the brink again, falling over, just there. With you still shaking above me, I spread your ass and press my finger inside again. I feel a jolt and I search your eyes. I see that they are wet with monsoon tears. As we cum together, you are shaking and crying. You start to apologize and then you say that you aren't going to apologize for crying. My legs are shaking, me still inside, holding you as you sob into my shoulder. Your tears are mixed with sighs that become a laugh. "It won't stop," you say, your body moving and twisting for minutes over me until your pussy squeezes my now-soft cock out of its home.

She rolled over next to me with her head on my chest and said, "I am too sad to leave. Will you come over tonight? I'll ask M to invite you guys over for dinner."

Tears were welling.

"I don't want to leave yet. Can we stay just a little longer? What time do you have to be home?"

"I told Elle I'd be home around six p.m. Fuck. This sucks."

"I wanted to say something to Elle on our walk today. I almost did. I told her that things weren't going great with M and me and that when we divorce, she would be the only one I'd ever trust with the girls. I couldn't leave them with just anyone."

I tried not to make the questioning face I always made when she spiraled on this subject. No matter how many times we had this discussion, or one like this, I could never convince her that she wasn't abandoning her girls. No matter what I said, she feared that Mike would find a way to keep the girls from her. In her eyes, she would be out, and someone would come in to replace her. She reasoned that she could live with that reality if the replacement were Elle. Elle would understand and wouldn't stand for a mother being kept from her children.

Kat continued, "Do you think they will ever get together? It would make things so much easier. Elle, I could trust her with the girls.

They have to know, right? Everyone knows, don't they? I feel like they have to know."

I recited a quote I'd heard a dozen times: "People see the world according to their own limitations." I stroked her hair for a moment and then continued, "As Mike and Elle often say, we are too much. And we really are. Maybe that's why they can't see us. We live in the clouds. But, any one watching, any one *too much* like us, they know. How could they not? It is always you and me and always M and Elle. But no. They don't know. If they did, we'd never be able to see each other again. He doesn't strike me as the type that's good with sharing. He won't see our relationship as we do, he'll see it as a personal attack."

"You don't think he'll understand?"

"He definitely will not understand. I mean, if he really thought about it, he would see that it makes sense, but he would never allow himself to get there. He won't want to. Where's the benefit for him?"

Kat countered, "But if we could only get them to see that they are better together... During my last trip to Mendocino, I told my mom and my sister about us. I was afraid to tell my mom, but Mary can't keep a secret. I figured that it would be better coming from me. Financial worries aside, she didn't have a negative thing to say about us. She said that she always knew. I didn't give her all of the details, but I did tell her that we are true partners and best friends, that we are in love, soulmate love, but we are having difficulty making the split. Then I said that Elle and M really seem like they hit it off. I added that if we could somehow get them together, they'd see that we could all be happier. She said that she knows a few couples that have swapped. No divorce, no lawyers, no awkwardness. They were just mature about it: 'We belong together, it's obvious, life is too short, let's change things up.' Could we do that? Do you think they would? They really do seem like they belong together. Don't they?"

"They do. But, unless they come to it organically, it won't happen. And at the rate those two moves, it will never happen."

"I don't know. Maybe if I tell her, or if you tell him. Would you talk to him about it?"

"No way. Not happening."

She sighed and smiled a mischievous smile ...

"Do we have time for one more?"

"Time, yes? Can I ... five minutes after I just came? No."

"What if I do this ..."

***

The next day, I wrote this:

Kat,

The magic of bones and bruises and oceans and You.

I am like the bruises I've left on your body: solitary, temporary. Something to be healed from and forgotten when you have settled back into your bones.

The bruises *are* fleeting evidence of something deeper, something permanent we share. They rise as if they've been waiting for me. I believe they have. Your bones know this, for I have felt them shake. But the evidence fades all too quickly, allowing the business of life to twist and obscure the depth and meaning of our connection.

The bruises, I feel I've conjured them, caressed, chanted, begged them to rise. I maintain them as long as I am present. But I am not present often, not often enough.

I am a far-off land. Across a wide ocean. Visited with a love that shakes off the cold, the tired of the usual grind, the consistent grayer existence.

They are loved for the romance of change, a rejuvenating jolt, and temporary danger, but they are never *home*.

And so, the distance of time, of oceans, will cloud sweet memories with the consistent gray, and the letting go of me prevails as the untended bruises fade away in my absence.

There is a price for all magic. Mine is high. In every moment I can feel you in my bones, our potential, and the loss of time-this life slipping.

Anything, always, to be near you and to let you slip away and come back as many times as you will allow.

Because I know, too, the price you would have to pay, and this cost would only tighten our bond. Those that would be left in the wake if you chose to cross that ocean. The guilt you would feel for chasing a dream when others envy you for your reality. I cannot ask that of you despite my selfish rationalizing— the, "this doesn't happen every day," the "the depths of these feelings aren't felt by normal people" (we *are* uniquely fitted, I know this), the, "we lift each other up" - open each other up. I know you feel the true soul magnetism that allows us to hurdle over the gaps in time and life that have kept us apart, the "loving someone as a true equal," not to house each other, but to support one another, wanting to see each other run wild and succeed, challenge the world.

At base, it is a dream. One whose reality would depend on us being enough for each other, because it would be us against the world. In this dream, I would conjure bruises every night, remind you of them every day, curl up next to them and trace them with my kisses, fuck you like tomorrow was not a certainty (we still pretend it is certain, don't we?). Hold on to you as long as you would allow.

Do not worry, I wouldn't worship you, that is too much for anyone to bear, but I would worship what *we* would become. I would tend the fire of our relationship with the passion of a zealot because it would be (it is) sacred.

But the weight of living on an island is too much for many. And I understand the doubt that this creates. But when we fuck, I fuck you like today is our last day, because we *are* running out of life. This is it. The only life we will know. And this is the other side of the price of my magic - feeling the uncertainty of our time in this life. If we had one day, one week, a month, a year, ten years, how would we spend these days?

I have this pseudo-spiritual (bullshit?) thread running through me that haunts. It scratches to get out in my quiet moments, begging me not to leave anything on the table, to wring everything out of this life.

And you. Everything feels different with you. It *is* different. Deeper, wider, brighter, wild, scary, untamable, addicting, uplifting. You would be (are) too much for me to leave behind. So, I will never abandon even the smallest scraps of you that I can gather.

Life changes. And maybe there will be a day that this makes sense. It doesn't now and that is OK. It has to be OK.

I will continue to dream that we will run wild together someday.

And I will conjure bruises, the only fruit of our connection, whenever you allow. I am not going anywhere - not without you, anyway.

Thank you for your manifold gifts, for giving me the courage to be this open with someone, for allowing me to love fearlessly and without shame.

I love you with every fiber of my being.

Xoxo

Kat replied,

I can still smell you and it torments me. I know we are meant for each other; I know this to be true. At times I tell myself that the emotional turmoil would be temporary and in the grander scheme of life, happiness and being with someone who truly sees you and understands you is essential to being. Then the emotional side rips through when I play with the girls and I wonder, for the millionth time, whose happiness is worth more... But wouldn't they benefit if I was a true expression of myself? But what if they didn't and instead were tormented by being brought up in a split family? That is what is in my head, but I never want to say it aloud because then I cry when I just want to be held by you, to kiss and hold you. My desire, yearning, need, whatever this is for you is beyond my control and offers a life of heightened joy. I want to know the potential for love and sex and life with you.

I miss you more than ever. I want to hold your face in my hands and kiss you.

Following Clues: Awkward Hands Inspired

Each time we met, the awareness of our situation, our lack, our need for rain, became apparent. It was as if we flooded the soil all at once and because of drought, it was ill-prepared to hold the water. It didn't satisfy; it made us needy, it reminded us of what it could feel like to be satisfied, it made us hungry for more, it made us angry with life because it showed us that all of this was actually possible. It showed us what we had been missing all these years. And now, walking through our respective doors, crossing the threshold to our others after we fucked our way to and from the cosmos, a kiss on the cheek, smelling like condoms, sweat, and radiating fuck. "How was work, babe?" We hated the lies, our distance, facing our others. And what's more, I discovered that our post-fuck beaming light of joy was contagious. Ill-advisedly, on these post-fuck nights, Kat would nudge Mike to invite us over. She "needed to see me again," she'd say, if only from across the dinner table. She needed to touch my foot under the table "just to see me smile." On these nights I learned that our others could sense our energy. They could smell the pure animal fuck lighting our aura, how Kat walked with a sultry gait, how I smiled at everything, how we even beamed at each other when we should have tried to play it cool. Our world was different and for one night, so was theirs. We'd endure these dangerous nights as best we could. We'd attempt to dodge the falsely buoyed advances of our others. Then, the next day we'd be safe, back to a week of going unnoticed at home, performing our mundane daily rituals with our others until Kat and I met again. On these days and nights spent fucking for hours in poorly lit hotels, when we returned to them, they'd sit closer, place hands on our backs at dinner, lean in to kiss, stare longer as we clinked glasses. They were drawn to us. Then when we found our separate beds, two miles apart, in the pitch of black, under the sheets, their hands would search for us behind a hollow act they used to know.

If Kat could feel the post-fuck awareness at home, she never spoke of it, but I couldn't take it. I needed to tell her that I felt it on all sides, from both Elle and Mike, and it was too much for me. I needed her to know. I needed her to tell me that she'd do what she could not to give in to the awkward hands. I sent this email to Kat:

K,

    I feel like the Others can sense when we've been together. They don't consciously know what is happening, or why, but when we return home now, newly ignited and reeking of unbridled fuck, they can pick up our scent and they are drawn to us.

    I see it when you invite us over after I've been inside you.

    I imagine that the scent we trail is perceptible to the Others, even when we are lying in bed emailing stories and texting odes of love over the two miles that separate our homes.

"Who's that?" he asks, seeing your phone light up again.

"Work," you lie.

"Again? Doesn't any one take a night off?" Preferring that others don't take your time (even if he doesn't want it).

"Almost done," you lie.

"Where did you get those bruises anyway?"

"The girls. Olive scratching at my neck. Oh, and this one ... I tripped on the box of crayons."

I have seen it here and imagine it to be so there.

This scent, however, isn't for them. There was a time when, had they acted, moved, struck, done something, anything before Us, before we knew what we were, we could have found this scent with our Others and let them have everything that came with it, but no more.

They move like mountain climbing tourists, worried, slow, and unsure, but we are Sherpa moving with the mountain, understanding Her winds, Her temperament, Her depths and danger.

We understand the ecstasy of traversing this realm.

But, tourists or no, they have our scent and their lizard brains tell them things their minds can't understand and that ancient primal part of them wants what their conscious mind cannot even conceive.

And they lay quietly in the dark, unmoving, to test the terrain. Will she move to me as she once did? he wonders. And when she doesn't, his hand slides to her side, quietly asking permission. It rests at the hem of her night shirt, knowing what lies beneath. When she doesn't move as she once did, on occasion his hand will "accidentally" glance across her breast, hoping to call her forth, because he knows this still moves her... and depending on the night, she can't pretend that it doesn't.

And when I hope to fall asleep quickly, or breathe so that I appear so, at times her hand falls awkwardly across my chest, quietly asking for permission...

... There have been slips, clues that you have left me to find - the secret code of the unconscious mind - and in these slips you have complained that you've been "left alone again, been overlooked again. Trust me, he doesn't see me," you say.

When you do let these words slip, one might be convinced that you aren't complaining that I am not there with you, but rather, you seem to be complaining that he has missed yet another opportunity, that despite your openness, your moves, the awkwardly sexy way you slink about in the bedtime hours, you still haven't been seen by him.

It is that he has left you alone, again. That he still doesn't see the *opportunity* before him. That is the word, right? Opportunity. And what I hear you saying in this slip is, "I am available, I am here, but I am not being fucked as I should." You aren't saying, "I am alone without you," you are saying, "He is home, and I am naked in bed, but don't worry, he doesn't know what to do with me." A subtle difference, but one worth pointing out.

I know that you are open and free with your body, but it also seems that behind your words you are screaming, "Will he finally get it? How the fuck is he not getting it?"

And because this is so, because I've read the clues – on these nights they smell the fuck and sometimes we let them touch – I don't want to say the words – I can sense how you've wished for him to flip the switch, so that he could suddenly see you with my eyes, hold you with my hands, kiss you with my mouth, and fuck you with my abandon.

I imagine you lying in bed naked, texting me in the dark. His leg reaches toward yours.

And if he falls asleep, you reread the words, the stories, and the poems I have written you, but when he doesn't fall asleep, he can sense the emotion our words have stirred in you and he can sense the changes in your body, the wet that I have made for you. So, he waits for you and when you pause, his hand reaches out...

I have artificially tethered this dance.

We should leave them or stop.

This isn't right. When his words fail to reach you, mine do, and when his eyes fail to see you, mine do, and when his hands, mouth, cock fail to make you feel alive, mine do, but in this half-existence, I am only a balm applied when the days have been too long, or his touch too awkward.

I falsely buoy this dance, this torturous menage-a-trois (a-quatre).

If I weren't here to balance your needs, willing to wait, there would eventually be another Johannes of Edinburgh. There would be someone else to see the flash of life in your eyes, your openness, your moves, your beautifully awkward and sexy way - only this time, Edinburgh would end differently.

You'd fly home thinking about authenticity and openness... you wouldn't tell him what you did, but you'd leave him because you'd feel like a whore, and you'd feel like you had no choice.

But I am here, too close, too open, too understanding, too in love - fulfilling all the needs that he ignores, but, unintentionally, providing you an infinite timeline to come to grips with what to do with your children as we manage our infidelity.

And as you lay in the dark together with the time, I have bought you, he can sense when I have moved you and his hand slides to your nightshirt.

In return, Kat wrote this:

I silently sobbed for the last two hours. I thought of moving downstairs away from M to have space for screams, but I was frozen in place. Tears masking my vision. Sniffles that gave way to empty screams.

Unable to fully appreciate anything because of the guilt, the lies, the falsity of the life I lead. I don't know what I am doing. With you I see passion, life, potential, and I am excitable and passionate but here, here in this house, this gray existence is all I have known. It is what I am used to. Is that a reason to settle?

I am constantly afraid of being unmasked. Exposed. For a fraud. And a liar. A cheater. A whore. A terrible person and horrid mother. I keep saying I need time to think. But the reality is that when I have time, I waste it. I do nothing of worth or value.

And you are right. You are the eyes, the hands, the words, the soul that gives me life. And I am most certainly not worth it. Trust me, says the thief.

You read the world around you with an accurate insight into slight movements and emotions. You deserve more than this double life. You sense the reality of a situation and scene.

Perhaps it is because we lead parallel lives that you capture the heartbreaking chill of my nightly routine. Or perhaps you have a superpower to reach into the depths of my life and draw the misery and hope out of the scene. I am forever indebted to you and your words, your openness. Your hands. Your eyes. Your love.

I feel you as the moon rises. On a chilly night. When the waves reach shore. When I am driving. Reading. Dancing. When I breathe. I feel you in my shaky inhales. You are with me everywhere. We will be together.

I promise.

I love you to my bones.

A Beautiful Cage Indeed

When summer fades in Southern California, it stretches out far and slides into the next, like the shifting dunes just beyond the cities. The desert blends into us such that it is hard to know where the line dividing anything might lie. Like the summer sand, it stretches beyond our line of sight, leaking into months where it has no business – September, October, fading into the feet of November, how the hell is it so miserably hot in November? November was when Kat and Mike moved back into their house, at the end of the never-ending summer, where things were still drying up and baking hard into the ground, when even the thin air, like Kat and me, gasped for something more.

The house was amazing. Shining white stucco, beautifully blended with the existing hundred-year-old windows and doors. Mike did most of the work. His father helped when he could. It wasn't lost on me that as a friend (was I still his friend?), I came over and helped work on the house a few times. I helped them hoist the giant beams that supported the second floor running directly under and over the master bedroom. My gloveless hands unwittingly sent curses and bad blood into the grain of the wood, into the nails, and it crawled into the struts, the drywall, I am the drywall, into the baseboards, the hardwood flooring, and back again. What the fuck was I doing there? ... Fuck, I was in love with his wife, and I was there hammering nails into the cage he designed to keep her.

It was a beautiful cage indeed. It was beautiful and perfect, and a dream come true, a sure sign of Mike's dedication and hard work. All for the family. And it was suffocating Kat. The walls were too clean. Too white. They made Kat's eyes hurt and her brain scream. She liked the unfinished floorboards in the original house, the half-sanded hardwood floors, the quirky cabinets that never closed properly, the old grate in the floor. He liked the new faux Deco fixtures, the perfect edges, the tight seams, the perfectly white stucco that sealed against moisture, and the pristine white walls that told you never to touch. Kat thought, if Ibsen had lived in Southern California, this would have been the house for Helmer and Nora and that hundred-year-old door with the leaded glass would have been the door she slammed. It was true Southern California perfection in Spanish-style architecture. A pristine white box with a sturdy, tight lid. A shining symbol of the nuclear family. Literally built by the hands of a doting husband with dedicated rooms for all. "This room is for the children," he offered. "Kat, this is where you will work," he directed. "I'll be in the garage," he instructed. "After you put the children to bed, we'll sleep here," he might say without any of the innuendo she deserved. The story, the implications, the roles, were all defined by this space, and they seeped into every pore, twisting Kat's mouth hard and tight as she received her obligatory "let's see if we both survive the night" kiss from Mike. It stung her heart as she coldly repeated the words he offered, the words that we both moaned quietly to each other that one night in the front seat of her car.

Our others were the kind of people who, despite their settling, maybe because of the settling, wanted to stay together at all costs. That was what people were supposed to do, right? That was what those gospel doctrines of gender roles and coupling told us to do. Most people know what we are *supposed* to do, but few know what we are supposed to do when our hearts prefer things not wrapped in perfect white boxes. Kat and I knew that we were *supposed* to want the roles our others envisioned for us. Sometimes, early in the morning, all wound up in the love and business of our children, we even wanted to be satisfied by those roles and expectations. The struggle of this duality for us was apparent in our early "I love you and I hate you" foreplay, which meant, "I love you and I can't stop. You have opened a world to me I never knew existed, and now I can't go back, and I hate you because I love you."

I love you. I hate you. We knew that life would have been much less complicated if we could've quietly fulfilled our roles, but we both independently discovered that we felt tied down and held captive by the roles we were forced to assume. We resented that the roles required us to shift how we defined ourselves by what we did to survive. For us, and the ghosts who loved us, these roles in no way defined who we were. The idea alone cheapened life.

The roles took too much from us. We felt the crush of being identified by who paid the mortgage, by the jobs we held, the strain of only being known by our occupation at dinner parties, to talk about them ad-nauseum, and with enthusiasm, because that job is who you are, and fuck, fucking parenting roles, the sacred, inescapable, revered, everything for the children parents, we *are* supposed to be this, right? We want to know who feeds the kids, who folds the laundry while catching up on a TV series, who mends the fences, who straightens the house, who tucks the children in, who washes the dishes, who has the larger bank account.

If our others only knew that there were those that didn't want to *be* their job, that it was possible to love but not be defined by their children, that some of us felt trapped by those expectations, and just to make it through the day, some of us would sometimes attempt to escape those roles. We might wander into a bookstore for a few hours to find a book that imagined a life we weren't brave enough to make on our own. Or we might sink into a bath with thoughts of past lovers until our bodies shriveled and the water turned cold, and the children banged against the door. Or we might jog every morning to the recurring fantasy of running away to Scotland, or sweeping someone away on the handlebars of a bike to laugh uncontrollably. Or perhaps we just sit on our front stoop alone, because we need a moment to cry. I did all of these and more.

Even temporary escape was not something our others seemed to understand. Their default for finding security within a well-defined framework limited their empathy. They knew their roles well. They held tightly to these roles. The roles gave them shape and purpose and allowed them to set boundaries, to find certainty, to build the walls of their doll's houses. If the conversation at a party strayed too far, actually at all, into the provocative, showing even the smallest attempt to really get to know someone ... For example, "Have you read *Tropic of Capricorn*, or *Henry and June*?" Asking, "Do you read, are you a romantic, what are your ideas about love, sex, and marriage? What do you think of freedom, sexual freedom, and equality?" And if one were to form an opinion of these people based on their ability to respond in an open adult dialogue, questioning the systems that had frozen them into mindless creatures only capable of thoughts and memories that captured the headlines of the latest news scroll (because who actually reads the articles?). If one were to balk at their flaccid opinions. "Books? Do people still buy books? Isn't that what our phones are for? And poetry? Corny! Come on, you can't really be into poetry." The scolding eyes of our others would tell us that we had disappointed. The eyes would say what the mouths in the car ride home would repeat.

"Why can't you just be normal?"

"Why can't you just let things go?"

"Do we have to do this every time?"

"The roles are easy; we are our jobs, and we are parents. The end. This is what I am and just in case *you* didn't know it, this is what you are supposed to be. And if you aren't sure about it, you could ask anyone at the party. Just listen, babe. Everyone knows, how is it that you don't? ... (long, awkward, disappointing pause) ..."

"Why ... why do you always do this?"

The boundaries provided by these roles lent a certain type of peace of mind. They certainly provided Mike and Elle that peace of mind. The definitions of each role in their purest versions were the walls that protected them. They helped keep other people out. They helped keep certain people in. They reduced risk. People who bought factory warranties loved this shit. "If your spouse gets out of line, just give us a call, activate your warranty and we'll shame your spouse into becoming the person you always dreamed they'd become when you first married."

Kat and I were not made for warranties. We were romantics, Victorians, dark emo rejects of the late '1970s CBGB, we were the raw power of the MC5, we were of The Lighthouse, of Miller's Tropics, of Nin's Delta.

One day while folding laundry Kat wrote:

Anna Karenina. This was one of my favorite books. I love the copy I have. The smell of old books... I love how we have that in common.

I'm watching the TV series loosely based on Anna and the count. It's awful but it reminds me a bit of us, when you come to the house. The love affair that is almost entirely symbolic and lived out through words, glances, subtle furtive touches. "You deserve to be seen, desired, to live," says the count to Anna. You have said this a few times, what is a life without passion? We are lucky? Fortunate? Destined? To have found each other. To have recognized the potential and unable to suppress the obvious connection. Connection sounds so trivial. Connection, love, these words fail to grasp the entirety of what happens when I see you, feel you, touch you.

Is it strange that I sometimes think of having a baby with you? To be clear, I do not want to have another child. It must be a biological and emotional urge. I was imagining your profile while folding laundry today, watching the show. I imagined that you were watching with me and had your hand on my leg. Running your fingertips up and down my thigh. I love you. I miss you. I feel you. See you. Hear you in the moments in between.

And you are loud.

When you laugh, I feel the deep reverberations ripple through my chest and into my abs, causing me to both laugh in response and immediately need to press myself against you to stop the reverberations or hold onto you before they overtake my entirety. I want to curl up inside the smile lines that frame your jaw and kiss each side slowly to make them part of me.

I don't know what to do with this longing and this frustration. One of these days we should talk. It's hard to give up the few moments we have for that sort of talk... It's not so difficult, I suppose. It just requires strategic maneuvering and stable emotions... the former is not my strong point unless I spend time planning and the latter needs a bit of work...

I think of my lips on your neck just under your ear. I love biting your earlobe and seeing your lips draw into a smile. It does something to me and I just need you inside of me. Something happens to the world when we are joined. It becomes clearer and disappears at the same time. With my hands on your chest, feeling your heartbeat and the pulsing between my legs... it is as close to heaven and Zen as I suppose I will ever get.

I hate when we have to part. There is never any time. I don't even know what we would be like if we had time.

To many more moons...

I love you soooooooo much

K

We were Anna and the count. Both simultaneously. Both not believing in the bonds of marriage, wanting to test, to flirt, and lean into someone (whoever we chose), wanting to be pursued, to be seen in such a way that validates, that amplifies, that fuels dreams and fantasies. Both wishing that we were strong enough earlier in life to consciously recognize what that too-small voice was incessantly chirping in the base of our skulls: "relationships should be earned every day, not guaranteed by a piece of paper, or chained by the specter of children." Like the count and Anna, we both pursued each other because somehow, we managed to hear the other's shriek above the noise of life, of work, friends, husbands, wives, too white walls. So, yes, here in the perfect white box, in the Doll's House, in the presence of our others, we lived in a symbolic state, through subtle words, subtle glances, quiet smiles, furtive touches in the kitchen and under the table. Each time we met in the presence of our others, we proved that we could survive this way for a few hours, in the classically quiet, almost never realized romance that the count and Anna might have recognized as proper love making. A shudder at the touch of an elbow in passing held with a lingering eye, or of a foot under the table, capped with a muted smile. Eventually, however, dinner would end. Mike would tend to the fire pit outside, Elle would begin washing the dishes, I would take my time flipping through Kat's records and she would disappear upstairs. This was when we'd very often, almost always, aim to make Anna and the count blush, this was when we'd venture into the not-so-subtle art of love making and we (de)evolved into pure unadulterated lust.

K: (Photo from their bedroom)

Me: Ugh. You turn me on so much. Shame on you, I am getting hard in mixed company.

K: You do know that I love your cock

Me: When it's in your…
K: Pussy
K: Ass
K: Mouth
K: Against my tits
K: When I feel it between my thighs
K: (Photo)
Me. Fuck
Me: I need you
K: I need to feel your weight upon me
K: Tomorrow morning. Jog. Six-forty-five a.m.

The next morning, I parked about a half mile down the street from their house, just past Twiggs Café, and she jogged to meet me in the backseat where we made the palm trees that lined the streets blush.

We Should Have a Witness

Kat's sister took a temporary job in Fort Bragg and asked Kat to watch her apartment, to water the plants, to check the mail. No one gives up a Pacific Beach beachfront apartment unless they have to. Kat timed watering the flowers and picking up the mail with my schedule and her period. At our Friday night dinners in the Doll's House, in between bites, Kat would say, "I'm running the cliffs tomorrow, what do you guys have going on?"

This was my cue. "Cool, I wish I could do something like that, but I've gotta work. What are you all up to?" I'd ask, nodding toward Mike. "Brewing a beer." Yes, he built houses, worked with wood, and brewed beer. "How 'bout you?" he'd ask Elle. "Sleeping for as long as the kids will let me."

"You guys should come hang out around the firepit tomorrow," he'd add. It never failed. Every time. Every time Kat and I fucked, Elle and I were invited over.

The next morning, I parked on Cass just in front of Leilani's Cafe, reasoning that if I had to run out of either one of the apartment's doors, I could scramble unseen to my car. I walked my 'I am fucking your wife' walk up to the courtyard and I knocked on the door, still imagining Mike might do what I would do if I knew my wife was alone in an empty kid-free apartment. I'd drop the kids off early at the parents and surprise her with a visit. To fuck her in all the rooms and all the ways I couldn't when I lived there surrounded by people. And because I could never quite believe that he couldn't make those sorts of connections, I worried a lot. I'd ask Kat if she thought it was possible that we'd have a visitor. She'd laugh. "Trust me. You have nothing to worry about."

Saturday, seven a.m., shoes, socks, sports bra, yoga pants on the floor next to a huge pink balance ball Mary used while she painted. She threw her arms around me, and I reached behind to spread her ass while we kissed. She was naked and wet and laughing, balancing on her tippy-toes.

"Did you bring me coffee," I asked, not yet letting go.

"I did. I went to Black Market Bakery, we also have a doughnut and a bear claw to share," she added as she led me away from the living room to the futon that she and Mike slept on while he built the Doll's House. We stood in front of the bed and kissed like we did after Soda Bar. It was all mouth and sighs fading into laughs as I pulled her hair behind her ear to find her neck. I licked the salt and bit the bone. I pulled at her ass gently, separating, then diving between.

"I need you inside me." A phrase she repeated frequently, of which I never tired. She dropped on top of the bed, digging the heels of her hands into the uneven mattress, her knees just on the edge, legs forming an uneasy open-ended triangle, and I spanked her hard.

"Fffffuck."

Again.

I worked on her ass to leave the bruises she required. Her pussy was pulsing, dripping, gaping.

"Fuck, god, fuck I love you."

And then I stopped.

"Come here, baby."

She sat up, appearing a little confused.

I led her to the kitchen where the back wall was covered with a giant framed mirror. I've heard that when men enter a room, they often size it up, gauging who they might have to fight, scanning for possible weapons; a beer bottle, a two-by-four, a knife. Me, I never saw enemies nor weapons when I entered a room. I saw potential orgasm landscapes, places I might fuck, or should, or if the timing were right, where I could: a couch, a balance ball, an ottoman, a handmade wooden dresser, a vintage coffee table, a rug, my rug, her kitchen, her staircase, her mouth, her tiny, pointed tits. And after many dinners at Mary's, I had imagined a plan, I dreamed a dream, to fuck her right there in front of the mirror and there I was naked standing on the filthy sand-splattered linoleum floor of Mary's Pacific Beach kitchen with Mary's sister, Mike's wife, Elle's friend, my lover.

I felt like a wrecker of worlds. A goddamn motherfucking manifester of fuck, but it was she who invited me in; my kind cannot cross the threshold without invitation. She invited me in and fell before my cock; and now, in this kitchen, in this mirror, her legs spread, her back arched, shoulders bent up to the ceiling, her hands to the sky holding on to the edge of the mirror where I searched for us, I only saw Kat, her eyes burning into the mirror.

Her hands twitched on the edge of the frame, and she arched her back to give me better access. Her pussy was ready, still wet from being bent over and fingered on her temporary marriage bed. I slid into her slow and steady, pulling out just as the head of the tip crossed the threshold, repeating over and over as I found her eyes in the mirror and when I did, we connected, and she rattled with shivering quakes. She dropped her head, letting her hair hang about her face as I fucked her hard through the convulsions. And when she was done, "Wait, wait, wait. Fuck. Wait," I stopped and slid her to the left so that she could rest her body over the sink where just two months before, I washed her birthday dishes and fantasized about eating her out on the floor. I waited, breathed, and then I started over, the tip crossing the threshold, then out, then I waited, then I counted to three, then I crossed again, counted to three and waited for her ass to meet me and when it did, I slowly buried my cock deep inside her. She let out a full moan. My release was kept at bay when I realized that the kitchen window over the sink was wide open. I could hear the neighbors next door talking, others maneuvering for parking across the street, I could see the neighbors in the apartment opposite us in front of their window washing their dishes, I could hear them clink, and I could hear Kat's moans reaching the alley across the street echoing back to me and I pulled her hair to arch her further, to deepen her moans, to settle all the way inside. I held for a second, two, three, four. She was trying to move – wait, wait, and I pulled her hair, thrusting, my hand pressing down over her tattoo – Queen, Kept Woman – and I held until we came together.

***

That night, as I sat around the fire with Mike, Elle and Kat, sipping beer, half-listening to stories about work, I wrote her this:

The Mirror

I waited to find your eyes
In the mirror
And I found them
Peeking through your hair
Mouth agape
As I drove into you again
And again
Your hands searching
The mirror
The kitchen sink
Your head bowed down
Between your arms
Feeling me drive deeper
My hands in your hair
Pulling back to reveal your neck
Your mouth
Your breasts as you arched back
I pull harder and see your form
Outlined in the mirror
And I slap your ass
I had to punish you
To thank you
For making me love you
Like I do
I saw you smile
As I left my mark

The sky was blue
No clouds on the horizon
The windows were open
In the apartment
Across the street
I hope the neighbors
Heard us
As you gasped and moaned
As we came together.
The way we fuck
There should be witnesses

Trying to Set Boundaries

After Kat shook the mirror and we defiled Mary's kitchen, I was feeling our pull more than ever. I was struggling with our double life. I asked Kat to meet me at Live Wire. Five p.m. on a Tuesday was a good day to "work late." As soon as our IPAs were poured, I rambled the ramble that I had been holding in my head, that I wrote out in my journal so that I wouldn't stammer and forget. I stared at the floor, my hands, the jukebox, my beer, and then I finally read the words.

"I have been thinking about what I should say, what I would say if I wasn't a coward, what I would say if I weren't a total fool. I can imagine you writing your last email. Your beautiful description of a morning with me, met with the reality of duty and tiny feet… I want to tell you that this is over. That we cannot do this any more. Not because I feel guilty, but because this isn't what I intended. I don't have an exit plan for imagining everyday with you, only to never know when we will live that reality. I kick myself for letting it get this far without having an exit plan."

I went off script and stammered, "I don't know… everything is hitting me right now. All I can say is that you affect me. You always have."

Back to the words on the page: "You are my plan. This is it. Me and you. I love you. Help me figure this out. What are we doing? We have lived in tiny moments. Dangerous moments. Dangerous because they allowed me to see what I guessed to be true: there is even more behind the veil. And I fell. I lost myself in the range of our possibilities and I dreamed and daydreamed and cried in my car and in my bed and in the shower. And yes, I hear the pitter patter of the feet behind the words in your email, but you do know children can survive this, right? I know that on a long enough timeline, we are in danger, I will ruin it, we will ruin each other. How do we survive this?

I am sure that I will be a coward and do nothing, just as I've done every time. I am sure that I will go on living by nightly text messages, emails, and the occasional clandestine meeting and hope that an answer comes to us. It is painfully obvious that there are these few choices: do nothing and die daily to be reborn each day by text message, pretend that this is just for sex when it isn't, end it by ending it, or end it by telling the world. As you know, I want to tell the world. I am ready, but I am scared. I want to be brave, and I rationalize being with you because when given this opportunity, shouldn't we pursue true love? That is what this is. We've said the words, felt the magnetism of our pull even miles apart at night, we've destroyed the world and rebuilt it as you shook over my cock. I want to tell the world right now. So, I want to end it. But I can't... fuck."

She thanked me for being strong.

"I just need time. I am finding my way. If it is up to me, I would keep us. What we have is worth it. I don't want to lose you. I just need time. I need to move the conversations from my head to my mouth. I need to tell him. I will find a way. We will be together. I love you so much."

You are the Storm

Say Yes to this Harvest Moon

Elle and I had our patterns. We were like a doomed math sequence: one discussion gave us two emails which gave us one fight which produced three weeks of awkward 'working at it' and four weeks of not working at it while wondering what the hell we were doing, and seven weeks of silence and waiting before I sent another email listing the eleven opportunities we missed, the eighteen ways I tried and the talk that followed that squeezed out another twenty-nine tears because she "just can't do this any more" and in the end we'd do nothing about any of it, for the sake of the pattern, so that it could repeat. It was brutal soul-crushing math.

Kat and I also had a pattern: we were pure Fibonacci, starting small and spiraling out into infinity. Everything was amazing, but at every quarter turn I'd email Kat, upset about our timeline and how we kicked the can down the road again. Originally, Kat had a painfully slow plan that never really materialized. Before I came along, to fulfill her duty, Kat used to try to close the gap in Mike's natural and manipulative distance. She'd attempt to soothe him during the day, to manufacture connection when he was awkward and moody, and then in the night, he'd wait for her to entice and instigate, to go to him, to prove to him… and she would. Now, however, she reasoned that if she just held back (holidays and birthdays excluded), if she just stopped reaching out to fill the gaps he manufactured, that he'd feel the growing distance and end it.

"We are all wrong. There is nothing between us any more. It is hard to even be in that house," she'd say. "I feel like *he* may end it soon," she'd say. Somewhere between all of these words, I'd peek through the cracks to find the truth. This was her fucking plan. A painfully slow, guilt-free exit. All so that she'd be able to say, 'he did it.' For once, it wouldn't have to be her. She wouldn't be the cause of the pain.

Fibonacci spiraling, I'd email about the can we kicked, and she'd respond by booking a hotel room to make it up to me. The email was the marker on the spiral and the hotel gave us the momentum we needed to throw us further into space. We'd stand in front of the stock hotel art and the egg-shell bureau kissing naked and wild, both marveling at our reflection because we were too much, and we loved it. I'd lay her down on the bed and kiss my way from her neck to her tiny breast to her belly. I'd settle between her legs, and she'd cry as she orgasmed from the too much of it all and we'd fall into each other's arms and lay there naked and panting. Then as we'd talk, she'd cry again, feeling the weight of her Doll's House upon her. And cry again because we were too much to lose. And again, we'd fuck because she would soon have to go home to be the plastic figurine, the robot mother, wife, automaton.

***

On this latest '*trying to set boundaries*' hotel stay, we were both feeling it. She couldn't get out of the bed. She was naked and curled up. I could see her back muscles tensing up as the tears fell. I was already late. We held each other. Cried. Kissed and cried some more. I should have been on my way home ten minutes ago. She was sobbing into the pillow telling me to go. I fucking hated this. I had to go. I had run out time and my eyes were stinging with the lies I would have to tell and the truth that lay before me in wet sobs. I left in tears and wrote this parked in front of my house:

Your tears...

I will never forget holding you in that moment for the rest of my life. We are bonded forever. You are mine and I am yours. I am tearing up now thinking about you laying there twisted up on the edge of the bed trying to hold it in so that I'd give myself permission to leave.

It took all of my power to leave at all. I hate that we had to part. I hate that we ever have to part. I wish I could have stayed longer, if only to hold you. Until tomorrow, my love.

And the next morning we met, like every other time: hotel in the evening, home to a night in bed with our others, then again in the morning where we pretended that we never left each other.

Hotel rooms are portals to another world. Walk into a hotel room, close the door and the curtains and you could be anywhere. When we'd meet in the morning, Kat and I would imagine ourselves anywhere but here in San Diego where we'd have to explain ourselves. We were everywhere... anywhere: we were in Barcelona, Paris, Venice. It didn't matter because we created the mood of the space. As soon as I'd walk in the door, we'd hurriedly and excitedly undress and jump into bed. We'd lay there with our eyes closed holding each other, her arm and her head on my chest, and we'd pretend that we woke to find each other this way. There was coffee, croissants, and laughter. The mornings were sacred and somehow lighter than our afternoon and evening meetings where we tore each other apart and shed our skins. In the mornings we were giggles and laughter, we were silly and playful. God, how we loved being silly, how we loved pretending.

Later that night, she wrote me this:

Sometimes I call you the storm

Because of the unpredictable strength

And pull you have on me.

I love storms.

My fondest, most reflective and transformative moments have been during storms.

They affect me as you do.

Once, I was home alone in Minneapolis masturbating in my room. I remember lying on my bed. My knees were up. My legs were spread open to my closet mirror toward a curtainless window. As I touched myself, I would stare out at the trees and see them bend with the wind.

As I did, the clouds darkened my room.

I turned my light on to watch myself in the mirror.

As I was getting wetter, I could feel the weather change. It was like a tornado was coming; the wind was now howling, but I didn't stop touching myself. I was losing myself to the wind.

The strength of the wind blew the screens out of the windows and the trees were leaning sideways and I kept touching myself.

My hips were lifting off my bed as my light flickered off, and when I released and came back to consciousness...

I just rocked and moved with the wind and bent like the tree outside my window. It was amazing.

I came harder than I ever had before, or since, until I met you.

I remember feeling how wet my fingers were as the rain pelted the windows.

The wind became a tornado that came in with such a force, as though to cleanse the space.

I have moments of clarity and strength when storms pass through.

Moving to San Diego may have been a mistake for me because we so rarely get storms.

Rarely, until we happened.

Last night I tossed and turned as the winds picked up and I wondered how the palms stay rooted even when they look like they are about to snap.

The hail scratched at the house and bounced in the street.

The wind blew a little, but it didn't feel like a cleansing storm.

It was angry but there was no release, no sigh afterwards.

It just stopped.

I wished for a snow storm, like those in Minnesota.

You remind me of the wind and the snow.

Snow is remarkably loud as it falls through the trees.

And when it is finished,

The world has never seen such silence.

Then I wished for a thunderstorm.

For the wet suffocating humidity.

Then you.

San Diego has no storms such as these.

Except for you.

You are my storm.

Comforting and refreshing and cleansing and unpredictable and a release like no other.

You are storm. A rebirth.

I read this, thinking of Kat fucking herself, fisting herself in front of that mirror, in front of that uncovered window. I thought of her love of storms and how the storm less San Diego, with its level days of bland consistent weather, reminded me of her relationship with Mike and mine with Elle. We were both storms. Later that night, our families walked together around South Park. We had beer and lemonade, and fried tots at the Station and then chocolate and chocolate milk at Eclipse. We all sat and laughed and played like the strange, blended family Kat wished we would all become. As the day was starting to fade, I announced that I had an art show I wanted to see. Kat said she'd like to see the show, too. No one protested. It was at a tiny gallery called Teros that specialized in local filth. We lingered and leered at the shapes on the walls, drifting, holding hands, contemplating infinity, pretending we were what we appeared to be as we spoke with the gallery owner and the artist.

After we parted, she sent me a message. She asked if could write her a poem. I wrote her this:

To Quiet the Storm that Blew Through the Door

you held your ground
hard shiny rock
edges turned up ~
what metamorphosis
could mold such angles?
this earth
holding on to the beacon
someone
erected to save you.
someone
send warning
a storm is coming.
has arrived.
this wind breathes hard like a lover
and sends waves and pulses
to beat against your breast
losing its brine upon your shore ~
breathing.
to crash
to spit its frenzy upon the earth
to lurch in
and reclaim its birthright
its soft earth
to take it back to the depths of the sea
to let it feel the sea as it once did
in days before this life ~
to show what it had forgotten in those long days
when it tried to hold…
too tightly to that light.

to let it feel the sea
naked
and calm
and quiet beneath the waves.

We wove in and out of our depths, not knowing how to deal with it all, feeling our pull was inevitable, unstoppable, unquestionable. Hearing all the small voices chirping in our heads and still trying to find ourselves holding on to whoever we thought we were beneath that faint but sure center hiding in the darkest pit of our mind, we knew we were destined to be together; we just couldn't figure out how to make it so.

When we do it... when we stop telling lies... what are you going to say?

I think we should keep it focused on ourselves. They don't have to know that we were already together. When we are together it will make sense, but there is no need to tell them that right away.

Right. We say our words, move out. Separately. Then we appear to find each other.

We are undeniable. Us finding each other will make sense.

The shitty thing is, we were cowards. We should have broken it off before we did this.

We were going to, right? But we were able to buy some time with our kids.

And we do love our others.

But we belong together.

What if you are asked to work it out?

Trust me, he will not want to work it out.

But if you are.

I won't do it. I can't. I can't do it.

I know that it is you and me, but saying 'No' to his face will be hard. You should prepare.

I know. I am practicing the words. I know who I want to be, and I can't be that person with him. It is for me. That is what we need to say. It is what I need to say. I don't want to hurt him. I don't want him to know that I have been lying to him this long.

Of course, this isn't about jumping from one person to another, this is about us. What else is there? And yeah, I don't want to hurt either of them.

What if you are asked?

She asked if I wanted an open relationship.

What? That is crazy. What did you say?

Uh, I don't know.

Did you say yes?

What? No, of course not. Something like, it is too late. I didn't know what to say, other than to say that it was never about sex. What I wanted to say was, I am not looking to fuck; I want to be appreciated, not ignored or demonized. I am looking for what I have with Kat, but of course I didn't mention you. I mean, it would be easier if I could say that it's about what I've found with you. This is it. It is all I've ever wanted. More. It is more than I could have imagined. An open relationship? It isn't about sex, it is about being open and honest with someone and baring your soul to someone and having no fear, no shame, no regrets, and p.s. that just happens to make for amazing sex, but yeah, it is hard. Like we've said, it would be easier if they could be who we need. They just aren't those people. We will be the villains for a

137

little while, but really, we aren't. We are doing something very difficult that shouldn't be this fucking hard. We are choosing to right ourselves so that we can be one-hundred percent of ourselves always, with our kids, with everyone, in all of our relationships, and we were lucky enough to have found each other when we were deciding to make that choice. We will always have each other.

Later that night, after journaling my thoughts, I sent this letter to Kat:

K,

To start again...

It is hard imagining all of the turmoil we would cause, but that is in part because we are trained to view love and relationships through a binary lens based on old fashioned ideas about who and how husbands and wives should be, ideals handed down to scrub the humanity from fathers and mothers, to keep us in those roles, to keep us from who we might become.

But we, you and I, are not binary. We are reimagining our lives every time we speak to each other, every time we see each other. And no, it isn't fair - none of it is fair.

It is difficult to think about what is fair, the trouble telling the world about us would cause, but isn't it more difficult to live a passionless life of "good enough?" Isn't it more difficult to spend our days dreaming and imagining how we'd be together in between the spaces of our stilted interactions with our others?

I know that our others are the innocent victims who never asked for this. We know this and have respected each other's space. But, in order to answer your email, I have to violate this unspoken treaty.

Thinking about the "consistent gray," I can't help but think about a line I've heard spoken proudly a few times by your Other, to paraphrase: "Gummy worms aside, in all of our time together, we have never gotten into a fight."

On the surface, that sounds lovely. Who wants to fight? I know that Elle would love this because she craves the smooth middle of everything. Nothing too high, nothing too low, staying away from the dangerous edges of life. But, for me, that is a life without color or texture. It is a fantasy created by those that made our masks—if you don't smile too hard, cry too much, or furrow your brow you won't shatter the illusion of the mask. It will stay in place as intended.

That comment, "we've never gotten into a fight," I always thought it a strange thing to be proud of. Does he not see that it stinks with a lack of passion? The stagnant swamp water settling and rotting in the smooth uneventful middle of life? One must care about something to fight. There must be passion. And, if there has never been a passion-fueled argument, this is evidence of a life in purgatory, being sentenced to an "OK existence"—the lows are not very low, but the highs aren't any higher than the middle you already have.

I know that you and I would argue. Surely, we would (we already do, don't we? Our passion for everything aligns us). If we were a real, out in the open couple, our arguments would be a beautiful sign of our strength, a sign of both our passion and trust.

To speak, to be heard, to be understood, to be validated and to have make-up sex—to fuck like today is our last day (or our first day), because as life would have it, and if we are lucky

139

enough, we will again argue and grow, shed another skin, become new again unto each other and the next time we fuck, it will be a new day and perhaps our last in that skin.

And I know it's fucked up to say, but this living a passionless coupled life, to me, is a sad waste of two lives, or four in our case.

So, when you ask about what is fair, I think about this. About living out my days holding back, pretending that I can hold all of this in. Pretending that when I snap at someone or pick a meaningless fight, that it has nothing to do with me trying to hold everything in for everyone else. I think about how long I can do this before I have to vent.

I think about you and your four-year cycles. Your need for some version of a girls' night out away from M. How you need time away from the roles you play to re-energize your spirit, to give yourself the energy to put those masks back on the next day.

Then I think about how these things, the cycles, the nights out blowing off steam, the holding in, they are only necessary because you aren't being true to yourself, because you have not selected a life in line with your needs, wants, and desires (with your Spirit). You have selected based on a false reality for a system that, when asked, we would both outright reject.

Don't worry, I am not suggesting that you wouldn't need a vacation from me or time away, you would and should have that, we both should…

I am moody and would need space as well; however, our time apart would not be to rekindle a spark of life that was being choked out daily. It would be to grow and spread the flames that we have helped each other maintain during the gray of life.

Perhaps, right now, I am your new harvest moon. And if I

am, and you are on that hill looking up at the moon, would you right now, in this life, choose to stay in Minnesota or would you throw caution to the wind to chase a dream in New York?

Your past...

Leaving for New York didn't end your life or your relationships, it enhanced them. Who would you be now if you didn't make that choice?

Your present...

Who have you been since your return? Are you, as Mike put it, a busy teacher, mother, wife, homemaker? Or are you the person I see: a person that wears those masks at times, perhaps a person that has worn them for so long that you have forgotten the person beneath the mask, despite the fact that you only agreed to wear them now and again in order to access the deeper pleasures in life?

Your future...

Who would you become? Who, if the role was not thrust upon you? Who, if Hercules hadn't tricked you into once again holding up the world, who would you choose to become?

Would you say yes to a second harvest moon?

Ultimately, I have no right to say this, but I don't want to sleep with her, and I don't want you to sleep with him. I can bear it, but I don't want to, it doesn't feel right. It isn't right. We are no longer cheating on them; we are cheating on each other.

But don't worry, I know where we are, I know that I can't insist on this. I know that, because of our secret, we have to continue playing our roles.

Overall, life is short, and I don't want to squander our potential. I want to say yes to the moon.

I want to read poetry to you while you take a bath.

I want to cook with you.

I want to fight with you and have make-up sex with you.

I want to sleep in the desert with you.

I want to feel you fall asleep on top of me and find you still there in the morning.

I want to seduce you while you read.

I want to talk about books with you.

I want to be able to touch you gently and lovingly when you walk by.

I want to whisper to you (in a room full of people) that I love you, that when these people leave, we are going to fuck on the floor.

I want nights of trying to fulfill all of your fantasies.

I want the freedom to guess at them.

I want to explore who we are together, find our furthest edges.

I want to watch movies with you, tangled up and twisted together.

I want to buy you a new toy, so that when I am not with you, you will think of me.

I want to say your name aloud the way I hear it in my head - full of love, desire, and passion.

Make a travel book of our exploits.

Find a place to rent to live out our cabin fantasies.

Buy you sexy lingerie.

Drink whisky with you while we read silently together.

Laugh in bed with you after you orgasm.

I want an anniversary with you – every August 27, into the small hours of the 28th, we'd lay in bed and watch Casablanca in the nude.

I want to get high with you and fuck under the stars at the headlands.

I want to dance with you.

To be the new harvest moon, Kat's symbol of change, her symbol of life beyond the ordinary, beyond suburbia, that which allowed her to envision escape from her narcissistic mother, and her hopelessly drug-daze-dysfunctional father, and her too young to be anything to hold her there in the Midwest sister. And now, to be that motivating symbol which allowed her to envision life beyond suburbia in Minnesota, to be that which allowed her to run to NYU where she believed she became her true self; where she insisted, she found authenticity, the self she still remembered when she locked the doors on her San Diego suburban home and poured herself a dram of Ardbeg while listening to the Ramones. Wouldn't she now, while the moon was asking, choose authenticity and escape her Doll's House?

The spirit of this and every new harvest moon was what Kat tried to capture in her four-year escape cycle. It told her to pack a bag and run, to get the fuck out of Dodge, to slam the goddamn motherfucking door and not look back. It told her to never apologize for refusing the bridle. To wrestle. To bite. To spit it out and kick a motherfucker in the goddamn balls for trying to throw the bridle over her head at all. It told her that she would not be caged.

And I was there, a new harvest moon. I was rising over the mountains on the edge of the desert, over a long straight black asphalt road all wide-eyed, moon-eyed-roadkill, over a carport, popup tents, vinyl floaties, a pool, and a jacuzzi in a house that we rented for my birthday in Palm Springs.

Road Kill Baby

We cut through the back side of San Jacinto on the 111 where the valley funnels southbound winds through giant Quixotic-three-armed-generators who push the winds out to the Salton Sea. Elle behind the wheel and our two kids lost somewhere between their headphones, and all I could do was think of how to manufacture time alone with Kat in our looming shared space. I was the Wastes and the winds and the dust-devils. I thought of us and how our time was running out, how I was the faceless coyote carcass on the side of the highway, and how these winds moved through the valley to wring the salt from the man-made irrigation mistake that shaped this sea just south of heaven, just south of Movie Colony, where even the stars had withered. It *was* there. It wasn't a false oasis, there was water, but it was false all the same.

Just south of this withering colony, salt and salted bones decorated the shore of a withered sea and they crackled like tin foil and grinding teeth. In days past, the salt choked the fish who turned up gray-eyed with their bloated and floating bellies, who were later torn open by the sun and pecked by flies who buried their maggots among their flesh. They decorated this shore with their thousand ten-fold ghosts telling you to find more fertile waters. This cunt valley squatted and dripped its toxic irrigation runoff between San Jacinto and Joshua Tree, and it ended at this wet sun-bleached underside. I laughed thinking of soccer moms and strippers paying for their bleachings for anniversary surprises and scattered one-dollar tips, and I thought, we are driving just upwind from the stinking sea of dying dreams where Sea View Avenue and Sea Mist Place wind through fantasies never realized, through undeveloped lots and trailer park hookup stations where you flex-hose your very own excrement into the earth, how the Valley ends here in a forest of rusted metal-sided motorhomes littered with gardens of gutted cars, the last refuge for five hundred off-the-grid hippies that drive down from Canada to dry-winter at Bombay Beach, and I thought I could live there, just south of heaven, in the filth and the stink and the rot as long as I had Kat.

In the blistering air conditioning, under the spell of five lagers, we ate and charcuteried and swam and when I wasn't surveying each room's orgasm potential, I set my sights on finding all of the other misfit toys of the desert. I exchanged underwater hard-ons for a trip to the record store. I decided it was time for an adventure. I wanted to get out of the house. In my usual way, I asked the gang: Kat, Mike, Elle, the kids, everyone, any one, I didn't care. I just wanted to go rummage about. I had a mind to look for some vinyl and this desert, this false oasis of modernity clothed in tan stucco, where the inhabitants busied themselves filling their specific lacks with New, was ripe for picking. Scotch was out for seltzer, tits out for silicon, wrinkles out for Botox, and vinyl and turntables out for streaming media. Here in this extreme heat, they didn't have time for appreciating the old ways, they were trying to stave off death because everything here was literally dying. Feeling the pull toward the center of the earth, they tossed aside the old ways as if this would buy them more time on earth. They tossed aside everything I treasured. I was pilgrim of the underappreciated, the desert romantic, disciple to the complicated, host carcass to anachronistic thrift-store effluvia. The stylized excess of it all, the too much of it, it reminded me of us.

Gin Ricky's, a Tom Collins, cold metal cups decorated with stars and metal straws and horses, and seagulls; a flat black tie under a perfect white collar, an old fashioned (no sugar), a godfather (light on the Amaretto) with a burnt twist of orange, a plastic flamingo, and a beautiful and outdated silver-blue gown matched with pearls packaged at a discount, grifted from a long dead vogue who never really knew what she had, don't you know, no one wears pearls any longer; a clutch with a ghost, a ring with a curse, a lawn jockey with a wink and a lantern, a paper umbrella and a slice of pineapple that served to hide the eighty proof; a cookie cutter in the shape of a cock and balls for those bachelorette parties; a coffee mug with 'Norma' glazed in its skin; a glazed doughnut, I felt like a glazed doughnut all air and nothing and sweet and then gone, almost entirely forgotten once out of sight, all forgotten but what you left on the corner of your smile; an uncut Caesar salad with the goddamn anchovies, a baked Alaska, a blue-cheese olive, no two olives, pierced in a glass of Boodles London Dry; and records, Stevie and Tom: 'Stop Draggin' My Heart Around', all Needles and Pins; and Iggy the Idiot; and Frank, and Dean, and Sammy, all of the Seven Hoods; Louis Prima, and Keely, and Sam – 'I've Got You Under My Skin baby, I can't let you go'; Masekela, and Kuti—that Afro-jazz that made me move, that made me want to fuck, fuck her right there in the kitchen in front of everyone, and Nothing, NOTHING was fucking trivial. In this space, too much did not exist.

I flashed to Mike and Kat, and thought of how he was like

the Palm Springs residents, unable to see the magic in all those little things I adored, all the things he had spread open before him all these years. Like all these desert residents, he wanted other than what he had, he wanted clean lines, he wanted order, he wanted Eve, or Kat like Eve (maybe Elle), guilted into biblical submission, he wanted someone on the hook for the Fall so that he could guilt her into submission, he wanted someone who knew how to manage the smooth middle of life, but Kat, my desert find, was wild, she was Lilith.

"Kat, are you sure you can come with me?" I asked. "He did not look happy."

She twisted up her face, looking annoyed with me for the inquiry. "I can do what I want."

We drove south down the 111 toward the sea that haunted me (the only recognized water feature of the Lost Soul Tribe). As I drove, I found her mischievous smile, then I watched her hands hike up her skirt. My right hand made her naked thigh its home. I tugged and pulled at her skin. She took my hint and pulled her dress higher and higher until she uncovered her naked mound. She smiled as she rested the tips of her fingers over her clit.

"No panties?" I asked jokingly.

"Nope."

In any other scenario, the stop light would have been painfully long. It showed no sign of changing and I was thankful. I was delighted by seeing her pussy this way in my car. I whispered, "Put them inside." She looked to her right and checked a large pickup truck and a goatee looking back at her. He spied her pouting face made for lollipops and throbbing cocks and she turned back to me with wet full eyes to ask permission. I nodded. Her legs spread wider, and she moved her hand south to dive into her folds.

Green light. Fuck. I had never been so disappointed in a green light.

I drove.

She fucked her pussy.

For miles as I drove, she fucked that pussy right there in my passenger seat. Her right leg tilted toward the door ever so slightly, her left knee pressed against the center console, and my hand held that knee steady as I drove. Her long black skirt was pulled up to her waist and she started laughing as her fingers dove deeper. "God, I'm so wet." It was almost comical how her wet never failed to amaze her.

She made herself wetter for miles until I parked, until we threw ourselves in the backseat, until my jeans found my ankles, until she hiked her dress up and spread her legs over my pulsing cock, until I pulled at her top to kiss the pink. When I was inside, we held still for a moment. In. Deep. Deeper. I grabbed her ass with both hands. She moved with me like a belly dancer. Her full wet cunt ground my cock like the boots on the fish bones of that southern sea. Until I crumbled under her grinding mound. Until I melted into her nipples, until we dripped sweat and tears, until she shivered cold, cold stinging sweat over my cock, until my cock cried into her cunt, until we both burned up in the car from trying to hold back. This was how we waited for Dale's to open at three, Kat telling me to cum inside her, me asking her if I could, she telling me, "Yes, please, please, cum inside me, cum inside me." I said some ridiculous shit, "Let me cum in you and make you mine," and she cried again, panting, "Yes, yes, make me yours, I fucking love you, cum inside me, please cum in me and make me yours."

And I did. I held her arms steady, and we stared into each other's eyes as we panted short dry breaths until we returned to our bodies.

Eyes still wet with tears, our bodies still dripping with sweat and cum, we walked the aisles at Dale's like lover whores who just got their fix, twisted up together like high school sweethearts, arm in arm, moving as one, never letting go. We waded out far into this new secret space, letting it mark us as we marked it; this place was now sacred. We let this moment sink in as we drifted out too long into the mirage, far into the void of love. There was the hum of a needle in a run-in groove, the smell of leather jackets hanging in the back awash with the vanillin decay that gave old record sleeves and old books their intoxicating scent. My right arm was locked with hers behind my body, her hips pressed into my ass, her left hand wrapped around my waist, her head nuzzled into my back, my hips leaned into the wooden shelf. My free hand dug through 'Patti Smith.' I could see us from above as if in a dream and it was beautiful and silly and romantic, and we couldn't stop. I had to wonder what Dale might have thought of us and just then the turntable needle popped to the sound of Petty's 'Wildflowers' and as she heard the tune, she climbed my back. I could just see her smile over my right shoulder. I kissed her cheek and she softly whispered in my ear, "You are dripping down my leg. God, I love you."

Book II

A Different Beginning

A Snow Moon and Cocaine Kids

My band was booked to play a desert rave in the middle of nowhere, in the middle of Ocotillo, just south of the interstate, so close to Mexicali that the city's one million low volt lights shined to outline the southern side of the wash just as the sun dove behind the dunes to the west. We were drunk and high, playing with fire that shot out of a stack of pallets, sucking on the fumes of motorcycle tailpipes that tore through the camp, the scent of those tailpipes flooding in awkward adolescent visions. I felt like I was fifteen years old wading in the wake of a billowing school bus, feeling aroused by the toxic and intoxicating exhaust. This was where I met Elle. She and I were surrounded by that exhaust in a forest of tall spiny cacti that wound out of the ground pointing, bending, searching for flesh to tear, seeking saviors to crown. I heard that they bloomed beautifully, but in all my years of living in the southern Californian desert, I've never seen them bloom.

Elle watched from the edge of the fire. She was beautiful, tall, her long dark hair framing dark almond eyes, tight blue-jeans, black top surprisingly full, bright red lipstick, pushing goth-chick vibes hard, full on Depeche Mode, OMD, Robert Smith groupie. She wasn't like the others, not like those tailpipe junkies and motorcycle groupies who wore their flat-brimmed trucker hats like east-county tiaras. She was beautiful, and seemingly unphased at not fitting in at all. I liked this about her. She was holding a red Solo cup watching me, watching the band. I spit ten songs into the mic as I bled pure fury twenty-something-angst down my bass. The set climaxed as I drifted on the fringe of the fire and blew Southern Comfort into the flames, all emo and spent, kicking checkered Vans into the dirt, eyes following jackrabbit tracks and fire-storm cinders. She told me that a guy at work gave her a flyer. She had nothing better to do, she said. She didn't normally do this sort of thing, she said. We leaned against a car and held praying hands to our Solo cups, staring at the flames, watching its smoke disappear into the sky.

I told her it was called the Snow Moon, hanging one hand from my pocket, pointing to the sky, knowing just how corny it was that I was obsessed with the moon. It was huge as it moved over the dunes, glowing with the most intoxicating pale blue-white light. We watched it move quickly over the sky and seemingly shrink, as coked-out kids on motorcycles used the parked cars like a slalom course. The crowd was moving in to inhale the exhaust, eager to see someone either make it, or not, over the jump positioned in front of the bonfire. Elle and I linked our hands to follow the moon, to move beyond the motorcycles, the lights, the rising cinders, and the cocaine kids.

"Snow Moon?" she asked.

"It's a funny name for a moon in a desert," she said with a laugh.

"It is."

That moon was named in some other land for a phenomenon never realized in the desert. It taunted the desert with its namesake, with its cold true meaning, which was found far, far away in someone else's droughtless reality. To other people far beyond these ridiculous thorns, these deep and sprawling dunes, these dry, dry washes, and these blistering highways, its name hearkened weather for a season we did not know here; here we didn't have seasons, we had the heat of need, desire, and want spoiling and churning into lack.

"Is there a bathroom around here?" she asked, tipping the bottom of her red cup to the moon.
I laughed. "You're standing on it." My red cup gestured to the sand, the Jesus Christ bushes of thorns, the car tires.
    "Come on! Seriously?"
    We kissed under that taunting, shrinking moon, and left the desert in the early morning to lay in our own beds. We soon found each other back in San Diego and quickly became inseparable. We'd walk to Rolberto's to split rolled tacos, or to the Ken Club where she'd order a vodka tonic and me a Guinness. We'd play pinball and Ms. Pac-Man and I'd stand too close behind her so I could whisper in her ear as she pressed the paddles and worked the joystick while I worked my cock into her jeans, hand sliding up to find her breast. We'd walk back to her house where I'd sit her on the edge of her high bed and kneel on the hardwood floors to bury my face between her legs, her feet on my shoulders, her hands on her tits; I'd fuck her until she threw me off with her violent orgasms. At night we'd find a karaoke booth and drink and sing, or we'd meet friends at the bowling alley and dive down the lanes and run back laughing. The next morning, I'd take her in the ass before her shower, leaning her over the bathroom sink

155

while we waited for the ancient water heater to do its job. Other nights we'd sit at the Red Fox Room and watch Shirley belt out Rat Pack classics until one of us passed out in the booth, then we'd fumble the key in her door and find our way to the couch where she'd take my cock in her mouth. After, we'd sleep tangled up in each other, and when I'd wake, I'd pull her to the edge of the bed, and I'd bend her such that we could both watch her take me in. We were live wires, in love, in lust, and we were inseparable. We lived like this for years, and then something happened.

It was like we slipped into an alternative reality where a less satisfied, all gray version of ourselves was living. There was distance where previously there was none, there was awkwardness where previously we had no boundaries, there was tension where we were once free. The bed was cold and dry like a desert night. I was hurt and confused, wondering what could have happened to us (I still don't know). Seemingly overnight, we had forgotten how to speak to each other. As exclusive non-speaking partners, we began to communicate in line with the roommate-roles we had adopted: a brief text to confirm an appointment, a note to share a calendar event, an email to say what we should have said at dinner. I wrote letters telling her that we had not been ourselves, that we seemed to be losing our way, that I felt like I was losing, had lost, my partner in crime, and I could feel glass breaking and nails dragging on asphalt when I tried to bring it up. She told me that she felt attacked when I wondered at how we used to be, how we used to be wild and adventurous, how we used to be romantic, how we used to have an evolving, growing sex life that was now dry, cold, gray. In response, she reasoned away my anxiety. We loved each other, didn't we? This was true (whatever that meant). She reasoned "this is just a rough patch." We both reasoned that it was so. The good times, the romantic dates, the wild nights, the hope for the future were still so fresh that it was easy to confuse that for our true coupled nature. So, we carried on carrying on when perhaps we shouldn't have.

We planned an unwedding in Vegas, fitting for this newly developing unromance and our burgeoning unsex life. Vegas: it was a compromise that bridged the gap between our early "we are wildly in love, and we don't need a piece of paper to tell us who we are to each other" sentiment and Elle's desire to please her parents. Like everyone who came to Vegas, we too came to find something, to change, to remove the masks that life had asked us to wear, to metamorphose, to forget the mask entirely. To be what we were not. This was what we were doing, asking this ceremony in this city, rife with kitsch, tits with tassels, sideburns with grease, ringing bells, music, and its flashing lights to lend us its magic. But we forgot that the magic of Vegas exists in its facade. Nothing there was real. It was a black hole of a city, its core pulsing the inescapable blacklight of need, want, and regret into its ready tourists. It was nothing but a waystation, a living mirage for the Lost Soul Tribe. Its $9.99 prime rib tasted like mush and ash, its $0.99 shrimp cocktail would make you piss out your ass, and the free cocktails would make you forget the mush and ash and the shrimp. And in the morning, while your head was pounding, its eggs were soup, its coffee acrid, its buffet bacon flaccid, but it didn't matter because its Bloody Marys were free. We came here for the *deal*, we came to forget, we came for the mirage. We got what we paid for. The ghost of this city, its dirty underbelly, the false oasis, it would rattle just beneath our skin for as long as we'd know each other, and it stank of cigarette smoke and new carpet and too much fruity perfume and too much musky cologne. It mirrored our marriage, a piped-in false reality that became a thief in order to exist at all. Whereas the city stole water from reservoirs so that we might enjoy its façade, we stole each other's time. Like anything thriving in the desert, it was a lie.

A Female Quixote

Looking back at this ill-advised arrangement, it was possible to see that a few months before our 'unwedding' at the Tropicana, where no one was invited but everyone was welcome, something did happen; although, I don't know quite what brought it on. It came on the way light changes in a room when a cloud moves past the sun. If you blink or are distracted, you might not know there was any change at all. It might escape you that everything in the room including yourself was now pasted with darkening shadows slipping you into the gray. The old reality devoid of shadows no longer existed, it never existed because this new reality played tricks on the mind making it virtually impossible to recall anything being different at all. But it was. I didn't blink. I saw the clouds moving before the sun; unfortunately, Elle didn't. But we were changing, no longer able to access whatever powers we had that allowed us to take care of the other in our early years, no longer buoyed by the dreams of the false oasis that supported us when we couldn't find the strength, and no longer in agreement over what was happening, or even if anything had actually changed. She couldn't see the shift and because she couldn't, because I was vocal about our growing distance and my unhappiness with it, she felt attacked and hurt and she pulled back even further. I suggested marriage counseling. She was offended, in a rage. "Are you trying to say that it is me? Are you saying that I'm the problem? You know what? You've got problems. Your family is so messed up and you know it. You're just like them and you think it's me? I don't need therapy, you do."

Her family didn't do therapy, she told me. They also didn't talk about problems. They didn't get emotional about things, they kept to themselves. Each day they were silent apart, and at night, silent together. From her stories and our interactions, I pieced together visions of Elle's teen years. Each night after a polite but quiet dinner, each family member would retreat to the room best designed for their needs. Elle, she was captive in her upstairs tower of silent suburban sprawl. She was becoming the female Quixote, educating herself on those things her parents thought best not to discuss via new wave and goth pop record lyric sheets. She'd find her reflection in the mirror, put on fresh lipstick, and sit on her window ledge to smoke and breathe in the words. This was where Robert Smith taught her about love and romance. She was lulled to bed and educated by "Close to Me," "Friday I'm in Love," "Just Like Heaven," "Six Different Ways," filling her head with ideas of *the one true love*. At bedtime her parents could have said "I love you," hugged or kissed Elle goodnight, but they touched even less than they spoke. Elle said goodnight to Robert and as his songs played, she dreamed her impossibly beautiful melancholically-laced love-dreams.

She thought that she'd find love in college and mistook any advance as a sign of love. This was the curse of the self-educated, isolated, female Quixote: her eyes were full of windmill lovers. She believed that when those boys advanced, with their cheap pick-up lines and their probing hands, that they too were in love. Read the lyrics. Dark room. A drink. You kiss, you fall in love. The end. She believed everything she learned in her silent tower and in college, it was all there: the lyrics, the boys, the hands. This education created an unfortunate connection between love and sex. What she learned was that her hope for something more than just sex exceeded the hopes of her partners. It was the tragic college drink-fuck-cycle: drink, attraction, drink, hope, drink some more, mistake an advance for genuine long-term interest, do a shot, 'let's get out of this place'; and, in the backseat of a friend's car, at a friend's house, after hours in the school newspaper office, hope to find a head or a heart on the other side of this fuck. However, more than likely, in the morrow find them gone, or no longer interested, or suddenly, oddly, unavailable, or newly awkward, unless they were wasted, but then when they were wasted all they wanted was to get under that skirt. She hoped that each one of those guys would be *the* one, at least something more than a few awkward nights anyway, but none of them were.

Soon after we met, she hoped that I'd be the one. I threw her for a loop by actually being interested. I thought I was the one. I really did. I thought we were something special, but it wasn't until years later in therapy that I knew what I was up against.

The Sea, the Rats, the Leather Swivel Chairs

After work and every weekend, seemingly all of Southern California moved west toward the beaches, filling the highways and offramps, looking for relief, hoping for respite, seeking refuge from the lack on the thin line of sand. The beach was the confluence of absurdity and lack. Where too much meets not enough. It was a place that wasn't beset with drought, but the visible water was only useful as metaphor, where the wet and the salt of the sea cannot quench thirst, but was a symbol for the unknown, our dreams, our latent sexuality, our slumbering sexual appetite, our too large to define unconscious desires. This was where Elle and I came for therapy.

The practice was set on a dreamscape. A thin northbound coastal line of sand populated with bellies on foam boards, surfers on leashes, dogs not, and taco shops and homies yelling go back to where you came from with their faces full of carne asada burritos and mouths foaming from Jarritos, and hodads crushing raw-onion stacked cheese burgers in shitty pickup trucks covered in Dead Head stickers pumping Tupac. The wet sandy boardwalk with its bikinis, dogs, and catwalk selfies; its too-tan men, shirts off, tattoos, white socks too high, kicking at the homeless. Someone on the boardwalk ledge singing *No*

Woman, No Cry and they don't even want change, no one had changed any more. They were just there to suck you off for a fix, or to play a song for a beer, anything to hit that pen, man. It was all too much and still it was not enough. This thin line of sand leading to the houses on the hill, not a mile from the ubiquitous west-facing sunset floor-to-ceiling windows reflecting only glare to obscure the too much of the sea. The bodies piled up here because this was something other than desert, but on this edge of the earth, we were the too many of the too much, of the lost soul tribe, we were Legion, we were the Southern Californian swine of Gerasene.

Driving down Mount Soledad, I saw all of humanity moving on the shore and I dreamed a dream of an oceanic exorcism. I could feel the ocean and I knew her story. She wanted to heal like she once did, but she couldn't any longer. Once upon a time, before all of Southern California brought its misery to these shores, the water was potable, and the sea was the widest, deepest, truest freshwater oasis. In the early days, the sea would wash us clean and fill us up again. When man first came to drink of the sea, she barely noticed the hard-angled crystals that sloughed off his body as she pulled the lack from his pores. And so on with the next and the next over a thousand years and a thousand more. But as time passed, there were so many of us. Too many. She tried to save herself by flooding the earth, but the lack made us clever. So, we hid in the highest mountain caves and multiplied and became more cunning and more clever, hard and angled like the crystals and dry and hollow from the lack. In time, with our clever ways, we returned to the sea. We sought out her thinnest edges and took without asking. Not having enough to drown the earth, she conceded. And now we've been coming to these shores for so long that we have forgotten that we used to leave them feeling pure, healed, and whole. We don't have the perspective to acknowledge that it was we who made the sea nothing more than symbol. So, each day thousands of us lost souls make this pilgrimage to the edge of the earth to perform this hollow cleansing ritual. We bathe as our ancestors once did, not understanding how we have polluted the sea with our lack-filled misery.

I woke from the dream and found myself standing in the therapist's driveway, listening to the waves, trying hard not to be early because I couldn't conceive of the small talk that one makes when the world is fucking ending. I saw ocean, red bricks, planters with birds of paradise, ivy covering those bricks winding up the arms of trellis onto the eaves, not quite reaching the top because even in La Jolla the sun burns too hot. The ivy was full in the shadows on the north-facing walls. I could hear rustling beneath the fat green leaves, and I imagined a nest of rats thriving just beneath the veil. I imagined how they survive: stealing dog food, living off of scraps, burrowing into the attic at night. I heard them scurry, I could feel their anxiety, I could feel their red eyes and I wondered how many rats I had living in the pit of my chest. I felt full of scraps. Papers torn to shreds. Full of fleas and feces. Beaten and broken. All shattered to dust. I imagined my bones bleached and crumbling under the weight of the sun. I felt all red-eyed rat beneath the ivy of my skin, and I wanted to puke fur and tail, all of me. I felt as though I was inside out as I rang the bell.

Early therapeutic revelations were more like a garbage truck spilling its contents directly into my waiting mouth, like a broken sewer line in the house, an oil tanker running ashore to cover everything beautiful, everything I loved, in black. It was clear that we weren't who we used to be. What's more, it became clear that she couldn't conceive of that way of being any longer. She had dug in and rewritten our history; she was locked in an asexual mindset, frozen against even the slightest idea of romance for fear she'd get pulled in from the quiet edges and lost in deep connection and vulnerability, the type that comes from bearing one's soul to another. The former fun-loving, outgoing, romantic and adventurous husband she used to celebrate was now adversary and villain. To fill in the cracks from Elle's new façade, to prove that we were normal, she borrowed loose facts and compiled evidence from friends holed up in sexless, romance less relationships to normalize our awkward exchanges. Sydney: Romance? Nope. Sex about once a month. Lauren: Sex? What's that? Meredith: Eh, once a week. Even Kat chimed in, and she too thought this was normal. "Sex? Rarely. He isn't interested." And another, Amy, she liked to drink a lot and got loud when she did. I overheard her telling Elle about her epiphany.

"All sex in marriage is performed in exchange for something. What are we? Whores? Fuck that. I don't have to swallow Pat's cum any more. He can't even jerk me off right, he's lucky if he gets a hand job."

Elle treated their testimony like gospel. Surely, *they* were normal, she professed.

***

In therapy, these conversations provided the ammo she needed to justify and normalize what we had. Balls deep in confirmation bias, Elle recalled that "back then" she just no longer felt like she *needed* to do anything.

"Needed?" Now I was hurt. I accused her of the ol' bait and switch, of feeding the ass for years on fat carrots until he was harnessed and then once secure, only dangling rotten peels before his nose for her life journey.

"So, all those years, all that fun we had, all the romance and crazy sex, that was to acquire something? Me? So, that was a performance? Is that what you're telling me?" She stammered and pushed back at the idea of faking it. *It* being our entire goddamn relationship, but she didn't have an answer. I honestly believe she had no idea what the reason was. What she had settled on was that she wasn't interested in romance, and she was even less interested in sex. The *why* became anything and everything. To be clear, she could have some sex, but that was it, just some. Probably missionary. That would do for Elle. She had no other needs. No romance. No foreplay. God, no foreplay, that would require openness and reciprocity. For fuck's sake, what if in exchange for cunnilingus, I was hopeful of fellatio? That would never do! She was not interested in romance, foreplay, or trying to keep the flame alive. I was formally instructed by the swiveling leather chair opposite me that a weekly horizontal romp in the dark was approved. She thought I should be very satisfied with that. Elle checked in with the therapist: Turned out that once a week is normal for a lot of people and a lot more than what many couples got. What's more, that "normal" that was better than normal for a lot of Elle's friends. So, she was satisfied

166

and said I should be happy too.

I was not.

"See, normal!" she'd declare while explaining that any lack I felt as a result of needs that fell outside of normal was a psychosis from which I alone suffered. She was locked in misguided binary interpretations, so every week I'd attempt to reset for us: the flame had gone out. I wanted it reignited and I wanted to keep the flame alive, to work on and cultivate connection and openness which should lead to romance and sex. She wanted to prove to me that we were *normal*.

The Whore in the Attic

To take a stab at this now polarizing topic, the therapist would cite the paradox of modern love: the Madonna and the Whore. I countered by citing our timeline. We didn't have kids and we weren't even married when she fatted me on fresh fruits and then changed the game.

"Yes, yes, I see, but talk of marriage had occurred. Elle was aware, we are all at least unconsciously aware, of the roles associated with that shift in status," she'd recite. I conjured visions: single college grad looking for fun becomes a married housewife looking for coupons. The therapist and I played Greek Chorus to the expectations associated with coupling, and the roles therein. We sang and swirled around Elle.

"Marriage! Duty! Work! Laundry! Children! Always the Children!" Elle used these words to fortify her stronghold. "Yes, yes, exactly," as she laid more mortar and brick fortifying her stronghold. "See? Normal!" I suggested that the model was a template used to *explain* behavior, that it was not a *guide for* behavior. "We decide who we are," I'd counter. We choose to observe the dogma of the average or not. I chose not. However, Elle chose to view the Madonna model as a validating guide that gave her permission to dig in further. She saw it as doctor certified, permission to pursue the average. The model became the justification for digging in, building walls, for being roommate, part-time dry missionary fuckbuddies. And the doc would reason that it was completely normal that she was processing the Madonna, stating that the issue "is that life is busy, you have these roles to fulfill for your family. It is hard to find time for romance and connection and as the relationship transitions into marriage, the woman feels she must embody the essence of the doting wife and mother." I thought to myself, didn't Ibsen write Helmer speaking these very words to Nora? And now these words of the lowest-hanging fruit were flowing through our therapist: "First you are wife, then you are mother. First you are husband and then you are father." What the fuck? Did our insurance cover Ibsen?

I set my mind for cruise control and drove east toward the heart of the city. I could see the curse of the Madonna looming over everything, shading each house I passed in its cold consistent gray. I imagined all of the Madonnas in all of the houses easing into the smooth middle of the night, where the whores they used to be during courting were tucked away tightly somewhere in the attic, just inside the trunk beneath a fading wedding dress and fading promises, their whore essence captured in fading photos of days long past, all boxed up tightly to hold back the ghost of the madwoman who would set beds on fire.

I could see millions of these unwittingly disconnected locking their bedroom doors against the pitter-patter of tiny feet, turning the lights out, dropping their flannel PJs to find the wet and the hard in the pitchest of blacks to perform their latest version of their mindless wedding-night ritual. These philistines, all fucking without pageantry, without ceremony. Hurriedly, because the little ones never sleep through the night. These horizontal corpses were more worried about making good time and straightening the bed when they finished than connecting, more satisfied if their sixty-forty sheets weren't marked with stain than finding themselves in the stars, more content to scroll on their phones as they wordlessly excused themselves to wipe the breech and the mast, more content to share memes than to burn the bed with pure unadulterated lust.

I thought of all the Madonnas taking their cues from the 1950's, fucking in the quiet dark. The partner shall avert their eyes out of reciprocal shame-driven respect! I protest, this was the 21st century; sex should be fun, a celebration, a way to shed the fuck-all of the day to reconnect, to create the space to allow you to remember why you were bothering to endure the incessant grind of life at all. The bedroom should be the Rollins Band, End of Silence front to back, raw, hard, harder, barefoot, bare-chested, with the goddamn floodlights on the entire set, so that you could see every glorious bead of sweat, every word sprayed into the phallus mic, every line in the face, every loose tit floating Christlike on top of the pit. This Madonna model was deeply flawed, maybe a little like this analogy, I don't know, I think it works. All I really know is that the language we use to describe these models, which serve to bind us in our unforgiving roles, is severely lacking. We let this happen because we are fat and lazy with the shit of the day, brains tapped and too tired to think beyond zeroes and ones. We mistake models like these for everything when in reality they are the thinnest filthy white-foam edge of the sea creeping on the shore leaving behind the true deep ocean of reality, so vast that its meaning is lost on us.

In our next session, I'd swivel my chair and attempt to recall

170

the rant I stored driving home from the last session.

"But, Doc, this model is lacking. We don't have to become the roles. We don't have to let them limit us."

"True," she would say, "we don't have to become the roles. That is for you to decide."

Elle would interject, "But it is normal, isn't it? To do that? I feel like everyone does this. Right?"

And the doc would give her what she needed: "Many couples settle into their roles, these roles." I was pulling my fucking hair out at this. "These roles, this 'normalizing' approach, isn't working for us, it isn't working for me. We are here *because* this isn't working."

Elle started crying. "But I feel like you are blaming me because you want something different from normal." I tried to stay calm.

"We are here because I am trying to connect with you. I don't give a shit about what is normal, or what other people do. I am saying I feel disconnected, so if this is normal, I don't want it." I paused while Elle dabbed her eyes. "And yeah, it is normal for people to assume these roles, to get stuck in a role, to use these binary models as guides for their relationships, but we don't have to. That's the point. This model explains behavior, it doesn't dictate it. *We* decide." Elle was still crying, stuck on *normal*.

"I feel like you want too much. Like I can never be enough for you."

The doc jumped in to define what I already knew with a question. "And how does that make you feel, Elle?"

She stammered, "Like, like I don't even want to try." And there it was, the beginning of the end.

171

The Organic Fallacy

As therapy progressed, in an effort to carry my half of the dying carcass, I researched how to rekindle desire and keep the flame alive. I watched TED Talks, read books, watched how-to videos for love, sex, and relationships; learned about love languages, styles, addiction, attraction, attachment styles; she dug and she dug. I was beginning to realize that she still couldn't see the cloud move in front of the sun. She didn't acknowledge the change, that she had changed. All she knew was that I was not happy. I was not happy that we went from having zero noticeable differences in our ideas of romance and sex, to years later sitting in twin leather rotating chairs (so we could all face one another), coming to believe that not only did we have major differences, but that perhaps we shouldn't have married at all. We went from a life where we manufactured opportunities for fun and adventure in romance and sex to Elle wanting everything to be "organic." Organic sounds great, but here as it was applied, it was a strategy. It was a clever angle that didn't require any effort considering the full-time aspect of the business of life. Organic, like don't email, text, nor talk about it. Organic, like get up at five a.m., go to work for ten hours, come home, try not to crack talking about the minutiae of the day, take out the trash, take someone to soccer practice, try to wrangle the family to circle the dinner table, eat,

172

clean up, pass out on the couch, brush teeth, lay on your back to see if any one reaches out to the other "organically," pass out either way, hope tomorrow might be more organic.

Organic meant, when we have time, we will find each other as we once did. When the day hasn't leached the life out of us, when the kids aren't crying for something, when work isn't calling, when your mom isn't visiting, when the fuck of the fucking day hasn't made it too fucking difficult to talk about the fucking day, when Newton's first law isn't the law.

We Live in the In-between Hours

Early on in our snow-moon days, I learned how to mark time with Elle. Our rogue-wave connection pierced through the consistent gray of life. Those memories, our songs of experience, outshone the overwhelming reality of the multitude of minutes that made up the doldrums of life. Without those long-past markers, in the time after, we just floated and drifted and died, existing but never tasting life. The world spins, but we don't move, and years pass and pile up without notice until the mirror tells us how sunken our eyes have become, how our faces sag, how our soft lines are now dug so deep that we don't recognize the shadows on our own faces.

As time passed, Elle and I found that we were stuck navigating the doldrums. We drifted lifelessly in these horse latitudes, not talking, not touching, not living, not dying. We threw everything overboard so as to prolong our existence in the drift. In the frenzy and the fear, feeling the steely eyes of my thirsty hallucinating other break me down into salty slabs of meat and rations of water, feeling I was in danger of being thrown out or cannibalized, I jumped to a lifeboat of my own accord, but the salty sea loves to torment: enough water for a kingdom, but none to drink; sails high, but no winds; floating, but the current refuses to push us beyond the cries of the drowning animals we have cast overboard and we are forced to watch them tread water until they gasp and sink. And I float, not with, but next to Elle.

In an attempt to battle the drift, the therapist suggested we name our needs, present them to our other, see what we wanted versus what we might "settle" for. It was suggested that we write an advertisement for a potential partner. This was mine:

I am looking for a person who wants to have an evolving, fun, and adventurous romantic and sexual relationship. I want to dance and laugh and take chances with someone. I am looking for deep connection. I am looking for someone who knows who they are and wants to teach me. I am looking for someone who wants to connect romantically, who wants to be turned on, who wants to turn me on, and is willing to find out how.

I will take care of your needs - if I don't know how to do it, I will learn.

Not looking for a quick hook-up or fix. I am interested in a long-term relationship that doesn't flat-line, so we will need to keep the flame alive even while we are not in the bedroom - up for emails/texting/sexting/goofy games/classes/dance lessons/ whatever. Anything to feed the flame.

My advertisement was not well-received. Elle saw it as an attack, a way of pointing out how she fell short. "All you did was list the things that we don't do and state that you wanted them. I feel like you are pushing me." She imagined that I had written it for

174

someone else. It wasn't an opportunity; it was an indictment.

I was baffled.

She never sent me one in return.

Picture Elle, settled into her confirmation biased fox-hole surrounded by impenetrable walls, misremembering who we used to be, forgetting that she had a romantic streak that was both enticing and sexy, and an animal streak that loved to fuck and be fucked, now believing that she was asexual. For me, all of this was pure lunacy. Hers was a becoming, I assure you, but whatever the case it didn't matter what she was, it mattered what she believed she was, and she was relieved to find that therapy approved of her very normal and naturally occurring asexuality. But the problem was in the question. The question of "Am I normal" is much different from "How do I cultivate romance, or how do I open up sexually, or how do I work to deepen connection with my partner."

Therapy was frustrating. It seemed to encourage the building of walls and digging in, but there was some good. My voice became clearer. It was less swayed by the hurt and anger at the slow-drip decay of my former relationship with Elle. I exchanged "What the fuck happened to us?" for "I feel that…," or "It hurts me that…," or, "It doesn't seem fair that…" and as we learned to speak again, we split up into individual sessions so that we could tackle our individual blocks without the prying eyes of our other. Over time, it became apparent to me that Elle worked on fortifying the walls that she had built to protect herself from the slings and arrows of her overly romantic husband. Discussions shifted from how do we keep the flame alive to "I just need you to give me some space. If only you'd give me some space." It was no longer about romance or the flame (was it ever?), it was about her normalizing self-preservation. So, I gave her space while I worked on the magic phrase that might gain me entry inside those walls. For the record, I never learned it.

Good Enough

The therapist saw my frustration building. For this sort of hang up, she brought out her secret weapon: "good enough." It was a very sound and disarming theory that turned out to be good enough for Elle. Consider what you have, she'd say. A marriage isn't just about romance and sex. It is natural that those things fade over time. You are a father to two children. You get along with Elle, you are friends, you are the breadwinner for your family. Consider the possibility that your romance and sex with Elle is good enough.

But I wasn't there to save a marriage, I was there to save us. Good enough? I hated it. That "good enough" existed at all, that it was poised to make sure we all found the smooth middle of mediocrity, was a crime against whatever accident created us. It made me want to rip apart those goddamn swiveling leather chairs. It made me want to fight. Good enough was a white flag in response to a skinned knee. It was quitting too soon. It was for cowards. And in this particular situation, good enough, when I remembered what it was like before we dried up; when I wrote, begged, cried, argued, fought for us to keep the flame alive because I saw this coming at us like a fully-loaded eighteen-wheeler blasting black smoke, five bricks on the gas pedal, steering wheel tied and locked, heading straight for us on the wrong side of the highway; good enough just wasn't good enough.

My well-documented call for change, or unhappiness depending on your perspective, became all the evidence Elle needed to prove I was the cause of our troubles. After all, she was still happy, right? She was satisfied with normal and good enough. That was what she would tell me, that our issues were actually just my issues. My documented and confirmed unhappiness gave her something to hold onto; she could point to it and say that I was not happy with good enough, which to her meant I did not love her, I did not love my family, and I didn't care about the kids (enough, anyway) to quietly and graciously take on the modern role of passive father. So, for Elle, the impending collision that she couldn't see coming, the clouds moving before the sun that she did not observe, the drying up of our relationship that she didn't register, all screamed that I was at fault. Consequently, her view of me twisted. In therapy, I became demonized, my drive for connection and fun and adventure in romance and sex meant many things, all of them bad. She'd say, "You are insatiable, always wanting. If you get something, you always want more." (She was not a fan of "yes, and.") "You might have a personality disorder, you are probably bipolar, definitely clinically depressed." *Swiveling the chair: "Did you know that he sent me porn?" Now she turned to me. "You are for sure a porn-addict. You are emotionally unstable, and you get so angry it's scary. I watched a video on toxic relationships; I'm pretty sure you're a narcissist."

I was a monster.

This confirmed it. We were no longer in therapy for the same reasons. I originally thought that the reason we were sitting there was to find a way around the mundane, the Madonna, and the good enough. I thought that we were looking for a way to manufacture what had become inorganic, a way to find a life that was better than good enough. It turned out that we were not negotiating in good faith at all. Elle was there to be therapist certified as a normal person wanting normal things. Therapy was an evidence-building exercise. It provided the clues that gave her permission to remain in stasis. She just wanted to be normal; her version of it anyway.

The real issue was that Elle no longer wanted the type of relationship we used to have. Eventually, she gave me the truth. The big chair reminded her, "To him." Elle turned and said, "This just isn't me. I can't. I'm just not into sex and romance like you are."

And there it was. There really wasn't much to do about that. We were both cowards and fools. Holding onto each other because we had two kids and on a certain level, we knew we loved each other, but we didn't let go because we didn't know what to do about deeply caring for someone that could never make us happy. Was there a model for that? We were scared, we felt we had zero options, so we continued, negotiating a decade away.

It was all the same putrid oozing shit. Elle and I were both standing at the finish line waiting for the other to cross, but neither one of us ever moved. We stood there negotiating our sad existence on the edge of that line, finding the smallest measurable movement and calling that real change.

Negotiating, I'd say, "I'm not sure how we're supposed to

generate and maintain passion in our relationship when we are alone together for an hour a day and dead tired most of those days. I need more than just nine to ten p.m. on the days we can keep our eyes open."

"To her. To Elle. You are speaking to her. You need to face her," so spoke the woman in the larger chair. *Swivel (south-facing).*

"What can we do to maintain our romantic and sexual selves under these circumstances? All of my past requests have been shot down. You don't want to go out, you hated the dance lessons I signed us up for. You don't want to connect with the tools we have; you don't want to text, and judging from the very brief and businesslike responses to my emails, you don't want to email either. But considering the limited time we have together, what else is there? What can we do other than hope that we can get through the awkwardness that has built up between us within the hour we have, on the one or two days a week we are both willing to fight to be together in the dark? You name it and I'm up for it, but I've struck out in all my attempts to bridge this gap. I feel like it's fucking crazy I even have to fight for this. What am I supposed to do?"

Her chair swiveled away from me.

"To him."

She didn't move her chair. She wasn't talking to me anymore.

"He wants too much. He's always pushing. He's always telling me that I am not enough."

We were sure to drive separately so that on the way home she could listen to the latest "How to be Normal" podcast and so

I could scream into my steering wheel. At night we'd lay there quietly in the dark, both on our backs, wondering if one of us might reach out to touch the other. While I waited, I'd think about how this forced and cold post-therapy ritual was in high contrast to our early wild nights when she'd wear a mini-skirt and I'd pull up that skirt to spank her before I flipped her over. These nights, these years (it had been years), more than likely she'd reach over and jerk me off while the fingers on my innermost hand were guided to spread her pussy, to give her the access and permission she needed to rub her slit until she came. The sheets would rustle and she'd finish herself as I dripped warm all over her fingers. Other nights might end with good old-fashioned penetration, but when that happened our sessions were minutes long before the soft was squeezed out by a small twitch, when before, in our other life, there'd be hours of hard and sweat and eyes rolling and lips bleeding with spasms that would have thrown the best of bull-riders. We had been reduced to a mayfly inspired fuck session where after entry, she'd rub her clit hurriedly, like the flurry of fluttering wings, until she came and sometimes I would, and sometimes I wouldn't. That night, we just lay there trapped in purgatory. I began to let go.

I tried to get the words out. I would say, "I was thinking... yes, you are correct, our last 'Last Shot' discussion was in January. The one before that was in June, the one before that in April. Not that any of that matters. The main thing is that recently I have been unconsciously pulling away. You're right, I have not been very present. I'm sorry. This is hard for me - living like, feeling like, my needs don't matter, like I'm trapped in a roommate marriage - I don't want to live like this any more. We need to either have our needs met, or agree that they will never be met and move on. I have been asking, talking, writing, begging for this for years and at our last 'last shot,' I told myself that this was it. I understand that it's hard to be 'that way' with someone who is distant, but in this 'chicken and the egg,' the distance came after years of me trying really fucking hard."

Her voice trembled, hands dabbing eyes. "I am so tired of this. We do this every time."

"I know, but I don't know what to do. As you requested, I pulled back to make space for you, and I waited and waited, but it seemed that all you wanted was the space, the less of me. For over six years, I have been trying to jumpstart this stalled relationship."

"You aren't the only one that has been trying." Her words shook.

"It feels like I am. I have asked what you would like, what we can do to connect, what you would like in the bedroom, and not only have you never asked any of that of me, most often you don't even bother to respond to my questions and when you do, you give me conditions and delays."

Looking out the window, "You aren't even here any more. You don't even talk to me," she sobbed.

"You're right, I am drifting. I'm slipping away because I have explained my needs and how I feel they have been ignored. You have demonstrated that you have no interest in being the person to fulfill them. So, my mind drifts in ways that I never wanted, but I feel justified, because I feel like my wife doesn't want to be the object of my affection and I certainly am not hers."

Notice the shift to third person? I was proud of that. You know, to really drive the point home.

"What happened to us?

She didn't speak. She massaged the hem of her cardigan. Receiving only blank stares and silence, I continued.

"In therapy I believe we said everything there was to say. And this is where we are - after all those times that we said 'this is it,' if we can't get it by now, if we don't open up to what we both want, we have to move on. So, this 'this is it' is my last. It took me months to get here. But I can no longer make you responsible for my happiness; I give up. I feel I have been beaten down. It has been years since we've really touched. Long gone are the daily morning calls to just say 'hi.' You don't visit me any more to talk; I let go of worrying if you'd come to bed with me; I no longer leave you emails, texts, or articles hoping that you will engage. We don't even kiss any more. Our private rooms in faraway cities have all floated by without a spark. And worse, my imagination and desire have been wasted. I know that this is only romance and sex, and we have built so much more than that. The kids are amazing, you're a great mom. We have a lot to be proud of and a lot of memories to hold onto. And if I have a regret, it is that I have used that word 'regret' in the past to try to pull you to my way of thinking. The pouting and whining about not being able to realize my romantically charged desires with my wife was a childish approach. I have no regrets about my time with you, only fond memories. And whatever becomes of us, we may no longer be lovers, but I promise, I will never abandon you. I will never abandon the kids. I think you know all of this. Thank you for allowing me to be a part of your life."

After years of working at it in couples' therapy, after my

night at the Soda Bar with Kat, I quit couples' therapy.

Romance aside, Elle and I were great at living together. We were very considerate roommates who loved each other and happened to have kids; furthermore, I didn't want to miss out on anything with Lily and Alex. So, as my affair began, I *was* ready to leave... At first, I stayed because Elle and I got along good enough (ha!) and early on, I sincerely hoped Elle and I would work it out, but within months I was only holding on so Kat could figure out what to do with her girls.

Kat's eyes would glisten, and she'd say, "I know you're ready, but I can't yet, you know that, right? Three and six, they're so young, I'm worried about what would happen to them without me there. He ignores Olive, and she has special needs, you know?"

"I get it. I do. But, seriously? Ignores her? What do you mean, he ignores her?"

"She doesn't get what she needs from him. His whole family is that way. They love Milla, they dote on *her*, but they ignore Olive. He doesn't have the patience for her. I swear, it's borderline abusive."

"Seriously?"

I mean, I had seen the way Kat and Olive clung to each other, but I never put it together.

We sat quietly for a beat, and then I asked,

"But, seriously, Mike abusive? Come on."

"I am serious! I can't trust him, or his family, with her. I have to figure out what I can do about this before I leave him."

She'd read my face. She could see me looking out beyond the horizon and she'd say, "We will be together. I promise. It can't be any other way. You are in my dreams. You are in my bones."

"I know baby. I can hang on for a while longer. I just hate the lies. It's fucked up to say, but I love Mike. And Elle, I mean, we're only married on paper, but still, I love her, and I know you do too. I just don't want to lie any more."

She'd say, "Soon. I promise."

I shouldn't have agreed to hold all of this in, but I did.

Book III

The Four-Headed Romance

The Vermin & The Dinner Parties

Die Verwandlung. The Metamorphosis. Early on in our relationship it was Elle who metamorphosed, but oddly I became the *Ungeheures Ungeziefer*, the tremendous vermin, spending much of my time writhing around the floor cuckolded to apathy. I was so lost, so transformed by this new silent paradigm that if the scraps I was fed weren't so rotten, and if the horror on the face of my keeper-other who fed me these scraps wasn't so apparent, perhaps, no, not perhaps, I would have settled for much, much less in life. However, the joke was on her. I died on that goddamn floor waiting for those scraps, died from tearing the bark off of my own organs to feed our dying, dead, ghost spark. The slow metallic-earthy burn of my liver, the ashy asthmatic underdeveloped lungs, the bulging intestine, the cracked and breaking broken heart. When there was no more of me, when there was only dust and ash, I'd wait each night to go where the dead go. I waited for Charon to ferry me across her River Styx, to take me away. But when Charon too abandoned me leaving me on the shore with the living, I came to realize that I wasn't the vermin at all, I wasn't what she saw through those almond eyes: vermin, leviathan, taker, insect, narcissist, monstrosity, ungrateful, uncaring, nothing-is-good-enough husband—this wasn't me. That was who she had to make me in order to reconcile *her* metamorphosis, in order for her new asexual life to make sense. For, if I was anything less than a monster, she'd have to answer for who she had become. So, Elle projected her version of who I was upon me, and it became so. I wasn't what she made me, but that dynamic did heighten my senses. I too was becoming. I was changing with my environment, learning that I would have to find what I needed to survive elsewhere. I was becoming a quiet observer, a gatherer of facts, a beholder of twitches and tics, a witness of want and wishes and dreams, and lies and lack. Like the deformed totem creatures Elle carved for me, I scurried away when she came into the room preferring the comfort of the low shadows. From this perspective, with my forty-seven bulging eyes, my thumping thorax, and my notched antennae, I learned to see life differently: alone. When we sat with our cross-paired dinner partners Kat and Mike I could sense everything: the fear, lust, anger, anxiety, distance, jealousy, barren-want, worry, dread, shock, lust, fuck, romance, and lack. It would vibrate through my thorax as we four teased and slid between matched and unmatched partners, it would reflect in my forty-seven eyes as we slid between our marriages, and it would twist my antennae when we all sat there and became what the other Others needed.

Disgusted by the creature I'd become, Elle gave every sign that she was aroused by Mike; smiles came easy, sweaters were tight, eyes were big. After all, he was the picture of the not-so-needy, the conveniently distanced, the impeccably disconnected, the extremely too easy-to-look-at Male, the perfectly packaged club member edition sold completely devoid of all sexuality - just what every good-enough Madonna dreams of in a partner. Kat was right, they were perfect together. He came over to our house to give her hope, to remind her that these kinds of men actually existed in the world, to passively creep into Elle's fantasies, the kind of domestic fantasies where to gain favor, a real man works for sandwiches, averts his gaze, won't touch the hem, and sleeps down the hall.

But this too, this asexual-making-of-big-brown-cow-eyes at one another while fulfilling Victorian dating rituals, was still an affair even if it wasn't the type I would have wanted. After all, he didn't know that I didn't fuck my wife like I fucked his (I know, I know, he didn't know I was fucking his, but the idea was still conveyed). To cover all of the bases he was also engaged as my domestic foil, always fixing things, sometimes even at my request. Yes, fixing things, drawers and vents, making spoons and cutting boards as little gifts, even running over to the house while I was away to take care of my brother vermin, no cockroach was too big for him, nor too small for Elle. At this point, I owed him a lot. I wasn't sure, but I believed that it was he who gave Elle enough juice to rub her clit in the dark to the soundtrack of my steady breathing. He was a goddamn saint.

I had become decreasingly enamored of things, vents and doors, and Mike and Elle. I had zero motivation for the little domestic things and less and less each day for the big things: romance, our sex life, this marriage. The only thing I lived for in that house was the kids, so I let him fill in for me as I filled in for him. I imagined an '80s movie montage of our four-headed romance filled with hilarious cuts, mood set by the Thompson Twins, Hold Me Now. No, no, not that. The Cure, The Same Deep Water as You. I could see hands polishing wood, cut to me spanking Kat's ass, then Mike's woodcutting face followed by my sex face: Mike making rough cuts of wood for Elle's cutting board, fading out to Elle looking on pensively, cue sunset, Kat on all fours looking back at the camera, Mike shaping a spoon, zoom out of flames to reveal Elle sitting next to Mike at the fire pit, Kat swaying with me at a club, Mike fixing our ceiling vent, pan to Elle holding a screwdriver, cut to my face between Kat's legs, a pair of spoons crisscrossed in a handmade salad bowl, Kat's legs over my head, Mike running over to find the cockroach, laughing with Elle as she stands on a stool waving her dress, fade out to me on a bike, Kat riding on my handlebars laughing uncontrollably as we ride down Adams Avenue.

Have You Seen Me?

A few nights each week we four would test the boundaries of our four-headed romance. We'd dine on charcuterie and beer and laugh and talk. Our conversations, like our children, jumped from place to place, then disappeared for a time, only to pop up again somewhere unexpected. It was exhilarating and rejuvenating for two couples who found themselves drained in the daily presence of their other to be seen from a different angle. Long before Kat and I were fucking, we were pseudo-domestic and almost romantic partners. We'd often joke about how easily we filled in for each other; aren't we the myths we create, the dreams we let ourselves remember, the lies we cling to? We are what we cultivate. We were cultivating this at the dinner table, this four-headed romance.

It took me a while to put it together, but as our affair developed, it became apparent that Kat was orchestrating the dialogue at the dinner table. She was the central cog in a high-level Shakespearean drama that centered on romance and sex. Before we dined, on her weekly walks with Elle (yes, she maintained these during the entire affair), Kat would probe and purge on subjects concerning work, family, and Mike.

"He is just so rigid," Kat would complain. "All he cares about is that house. He works and sleeps. That's it."

Elle would ask, "have you tried therapy?"

"No, it's too late for that. I can't see myself married much longer. But I can't imagine another woman helping to raise my girls, no one but you, anyway."

Each day Elle would come home and report that Kat was unhappy. One day she asked me, "Do you think it's weird that she mentioned me helping to raise her girls? Is she moving or something?"

I'd say, "I don't know. You know how she is," throwing in a shrug. Elle would nod knowingly.

I would then add that information to the discussions Kat and I had. We discussed everything, *everything,* little by little in the hotel rooms we dirtied, on our walks at Sunset Cliffs, on our shopping dates at Vinyl Junkies, as we drank beer and ate cheese at Venissimo, as we sat together on her (his) front porch. She'd tell me her dreams, desires, and her fantasies and then she would tell me how Mike always shot her down and treated her like a child, if he acknowledged her at all. To explain how Mike was incapable of being the person she wanted to be with, she gave away all of Mike's secrets: the borderline psychological abuse, the anger, the manipulations, how he made love, or didn't, his ejaculatory issues, how he felt about sex, women, men. In between sips of beer, she'd cut him deep with quips like, "My mom thinks he's gay." My eyes widen, "oh," I'd say, and she'd continue, "I think she might be right. I think he even might be attracted to you. Sometimes it really seems so." I took all of this and Elle's reports as evidence that Kat was indeed leaving Mike soon. So, as we four sat and Kat steered the discussions toward the provocative, I realized I was too well-armed for these conversations. I had too much information and had too much to lose. I told myself to be careful, that I shouldn't give myself away. I saw it all unfolding. Kat had already had these conversations with everyone individually and now with the group present, she was hoping to find an ally in me to prove to our others that she wasn't crazy. This was dangerous.

On these nights, Kat would tease out the conversations that Mike thwarted in private. I think she wanted him to hear my opinion, to prove that she wasn't the problem at home. But I had no interest in educating Mike; after all, with Kat's musk still on my breath, I felt like we already shared a lot. So, while Kat teased, pressed, and tested the others on subjects concerning '70's bush vs. Brazilian waxing, polyamory, who would or wouldn't cross the same-sex boundary, subs and doms, the erotic, strip clubs, adult toys and the like, I held back, and she would send me wide eyes. Personally, I thrived on the furthest edges of the socially acceptable, and for different reasons both Kat and Elle knew this, but due to my silence, Mike assumed I was more like him. These edgier conversations were land mines. And I was surrounded. If I leaned too far toward Mike's more conservative views on sexuality and openness, Elle might give me away. But, if I leaned too far toward Kat, Mike might start to wonder at my intentions and Elle might think that I was taking a stab at her. I did a lot of listening and chin stroking.

Our dinner table conversations would often start out with Elle's obligatory, "Mike, these potatoes, sausages, hamburgers, whatever are amazing," and then trail off into something about beer or cheese or whisky; Scotland and kilts; where to retire; how to raise kids in this fucked up world. If we'd had enough to drink, we'd end up submitting some closed-door argument before the full dinner committee. Talks on art came up pretty often. Kat would find something by some local artist she'd want to feature in the living room and Mike would be less excited about the prospect. One piece in particular, the *Woman in Black*, came up in the usual fashion.

Kat said, "Mike hates the art I just bought, what do you two think?"

I stammered, "Uh, a reclining woman done in black with a giant red heart, hmmm." I teased, "I like it OK."

"What?" Kat protested.

Elle: "I like it. It's sexy without being pornographic."

Kat cast steely eyes toward Mike. "See, they like it! Can you believe he won't let me hang it up in the house? He thinks it's inappropriate."

I played along. "I can't believe it," I said with a pregnant tone, just before I told myself to shut the fuck up.

The painting was a little large and evocative for a living room piece. But I knew why she liked it; I knew why she wanted it hung there. She saw herself on the canvas, but isn't that why we like a certain piece of art? We see ourselves in it; we connect to a mood, or it tugs on a memory like a dream; or it somehow ambiguously conveys the essence of everything inside us, showing the world, on canvas, painted poignant echoes of our unconscious selves, our in-the-dark desires, revealing hidden lizard-brain pain, joy, ecstasy, hauling up to the conscious mind the fragmented minutiae that makes up who we are, but that we can't quite say aloud, that we wouldn't even know how to say, that we might not have even known we had to say until we are standing before the canvas with tears in our eyes. It gives the emotion of song without filling our brains with someone else's lyrical meaning; *we the observer* find, create, give the context and the meaning, no one else. That is why art on canvas is the hardest to understand, the most difficult to quantify and the deepest connecting medium. If one finds a piece that speaks to the soul, it will never be forgotten. All of that buried meaning hidden beneath the brushstrokes on that canvas, this is what Kat brought before us. The painting that Kat held, smiling, just on the edge of the dining-room table, contained her unobserved essence. It was the canvased version of the story that she had been telling Mike all those years. The story he couldn't comprehend. So, here in canvas form, Mike had rejected her again. He was incapable of hearing her story, and even though she was proudly holding the canvas asking him to consider the painting, Kat on canvas, he still couldn't see her. All her feelings about her marriage were confirmed: she was misunderstood, unseen, and unwanted.

It was a simple painting, a featureless woman done in all black, but laced with meaning. Black, the color containing all other colors, all possibilities, suggesting infinite complexity if only one were brave enough to pierce through the veil of the black. The woman was reclined with her right leg bent and open just enough to suggest the sex that we couldn't see, but that we knew was there all the same. It was asking us to consider the void nestled in the black. She reclined with a heart so red that even the blackest black could not dim its light. It was asking us to consider the passion, the infinite complexity of the woman that boiled just beneath her dark façade. It was indeed Kat; this was how she wanted to be seen, and this was how I saw her in all of her unobserved beauty and complexity. Each night I sat across from her at the dinner table, I could see that beneath her unassuming frame was a woman of infinite depth, with a burgeoning sexuality, and a burning heart lusting for life. I could feel her frustration at how others saw her, how they never moved beyond surface interpretations. People saw her the way Mike viewed the painting: a flat, unassuming, two-dimensional form not worthy of a second look. But I saw it all, I saw the depth and the potential, a forest of overlooked meaning sitting across from me in double as she held onto that canvas. I saw that when she was asking about the painting, she was asking, "Can you see me?" In fact, she wasn't really ever asking about the painting at all, she was asking, "Do you, does anyone, see me?" And because I did, she fell for me all the harder.

Still, I had to play the game. I couldn't tell anyone what I saw in the painting (I didn't even tell Kat. I wish I told her that night). So, I teased both Mike and Kat. "I love it, I could see it over the sofa."

"He said I could put it in our bathroom," Kat grunted to show her displeasure.

I teased again. "Yes, or that, I could see it in a bathroom or at the end of a long dark hallway."

"Stop!" Elle pleaded as Kat slid the painting behind a chair.

The painting disappeared from both view and future talks, but weeks later in an act of passion and perhaps subconscious protest, Kat sent me a video unintentionally showing me the painting's final resting place. *Video*... She pulls away from pressing *'record'* and smiles, leaning her head slightly to the side, hand on knees, knees and ass on master-bathroom tile floor, mind on me and the dildo I bought her secured to that tile. She was dressed in a black baby-doll lingerie set with white fringe. It plunged low and tied in the middle. She was beautiful, glowing, eyes wild, the tip of her nose flushed as it did in the throes. She looked into the camera and whispered, "For you," and she smiled one last cute but knowing smile before she became lost on some wide ocean. Her hands moved over the black and traced the lace, then hand over breast, then beneath lace, her head bowed, and her hair fell wild as her left nipple bent between her first and middle finger. She'd often start here. Breast gods appeased, her right hand found the black and lace between her legs. Overcome, her ass rose with the tide and settled back to earth. That hand disappeared beneath black and lace. Her eyes were gone, lost somewhere behind her lids. This was where she went to find me – somewhere in the stars. She rolled gently on her knees like a slow calm sea. Inching forward toward the cyber-flesh, she slid the black to the side: her eyes found me in the camera as she brought it (me) inside. She moved over the toy in small gentle waves, like it was filling her up with the meaning held within the canvas that pulsed in and out of view just behind her. The red heart of the woman composed of layered brushstrokes in black dipped in and out of view as she crashed back to earth. When she settled herself, her tongue found her teeth and she smiled. With her hands on her knees, she whispered, "I love you," and as she leaned in to press '*stop,*' I saw her full in double-form for just a moment. She was there, hung on the wall in black with that beating red heart and doubled smiling down at me from her knees.

What Do You Keep Under Your Pillow?

On other nights when we weren't talking about paintings that were really about sex and sexuality, we were literally talking about sex. One night's conversation centered around Kat's vibrator. It began as a discussion on how, what, and when to teach our kids about sex.

"Olive touches herself a lot in public and Mike tries to get her to stop. But I feel like that is kind of shaming her. I'm concerned he's going to give her some sort of psychological damage."

Elle: "She doesn't know what she's doing, right?"

"No." Mike added, "But she can't just rub herself right in front of everyone."

Kat countered, "I'm trying to have discussions with the girls about when and where it is appropriate to touch yourself. Have you guys had the sex talk with the kids?"

"That's his job," Elle said, nodding to me, "My family never talked about anything. I'm not very good at that sort of stuff."

"So, did you talk to Lily?" Mike asked.

"Yeah, both Lily and Alex, several times actually. They're still pretty young. I think it takes a few times for that sort of stuff to sink in, but I think having the ongoing conversation normalizes the subject," I said.

"You talked to Lily about masturbation?" Kat asked with big eyes.

"Yup," I sure did.

"How did that go?" Mike asked.

"It went fine. She told me she already knows it all. I said, 'Sweet, then this won't be too weird,' and I just went on about the importance of knowing yourself and your own body."

"Wow, that's incredible. He thinks that three and six is too young for that sort of talk," Kat said, gesturing to Mike. "What do you think?"

"Well, if they're already doing it in public, I'd say that now is the time," I said.

"See! I told you! We do need to know our own bodies. And no one talks about it. For example, I just sent my sister her first vibrator. Can you believe it? She's thirty-six and she has never owned a sex toy in her life."

Mike sat quietly and looked away as Kat began her probing monologue on the subject of how every woman should own a vibrator. It all poured out into a scene of pure irony; in the house of classic roles, as Kat spoke of mechanical cocks, "I keep mine under my pillow," Mike excused himself to tend to the dishes. His was a muted dish-cleaning protest to Kat's public manufacturing of provocative imagery. As the dishes clanked, we were essentially being asked to imagine what Kat might do with and why she might need a vibrator. I was imagining tonight's bed-time discussions: Kat reported them to me the next day. "Why do you have to bring that up in front of them?" And "Why do you need to keep that thing under your pillow anyway?" and

"Why do you need that at all?"

As she delivered her monologue, I could feel a smile forming. I attempted to dampen my enthusiasm for the subject, but I was being betrayed by the mounting images Kat had sent me using that very toy. It was a small, teal vibrator, with a white button that lit up in the dark, so that she could easily find the speed she needed even on the darkest of nights, all housed in a cute Tiffany-blue silken purse that tied with tassels. I was dying at the table replaying the images she sent me weekly. So many gliding, tapping, probing images. Images in her bed, under the covers at night (I assume he was asleep), over the covers, on the floor, on her couch, on the bathroom floor recording the more advanced maneuvers: fingers plunge into her pussy as she applies the vibrator to the clit. I was connecting all of the images and layering them with the words she would send me just before and after she fucked herself, all with Mike asleep, or half-asleep, or distracted.

I had a very open relationship with toys of all kinds, but considering the company, I reserved my true philosophy for more select company and presented a sort of disconnected polite agreement. "What's that? Every woman should own one, absolutely," I stated over the din of plates clinking. Elle sat in silence, listening, watching Mike. Elle and I had a dusty drawer full of sex toys, all kinds, all sizes, vibrators, dildos, leather straps, blind folds, plugs, clamps with chains, ropes. Elle was hoping that I didn't mention them, how we used them, more importantly, how we didn't any more, how it had been years. I didn't. Kat continued her monologue: "Every modern woman should keep a vibrator under her pillow. She has to take care of herself. And it isn't just about sex and orgasms. It is about health. Did you know that masturbation is actually healthy?" I nodded in thoughtful agreement as Mike left for the garage to grab a beer. While he was gone Elle and I played musical chairs, me out to flip a record, Elle out to use the restroom. As we danced this way, Kat would whisper to each of us about how "you know who," motioning to the garage, "is jealous of the blue toy." Kat was starting to look a little flush as she set the table for dessert. She leaned in with a piece of cake for me and said, "I'll send you something tonight." I ate dessert imagining Kat gliding the blue vibrator over her clit with the tiny light just visible under her sheets, a spot-lit pussy. How could he sleep through that?

***

Further reading on the vibrator chronicles: Later that week, on one of their walks, Kat told Elle that she and Mike had drifted apart. "We don't even have sex any more," Kat complained. "Marriage *is* hard," Elle would console. "It is and he isn't, that's why I bought the blue toy," Kat said with a laugh. "Come on," Elle laughed in return, "you guys have just been busy. You'll get back on track." "I don't think so," Kat replied, "Mike is so tired and disinterested that I don't even leave the room any more. Once I hear him sleeping, the blue toy comes out." Elle laughed. "You are terrible!"

Kat had told me this same story over a beer, some chocolate, and between several orgasms at the Double Tree Hotel, but for my version, she added that she recently woke him up with her evening orgasm and as he stirred, she drifted off to sleep. She added, "But after breakfast the next morning, I went to make the bed and it was gone. He took my vibrator, can you believe that?" she said, complaining of his cold and draconian ways. I later found out that Elle did not get the director's cut of this tale.

After these walks, Elle would often come home and give me the "she's crazy" report, running down the list of Kat's latest outlandish and often selfish (as she would say) ideas, her problems with her mother, father, sister, job. "There's always something, and nothing's ever enough," Elle would say. I noted how she never reported anything about Mike. Elle kept those bits for herself. But this, this story, the nighttime masturbation ritual, I didn't know Elle knew. She held onto it for a while, seemingly for future comedic effect.

To bring the Sleeping Beauty masturbation scene full circle, and to add a touch of humor and revenge to this game, one night, years later, Elle and I went out for dinner. We had a beautiful and surreal exchange sitting in a deep red leather booth at the Imperial House. We shared a steak while being serenaded by the Rat Pack. Frank crooned 'My Funny Valentine' and we tested our boundaries, talking in detail about our tangled past with Kat and Mike, mulling over her "Kat and Elle walk revelations," and all of her Mike revelations. We eventually worked into a joint sigh and a long pause.

After enough time passed, I said, "Tell me one thing I don't know about you."

She thought for a few beats and then smiled a huge smile and laughed a little.

"One thing you don't know… hmmm… OK… uh, you don't know… Kat and I had the same nighttime routine." She laughed about how she and Kat had the same fix for the "I can't sleep" problem. I noted but did not say that Kat's motivation for nighttime self-pleasure began as a fix for a distant husband that was augmented and mutated by my presence. Kat would tell me that once I entered the scene, her masturbation went from a couple times a month to at least once a day, and the nighttime ritual, when the mood struck her, became a test for her husband. She didn't call it a test, but that is what it was. "Does he see me?" It was a test he always failed. On occasion, she'd still attempt to entice the husband that never saw her. She hoped that he could be the answer that I appeared to be, and when it became apparent that he wasn't, the practice evolved into a full-fledged attempt to revenge fuck herself within earshot of the man who ignored her. Not quite the same motivation Elle relayed, but it didn't matter.

Upon hearing Elle's confession, I too smiled a big smile and I started laughing. Elle's face twisted.

"What? Nighttime routine?" I said, pretending that I had forgotten.

She laughed and said, "While you were asleep, I'd sometimes masturbate in bed next to you."

I should have played it cool, let it sink in, or at least let it look like it needed to sink in, but I couldn't. I had too much wine. I smiled hard at this and laughed some more.

"OK, OK, my turn," noting that Elle looked a little disappointed that I didn't linger longer on what she thought would be an outlandish confession. I steadied myself then looked at her blankly and started to breathe long and slow and even, and as her face turned up in the shape of a question, I said, "I knew the whole time! You'd go all quiet and listen to my breathing, wait a few minutes, and then… the sheets would quietly rustle. I was only pretending to be asleep." And this was just how fucked up we were.

She started laughing. "Faker! Why would you fake it?" I explained, "In my mind, Kat and I were the couple. I was trying really hard not to cheat on her, so I didn't make myself available to you. So, I'm curious, if you wanted to get fucked, why was there zero indication, why did you wait until I went to sleep? What happened to the asexual wife?"

She said, "That's just it, I didn't want to have sex. I couldn't. We weren't there. I was so closed off I couldn't even hug you, but I needed to sleep. It really helped. God, I can't believe you! You are such a faker!"

To Augment Thy Breasts; or, With These, these (hold them), I Shall Be Desired

On another memorable visit, conversation centered on the idea of a boob job. Elle and I walked in with hands full of beer and dessert. Kat was caramelizing onions at the stove; Mike was in the living room.

"Set your things down on the table," Kat said as she moved to organize construction paper and crayons. "What do you think of my portrait? Olive drew it." Kat held up the drawing her youngest made for her. It was an assembly of sticks and circles. Kat was laughing, pointing out that her breasts were as large as her head. "Olive is much too generous," she said.

I joked, "Maybe this is how she sees you, all boobs and brain? She never wanted to stop breastfeeding, right?"

"True, but still, these are huge." Kat went back to the onions as Mike came in the kitchen to greet us. "This does have me thinking though, I could use a boob job. I would like to fill out a dress better, or at all, or just not look prepubescent in a bikini." Elle looked at Mike who rolled his eyes.

"What? No," Elle said. "Why? You don't need a boob job."

"Right?" Mike interjected with the exclamation style question.

"Come on," said Kat. "I don't even have boobs." Hands covering her flannel-covered tits. "Look at these." I was. She always undid an extra button. One just a little lower than most might. I think Mike assumed that Kat's manner of dress was solely motivated by her feminism, by her decision to ignore the shame about our bodies, the shame that was taught to all of us, but it wasn't entirely so. Kat was in part saying, "this is my body and I am proud," but part of Kat loved to be objectified; she desperately wanted to be seen as a sexy woman. Whatever the reasoning, Mike didn't care as long as it wasn't done in mixed company.

Kat sat across from me at the kitchen table and leaned in. She smiled as she adjusted her flannel. In the V where others might have fastened a button, I could see her red bralette, the crest of her tiny breast, and the edge of soft pink.

"I should have *something,* right?" Angling toward me.

I took a more neutral approach. A motto was developing: 'one should not be too enthusiastic about the breasts of one's mistress in front of her husband' and so on.

"Well, as long as they wouldn't be comically huge, because much bigger than what you have would be really weird for your frame." In the reflection of the window, I could see Mike standing in the kitchen, motioning to Kat who was facing him, sitting just opposite Elle and me. He was pulling on his shirt. I didn't get it at first, but as the conversation continued, I could feel the wheels in Mike's head spinning as he considered me contemplating Kat's frame and how a boob job might look on her. I could see it now – he was trying to quietly signal "Cover up!"

I pretended not to notice and I continued. "My feeling is, if that is what you want to do, then you should."

Again, I caught Mike in the window signaling. Kat looked increasingly irritated.

Elle protested, "Of course you say that, you think everyone should get one."

Now it was getting hard to pretend not to notice. Mike was coughing and pulling at his shirt. Kat said, "Excuse me for a moment" and they both left the room. I needed a beer anyway. As I returned from the garage, Kat walked past me wearing a pullover hoodie. "A new look?" I asked. "I was getting cold," she responded mechanically.

"So, back to it. No Elle, I don't think everyone should get one, but I do think everyone who wants one should get one. There's a big difference there." I smiled.

The hoodie triggered me. I was feeling mischievous. That night everything was boobs. Two potatoes on the plate: "Kat, perhaps something like this?" I'd smile. Two beers held over my nipples: "I feel like I could have gone larger, what do you think Elle?" The ice cream melting in my bowl at the end of the night: "Mike, would it be possible to get these two scoops augmented?" I'd laugh. And when she'd had enough, Elle said, "OK. Enough boob talk, we have to get going."

Elle drove while Kat texted me.

K: he's pretty mad.

Me: Sorry. I was felling silly.

K: I know. It's not you.

Me: Why does he hate boobs?

Me: Who hates boobs?

K: He doesn't look at me and he doesn't want other people

to have a reason to look at me.

Me: I mean shit, why do I care? It is a little strange that you're still complaining that he doesn't look at you.

Me: I shouldn't be talking you into a boob job while you're with him.

K: I only have eyes for you.

K: You know I am only here for the girls.

K: They'd be for us, you and me.

Me: I know.

K: OK. Gotta put the girls to bed. I lalala love you.

Me: I love you.

And, as my head hit the pillow, I pretended I was asleep that night while I listened to the sheets whimper next to me.

The Dildo

"Mommy, I found a body part, I found a body part!" Kat laughed as she described how that morning her eldest daughter, then six, ran down the stairs with Kat's dildo in hand. Cyber-skin slipping, balls waving. Mike at her side during this retelling averted his eyes lest he see my reaction or Elle's discomfort. Kat let us know that her daughter was rifling through her bureau, found the cyber-skin dildo and proceeded to march around the house with it like a band leader. Smiling, she told all of us the story of how she was able to use this as another teachable moment. So, as Mike sat next to Kat and Kat spoke of the wonders of cyber-skin massage devices I was lost in the irony of this situation. Due to the distance between Mike and Kat and the zero distance between Kat and me, and my desire to make sure that she had something that could satisfy her, something that would ensure that the lonely nights she described at home weren't too lonely, I bought her that dildo.

Earlier that week, as I often did, I parked my usual half a mile down the street from the Doll's House just up the street from Twigg's Café. Kat sent me a text from their bed.

K: Photo*

K: Utah.

K: 10 minutes

She'd come down the stairs, the girls watching Peppa Pig, Mike scrolling on his phone, just back from his run. She'd take a sip of coffee, then she'd let him kiss her before she left for her jog. She made sure to let him kiss her then because it was pretty good odds that her mouth would likely taste like my cock or maybe even her pussy when she got back.

She approached the passenger door cautiously, searching for the eyes of the lookers, the people that peered out their windows looking for people who might be fucking in front of their houses. And she searched for joggers, people leaving for work, and the dog walkers and with one last look, left and right, she slid into the backseat. She hopped in and kissed me with the same mouth that kissed Mike just moments before. She tasted like the coffee he made for her: roasted walnut, cocoa, and green apple. She peeled off her clothes. I told her to lay down, that I had a present for her. She closed her eyes as she laid in the back-bench seat. She was smiling, already pulling at her nipples, preparing to be fucked and I lay the dildo like a crucifix over her pussy. She sat up, laughing. "What is this?"

I said, "I wanted you to have something at home to remember me by."

"It's so much bigger than my blue toy."

I told her, "Exactly, now let's get back at it, I have to get to work soon."

She bent over my center console and I filled her pussy with cyber-skin as I worked on giving her the bruises she required. After she came, pussy still pulsing from cyber-skin, she turned around and rode my cock until she came again. As she left, she tucked the fleshy toy inside the pink hoodie, the same hoodie

Mike would shame her into wearing on evenings he thought her top too revealing. Hoodie, red face, dildo: she jogged an absurd jog, smiling all the way home.

Once home she messaged me.

K: Dangerous. M was waiting for me when I got home.

Me: Yikes. Mother waiting.

K: Yes! Always. I had to run upstairs and hide it.

Me: I'm sorry. Maybe I shouldn't have bought that thing.

K: No, no. I meant to thank you

Me: I don't know. Was it too much?

K: Not at all. Thank you for seeing me.

K: You guys are still coming over tonight, right?

Me: Yup.

Me: See you at 5

Monogamy is for Dopes

As Mike and Elle cleared the table, Kat told us that at a friend's recommendation she had been reading *The Ethical Slut*.

I had already read it, but I said, "Interesting, what's it about?" Primed and ready not to give my opinions on the Single Slut; BDSM, sex clubs, sex parties; holding back all my insights and my expertise in Making Agreements: swinging and swapping, what one might do while traveling alone in their hotel room (ah Edinburgh), after all, educating educators dictates that conferences will be aplenty, and one should have rules for such engagements. I had met a few Unethical Sluts, I knew their ways, but would not divulge their secrets here; I had plenty of slut-based beliefs, looked forward to building a culture of consent with my partner. This book was in my wheelhouse, but as far as Mike knew, I knew very little. Elle, and soon Kat, knew I was a student of the literature of Eros and Civilization and the ancient ways of Bacchus, and the Maenad: oh, those Raving Ones, and Women, Sex, and Power; and Perel, and Anami; and from the archaic De Secreta Mulierum to the beautiful and poetic: Woolf, Dickinson, and Nin, to the extreme, the dark and the vile, but the sexual all the same, Marquis, Voltaire, to stories touched with madness: Giles de Rais, Lady Bathory's Gynoecium, I liked to be prepared.

Mike scoffed as Kat explained that it was a book about the many ways to be sexual, how to be safely open and unashamed, and in particular how to dabble in polyamory. And, not that it had any bearing on anything other than her desire to feel pursued, Kat thought that with the recommendation, her friend (a card-carrying man-hating lesbian) was looking to add a third woman into the mix. Kat loved to be pursued, but as she told us that night, "I don't have feelings for any vagina other than my own." She tried to contain a slight smile of satisfaction. "I am pretty sure Anna was coming on to me when she gave me the book, but I would never." Mike scoffed again as Elle listened on in silence. Elle let Mike take the lead on approving and redirecting the conversation. She responded in squints, big eyes, and with a thoughtful tilt of the head. I laughed a lot and rubbed my chin. "Interesting, very interesting."

As the discussion turned to me, Kat asked, "Are we supposed to be with one person forever?"

I deflected with the classic, "I don't think we are supposed to do anything forever. I was with someone before Elle and when she tires of me…"

Elle jumped in, "Pretty soon."

"And when she tires of me," I continued, making big eyes at Elle. "She and I will likely find other others."

Elle was like a hype-man at a Baptist church. "Truth!"

Mike was laughing.

Kat jumped in. "Yeah, but what about now, are we supposed to be the everything for our other?"

Clearly this wasn't about the book any more.

"I do believe one might call that a soulmate," I suggested.

"Mike doesn't believe in soulmates," she complained.

Yeah, not about the book at all.

"Neither does Elle." I cringed for offering that up, I was hoping that no one would ask me what I believed, and they didn't. Clearly, I did. I was lost in romance and the idea that there were no accidents.

"Yeah, no," Elle said to a nodding Mike. "Too much pressure. There are a lot of people out there. There are a lot of options that could work for any one."

Kat was getting upset. I could tell that she was irked that Mike didn't believe in soulmates.

Soulmates. It always got her, and it rubbed raw that sore spot between the four of us. Kat and I were soulmates, but goddamn, it sure would have been easier if we weren't. That conversation was affecting Kat. She was letting it all sink in and fill her up and she knew that I could see it building behind her eyes as I hugged her goodbye for the night.

On the drive home, Kat and I engaged in our usual parting text exchange. She wanted me to know what she couldn't say at the dinner table.

K: I'm sorry about all of that.

K: We are soulmates

K: You know that right?

Me: It's OK. I understand.

Me: You don't have to apologize. It's hard.

Me: And, yes, I know. We are.

K: Goodnight baby

K: xoxo

Me: xoxo

At the dinner table, there was a subtle interplay between the awakened Kat and the still angry at not being seen by her husband Kat. I didn't feel like Kat got everything she wanted from these conversations. She was being flirty and provocative, yes, but I could see something behind the furtive glances cast between Kat and Mike. She wasn't making loose spontaneous play, solely attempting to push forward the platforms of the modern woman. She was angling. I was really getting the sense from these conversations that I was being used by Kat to hold a mirror up to Mike. She was trying to get me to side with her, to normalize what he had earlier rejected. She was trying to prove something to him. To challenge him. Kat kept prodding to either manifest the fight that would cause him to call it quits on their sexless, passionless relationship, or have him finally awaken to her needs. Kat wanted nothing more than to not have to be the one to break up their family and now I could see all of this playing out before me. She was hoping I'd unwittingly help, that I would say half of what I normally might in private, but I never did. She hoped that I might hint at the normalcy of our erotic milieu, at least in the vaguest of terms. She wanted me to passively challenge him so that he might perhaps find the dildo and fuck her with it as I did. So that he might fill her mouth with his cock, as I did, as she applied the vibrator to her clit; to say, "if you get a boob job, I am going to fuck those tits and cum all over them," as I did; to say, "pick out a fantasy inspired by your latest book and we'll live it," as I did. I could see the slow drama unfold as she'd probe.

Birds of Prey

Kat loved to garden. I'm not sure which came first, her love of the earth or her obsession with her astrological sign which told her she loved the earth, either way there was no separation now, she was of the earth. Those that tend gardens develop a keen sense of the life cycle; everything is living and dying before their eyes. One must keep watch, or the sun will burn the soil and starve the seed. Crawling things will swallow silky leaves and steal flowers if left unattended and if flowers survive to bud, in time, birds will peck clean that which we leave to chance. They sit on their wires waiting, seemingly occupied with other things. One day there is a touch of green in a tomato, and the next there is a hole on its surface that transforms the fruit on the vine into a decaying host for maggots until it drops into the stinking fermenting mulch with all of its worms and flies, smelling of wet earth, wood, and decay. I was not of the earth, but I loved to sit with Kat on the stoop in front of her house to watch this living dying cycle play out in time-lapse as we shared a beer. I'd imagine Elle and I were of the mulch; at best we were a rotting maggot filled tomato. We were yesterday's fruit. We lived and died, we were the living dead, our organs turned to jelly in the earth to provide nutrients for other fruit. Kat and I were fat on the vine, existing in this shadow garden full of life and the lessons of beginnings and endings. We were so fucking high on the pure joy of being seen and validated by each other, so lost in our shadow garden, that we often forgot about the real life that bound us to our houses. We forgot the predators that ground us into the soil: work, children, time, insecurity, our others. We forgot the birds that hung on the wire, waiting. We forgot how they would swoop down to mark endings and beginnings if life were left to chance. How, if we weren't watchful, they'd remind us about living and dying and all the small choices we made each day that led to all our bigger choices. The garden, the birds, they were trying to teach us something.

It was late March. Kat was talking about planting her garden, planting her radishes, beets, and kale and how if things grew like they did last year, her garden would give too much of what no one wanted. Last season she had a swarm of beets, hordes of radish and mobs of kale. The growing of it was just an exercise, a domestically approved way to pass the time within the property line of her doll's house. It was a small annual vegetable problem that reflected her larger perennial psychological problem. Too much of what no one wanted served to others so that it didn't go to waste. I recalled radishes cut like red-ringed nipples decorating the kale salad, all full of earthy and musty beets that stained the bowl crimson red. They reminded me of when our hotel dates drifted too far into her early-bleeding days; she was sexy, metallic, and musty and my cock dripped red like the side of the bowl. Gardening was sex for Kat or maybe Kat made it seem so for me. Either way, it was there on her stoop where we let our hands drift to find each other's thighs when the birds were away, where we'd wait for our others so that we might all have dinner

219

together.

Elle and I sat at their dinner table, trying not to talk about the obvious as Kat made small talk apologizing for the store-bought salad. Elle wanted to say something. No, she wanted me to say something, but I wouldn't. I couldn't. I knew too much. Besides, Kat had distracted me again. Her feet found me under the table and beneath her smile and glowing eyes, I saw black lace behind an open button on her blouse. I was thinking about how I'd love to devour Kat in that garden, in the soil, over the planter boxes that Mike made for her, against the garage, but Elle called me back, breaking an awkward silence that had everything to do with the fact that we all knew Kat was recovering from an abortion. Elle said, "It must be hard, for both of you. How are you holding up?" Mike didn't say anything, but looked to Kat. She said, "I'm fine. I'm doing better now." As Kat's words trailed off, Mike reached out to support Kat's back, and I couldn't fucking take it. I saw her adjust in her seat as if telling him that she didn't want his hand there, but I was losing my mind. I left the room to get a beer, to cry a little, to try not to fucking tell everyone everything, to try not to put a hole in the garage wall. Mike thought I left because I was a good man, because I knew that this talk was better suited for ladies. Elle thought I wanted to give Kat space to *really open up*, but they didn't know anything.

Two weeks before that dinner, I received a phone call from Kat. From the tone of her voice, I thought we'd been found out.

"Can you talk?" Tears coming through the phone. Sobs. "I am a fucking idiot. So stupid. Irresponsible. I, I, I…" More tears…

"What's going on?"

"I don't know what to do. I need to tell you something."

"What is it? You can tell me anything. No secrets, right?"

"I'm pregnant."

"Fuck…" And we were both silent. I waited too long to speak. When I did, I said, "I'm sorry. OK. Are you OK?"

"No. I'm not. I'm not OK. I can't believe I put myself in this position."

"We did it, not just you."

"I don't think it's yours."

"That's an oddly confident response considering what we've done."

"I don't know. I…"

"You told me you two barely have sex and when you do, you use condoms. Besides, whatever you do at home, we both know it could still be mine."

"Yeah, but… I don't know… I just can't think about whose it is right now."

"Does he know?"

"No, you're the first person I called."

Silence

"How could I let this happen?"

"Honestly, it doesn't matter to me. I just need to know, if are you OK? Do you need me to meet you somewhere? What can I do for you?"

"Nothing, I guess. I just needed to say the words. I'm feeling better now. I just needed to tell you. To hear your voice."

"What can I do for you?"

"Nothing. I don't know. I guess I just need to think. I have to go. I'll call you again soon."

"I love you. Call me if you need anything."

I was losing my mind thinking about the pregnancy. We were fucked. Over. Done. Our life of constant connection was gone. I didn't know when we'd see each other next, and I didn't know who we'd be for each other when we did.

Over the next week, Kat and I exchanged text messages. She told me, regardless of what any one thought, she wasn't going to keep the baby. I was relieved, but I didn't want to seem so. I tried to keep my feelings out of it. If it was his and they kept it, we were over. If it was mine and she kept it, life would get interesting really quick. She told me that we couldn't be us any more, not right now, not while this was happening. She said that she just needed a friend she could count on. That she needed to examine her life, she needed to deal with this. She needed time to tell Mike. There was no way he couldn't know. "I can barely keep it together at home," she said. "Even if I took the pill right now, he would eventually sense that something was going on. I am a mess."

I reasoned, "I know. You have to tell him. Obviously, he will assume it's his." As all of this was settling in, I understood that in the midst of all of this, we couldn't go on as we were.

"I just need space to tell him. It's going to be hard. I need time to think so that I can do what needs to be done about it." I said I'd go with her to Planned Parenthood, that we could get a hotel room and take the pill and just watch a movie and cry. She didn't want any of that; she wanted to cry alone in the bathtub and under her covers; what she really wanted was to have the baby, but she couldn't, so she wanted to feel all of the pain all at once. She wanted to punish herself.

"If you need anything, just call. I will be, I am, here for you."

"I love you."

"I love you. No matter what."

Over the next week, I was there... texting, emailing, on the phone with her. I became the non-romantic support system Kat needed: therapist, understanding other, the receptacle of her tears. I felt like a distant friend, a confused and former lover, I felt lost, and a little sad, no, very sad. I had no one to talk to. I was fucked up, twisted up, but I was all warm smiles and hugs for Kat. I would be there for her regardless of whose baby it was, but I was beginning to feel the strain. I couldn't speak a word about it until Elle and Kat met for their walk. When Elle returned, I got the report about the news I had been sitting on for two weeks. "Kat's pregnant," she said. I had to look surprised. "Mike wants to keep the baby. She doesn't, but to his credit," Elle said, "he's letting Kat make the decision. And, get this, she is mad at him! Can you believe that?"

"Uhhhh..." I had to think. Fuck this was weird.

'Well, don't you think that is a little strange?" she repeated.

"If I remember correctly, they had an agreement," I said. "They had settled on no more kids. Right? They said, after Olive, they were done."

Elle said, "Things do change, you know."

"Right, but I'm pretty sure he knew she didn't want another, so is it weird that she is mad at him? I don't think so. They had plans. He knows why she doesn't want to keep it."

"But now he wants it and he's letting her do what she wants. What more could she ask for?"

I had to play it neutral (a little too late)... as if I wasn't in love with Kat, as if I wasn't dying inside because we paused (stopped? ended?) our relationship, as if it could be his; thinking about what that would mean, as if it might be mine and what that would mean.

"I know, but still, they had plans for their life."

She, I told myself, she had plans.

"Plans for their two kids, a plan for retirement, a plan they had made together," I said. "Everything would go out the window if she had another baby at her age. I think it's kind of fucked up that he changed his mind."

This was not neutral.

"I mean, think about it, he knows that she doesn't want a baby, so he changes his mind and gets to enjoy the luxurious position of saying 'I let my wife decide' while feeling none of the guilt associated with the abortion?" I said it in the form of a twisted-up question, but it wasn't.

Elle wasn't having it. "You always defend her."

"I'm not defending her; I am just saying that this is some highly nuanced control shit."

I cannot stop myself. Fuck neutral. Now I am mad at Mike.

"Think about it, either way he would get what he wants, another child and his wife housebound for a few more years, or the powerful gift of guilt to call on and use for eternity."

"I don't know," Elle said, "I just don't think she should be mad at him for wanting to keep it and letting her make the decision."

Arguing with Elle about Kat's looming abortion was a total mindfuck, but it was still less difficult than my visits with Kat. I was a wreck, but I tried to hold it together for her. We met on 28th

Street and Beech in South Park right around the corner from where we'd fuck in her car after going to Hamiltons. She was wearing Mary Janes, black tights, a rust-colored dress with a white and cream pattern, topped with a white sweater. I was lost for a moment thinking about that dress. Last I saw it was at the Hilton in Mission Valley the previous month. I was cursing myself for thinking about how I hiked that dress up over her ass as I kissed her and how I pulled at the tufts on each shoulder to reveal her breasts. I tried to shake the image from my mind. I let myself off the hook by imagining that thinking about sex while pondering an abortion was like thinking about an abortion while you are having sex; it was a distraction that allowed for better performance. I wanted to break down. I was on the verge of tears, but I was trying to be strong for her. And I hated myself for imagining an alternative reality where Kat and I could slip away, where it was mine, where we could find out what it would be like to just be the two of us before there were three of us. All the while hating every fucking inch of myself for imagining a reality where I turned my back on my family. And we were just sitting there. Not talking. Not touching. Kat didn't want to be touched. She didn't want to look at me. I was beginning to wonder why she asked to see me. She stared at the trees, leaving my eyes to wander off into the hideously ironic, empty, childless park looming just behind her. Goddamn, why did we meet here?

Our conversation played eerily like our first phone call. It was a testament to how we didn't even know how to talk to each other any longer.

"I am so stupid."

Her chin knots up and begins to shiver

"I can't believe I let this happen."

"Come on," I say, "you weren't the only one in the room. It wasn't just you."

"It isn't yours."

"Wow. OK. I know you're mad, but are you mad at me?"

"No. I'm sorry. You're being too nice. I don't deserve you. But it isn't yours."

"Ummm, I do know how calendars work, I know where we were right around Christmas. That's when it happened, right? You and I were together a few times. And I will assume you had a later rendezvous with Mike. It was the holiday. I understand. Probably that night you sent me those photos from your mom's." She stared. "It's no big deal. I am just doing the math. You know I don't care about any of that."

She is bawling. Shivering. Looking through me.

"Look, I know what happens at home. I'm not mad. I don't care. We're both doing this. We knew we'd both be with our others. You told me that you always used condoms at home. Now, I can guess that wasn't entirely accurate; and I don't fucking care. I love you. I will be here for you through all of this."

I reach for her hand. She lets me touch it, but she does not reciprocate. She is cold and lifeless.

"I can feel my body changing. It has only been a month, but I can feel it in my breasts and my gut. I love being pregnant... I loved it. I want to have this baby, but I can't. Don't get me wrong, I have wondered what it would be like to have your baby," she reminded me, "but we are never, never having one. I already have the two girls, and I am too old now. I have a career to think of, and if I ever want to retire... I am so fucking selfish."

226

I stroke her forearm.

"I am a whore and a liar and now this. How could you still love me?"

"I told you, I don't care. It doesn't matter whose it is. We can do this together."

She hangs her head.

"I don't deserve you. I'm sorry, but I am so mad at him (*she doesn't say his name*). He's leaving all of this to me. The thing is, in his mind, this is one hundred percent his baby, and he is just leaving it all to me. He didn't even offer to go to the doctor with me."

Fuck.

"Don't worry about it. I understand. I'd be mad too. But we can do this together. Tell me what you need."

"I took the first pill this morning. I just need you to hold me."

I held her as her chin knotted up on my shoulder, as I looked out over an empty park, as airplanes carrying other people to other places flew overhead. We sat there until she started to feel sick. "I have to go home and lay down," she said through her tears. As she stood to leave, I was sobbing. "I wish I could be there with you. I'm sorry for all of this." And I sat and stared at that goddamn park until the sun set and it was too cold to stay any longer.

I survived in the shadows wondering if I'd ever see her again the way we were, the way we used to be before this "ordeal," as she called it, and then Kat sent me a text. "I took the last pill. I just wanted to say that I am so sorry for what I have put you through. I love you. You are seared into my skin. You are my bones. My marrow. Can you make time today? I hope so… I have a reservation for us at The Atwood."

"Yes of course."

"Fair warning, I'm still bleeding. A lot."

"Noted. I just want to see you. Tell me what you need."

"I just need you to hold me."

The hotel was a stale haunting reminder of what had just occurred. It was lit with that hazy sort of white that lights pharmacy aisles and doctor's office waiting rooms, the kind that makes us unrecognizable to ourselves in a mirror, showing us things, we don't see in other lighting. It illuminates, yes, but it also mutes and distorts; it has a weight about it that subdues a room, it settles like a collective hush that pours out from the fixtures. The hush hints at a parallel reality that scratches just beneath the surface. One in which, if we held up a light to the mirror, just at the right angle, we'd be able to catch a glimpse of the life that we should be leading, if only we had the courage. The room was taunting, cold, and lifeless, an empty shell waiting for someone to give it meaning and we did. That day, for us, for Kat, it was a post-abortion recovery room.

We didn't speak. I turned off the lights. I set out two coffees and a bar of chocolate on the nightstand, I kicked off my shoes and crawled into bed with Kat, fully clothed. She was crying before her face found my chest. We held each other. And we cried. We cried for so long that I could feel the walls sigh and the ghosts on the other side of that hazy light crying with us. The room became the oasis we needed, and we were seared onto each other's skin, we were inseparable and undeniable, and we had metamorphosed into the embodiment of the poetry we wrote for each other.

You are my bones, my marrow, my blood, the moon, the sun, my love, my best friend, my true love, my soulmate…

We spoke in poetry because we were poetry: beautiful and tragic and complicated and full of the minutia and the full magnitude of the joy of life. Writing these words here… I can hear it. "Who really speaks like that, right?" But that's just it, we did. I do know how these words sound. They seem humorous at best, but they aren't meant for you. They are for her, for Kat. This is our language. The language I know. These are the words I've been given to explain what is beyond me; even so, I know they are of a banal poetic tongue that went out of favor long ago with powdered wigs, spats, and ascots; comical out of context, laughable to the practical observer, unbelievable to the cynical, ridiculous and unimaginable outside of the space we created when we were alone, and yet, they were honest and authentic and real. What's more, here on their own, even these words for poems and retro-Victorians *aren't* enough, they just aren't. They are but an anchor; she and I are foundation and frame and form.

And we were more, much more.

Like those words, these words, we were a true anachronism.

***

When it was all over, Kat wrote me this:

I am up. 2:43 a.m. Insomnia has taken hold again. Rereading your emails and writing. Drinking Ardbeg (our whisky).

I was in love with you long before Xmas. I realized my need and connection to you during this ordeal. I keep coming back to what you wrote me: "You don't want to sleep with her, and you don't want me to sleep with him." And then it happened. This happened. I then had to retreat to this place of reckoning. I wasn't ready for it. I felt the same as you did. Those words hit home, but I couldn't say them. You have an uncanny ability to write me words that I have saved as drafts... unsure of whether I am allowed to say these things. I am afraid of scaring you away.

This song makes me think of you. Well, us...

Sing me a song of a lass that is gone,
Say, could that lass, be I?...

I listened to the 'Skye Boat Theme' on repeat (along with Ani DiFranco) when I was going through the abortion. I should probably go to therapy...

You never wavered. You never changed who you were to me. It never changed who you are or what you meant to me. When I asked if you could just be my friend, it was one of the hardest things I've ever said aloud. It wasn't what I wanted. It was what I thought I should do. I was wrong. I love you. I have always loved you. To many more moons.

Book IV

Untangling Comes with an Act of Love

A Night Under the Stars

An Evening of Obligation and People-Pleasing

Palm Springs for her birthday.

While everyone slept, I surrendered to my 3:14 a.m. insomnia and wandered the house. The house seemed empty. Not a sound. I found the black glass leading to the pool and I could just make out the stars reflected in its mirrored surface. It was asking me to move to the back yard. I slid the door to find the warmth of the night a welcome contrast to the cold airconditioned house. The night air hugged, warm and weighted. I positioned a lounge chair under the sky to count satellites, maybe to find our star.

One... two... at two satellites I fell into a dream.

I was like Alexander, needing insight into my siege on Tyre and I was Haruspex demanding a kill, and I was Desert Hunter of the Lost Soul Tribe combing the wastes in search of prey that, like me, knew what it would find when it followed the tracks of the desert rabbit. In the dark new-moon sky lit only by stars and satellites, I found a hungry coyote digging and snapping at a burrow just at the base of the Crown-of-Thorns bush. I stole her and brought her to the tiled floor of our Palm Springs rental. I tore open the beast while everyone slept, my mouth full of fur and breast of blood. It is all in how one interprets the entrails when spread upon the tiled floors.

First, I found the eyes and they told me Who, one hazel, one green, two dots in the right eye, one for each of us. I knew these eyes; I'd seen the hazel shake above me.

Next, I pulled free the intestine to measure the length; this would tell me When. It was unbroken. Soon.

Then, I ran the length to feel the seeds and the shit, to know the true foul smell of What we were doing, and it smelled like aged berries, half-truths, and lies. We had a choice ahead.

Haruspicy in hand I examined the liver, the source of romance and desire; it doesn't lie. It is full and smooth and fat. I take it in my mouth, and it tastes like blood, and warm cunt, and metal like when my face has been between her legs just after her period.

Last, with head in hand, gravity opened the jaw. I found the tongue to tell me How, and the teeth grinned, and the snout snarled, and the carcass spoke these words: "Ask her this – are we closer or further away?"

I repeated, 'Are we closer or further away,' and as my mouth moved to muzzle, I devoured the tongue.

In the morning I found this email from Kat:

I was in an immediate state of comfort and calm and yet anxiety tonight. So much of me is calm and true when I am around you, but much of me is trying desperately not to get caught looking at you, but longingly aching for a glimpse of you even in the mirror. I want to grab your arm and kiss you.

I know that there is no denying it. It is a matter of time. The "fuck it" moment will come. I know myself and I know that when I am tested, I am strong and can remain steady. I want you to know that I have made a plan for myself. Milla told me that she had a nightmare that I left and did not come back. My heart broke and sent shock waves through my system. Both she and Olive can sense what I know: that we are destined to be together. I am saying this because the "fuck it" moment could come without warning.

I will make sure my girls are taken care of, and then I will take care of myself. I need to make sure that my kids have a solid foundation. Then I can be free. Then we can be together.

I can sense my energy changing. I know where I am headed. I know where *we* are headed. I love you to my bones.

***

On our first night in Palm Springs, the night before I dripped down Kat's leg on our Dale's Records excursion, we swam in the pool's blue water at night, smiling to each other as we gauged who might be looking out from the house. Our hands reached out under the waves, happy to find our first chance to touch each other in over a week. We'd breach and we'd clock the shadows that preferred air conditioning and mobile devices to the dry winds brought on by the sun falling beneath the mountains. Silhouettes moved slowly inside, never venturing near the huge sliding-glass door. The lights were on in her room, the one where the French doors opened to the jacuzzi. Mike was inside with the girls, Elle was on her phone, the kids were on their devices. I swam up behind Kat and pulled her bottoms to the side, her pussy underlit by the light at the bottom of the pool, and we were left undisturbed to watch the stars begin to peek through the sky. The vast dry distances we endured each week in our normal lives left us to find each other, heart peeling like dried cracked lips, brain flaking like sunburned skin, liver burning and exploding like ants under a magnifying glass, we were so thirsty for each other. I told her about my dream, and I asked, "Are we closer or further away?" Her head tilted, not understanding why I needed to ask *when all of the evidence pointed to closer, only to closer, always to closer, closer now than ever, so close we could taste the pain they would feel when we finally left on the Day of No More Lies.* "Closer." She smiled, kissing me before we swam apart.

We were each other's balm for the dry nights at home where our others cast us aside, where we had reasoned that what we were doing, fucking in this pool, falling in love, writing poetry, exchanging stories, dancing to records, fucking down the street from her Doll's House in my car so that she could get out of the cage for a little while, long enough so that we could both endure another week of trying to justify this; wondering if we left now, would we have to sell our houses, displace our families? Would it crush everyone under the boot of our love, was it worth risking in order to be the authentic versions of ourselves? To be one hundred percent ourselves all of the time, but only with our children fifty percent of the time? Wasn't that better than being fifty percent of ourselves one hundred percent of the time? Children do feel these things; they unconsciously learn our patterns, our phobias, the soul-crushing compromises we make in the spirit of "good enough." If we stayed, if we didn't choose true love, we felt that we'd be teaching them to make compromises we'd never want them to make for themselves. Just like the desert of Southern California leeched its lack into us, we'd leech ours into them. Worse, now, here, feeling that we weren't crazy, that all those too small voices that pumped their "good enough" poison into us, our fucked up parents, our narcissistic siblings, our disconnected-automaton others who chuckled at these silly Victorian ideals of romance, true love, soulmates with such vigor that they made us believe in the days before the Soda Bar, The Casbah, Dale's parking lot, that they were actually correct, that what we dreamt of at night, wrote about, read about, and fantasized about, wasn't possible. They mocked this fairy tale vision. But here we were, so deeply in love and tangled in friends and kids that we justified hanging on this way for a little longer, pulling everyone else along with us. We said that it was to reduce their pain and in waiting, Kat and I survived on the smallest crumbs and in-between moments.

Elle would later tell me she read, "affairs aren't always what they seem, that they generate their own excitement with the sneaking around, the adventurous meetings, the constant texting, the sexy photos and sexier videos" … But I disagreed. Sure, Kat and I needed the connection. We drank our messages as desert wanderers dying from thirst might lick the dew off the fronds of the Pony Tail Palm. Our tiny drops sustained us, but it wasn't enough. We were in pain; whatever the thrill, it was washed away daily, diminished a thousand-fold by our distance. We were dying a little more each day from knowing who we were together, from feeling our electricity over our distance in the small hours of the night, but then living a lie; feeling that electricity, but then filling the sheets next to our others, to be present with them, but not too present. Early on, way too early on, we had fallen so hard for each other that we had to live off the poetry inspired by the full moon and the night ocean. It was all we could do to endure the fact that we knew we were still sharing a bed with our others. It was all we could do to deal with the shift, when we felt the all too ironic sting of shame for cheating on each other as we performed our infrequent and awkward duties with our others at home. Anything, even *that*, to maintain the lie at home.

***

Kat wrote me, true love never loses.

It doesn't. I know that we will be together. And for some reason in my head and heart, we have all the time in the world. Maybe because of this I procrastinate. I am 100% wherever I am. I try to be there 100%. But this is about us. I cannot explain to you in words how I feel about you. I am drawn to you. I belong in you, with you, on you, near you. I know I do. I know we are made of the same stardust that is trying to be whole again. It feels that way when we are together. And when we are apart, I spend a good portion of my day thinking about you. Feeling you on my skin. And it is absurd how challenging it is getting. I can't look at you in the presence of others without my whole face lighting up in what I believe looks like and feels like an aura of pure happiness and joy. I don't know what else to say. I love you. More than you know.

- K

Those words, and so many others like them, gave me life. In the days leading up to Palm Springs we were dying from lack, our words becoming urgent and desperate: I need you; I want you, I can't live without you, just a little longer, we will figure this out, we have to figure this out. In Palm Springs we were insatiable and dangerous, and we were getting more dangerous by the moment. We'd kiss in the kitchen, finger in the hallway, send photos from the bathroom, and worse (better?). The next morning, while our families played in the pool, I excused myself to use the poolside bathroom and she followed only seconds later, somehow registering my wordless signal. We were so thirsty to fuck that we leapt into each other with such force our teeth bumped as we kissed. She lifted her left leg to my waist, and pulled her bikini bottom to the side and we pressed our bodies together. We both came silently with our faces mashed in the reflection of the mirror to the cacophony of our families in the pool. She repositioned her top and laughed, "I love how you fuck me." I kissed her then motioned to the shower, I said that I'd buy her time. She refused. She preferred to know that I was inside her; she loved to find my stains between her legs when she changed. She walked out and settled into a lawn chair like a movie star, one arm folded over her head, the other holding a popsicle she grabbed on her way out to the pool. She licked and slurped as it ran down the wooden stick. I saw her smile like she was replaying our exploits in the open air. She was so picturesque I stole a secret photo mid-slurp; I still look at it from time to time.

So, after the pool lights, after the bathroom, after I drove and she fucked herself in my car, after Dale's Record Store parking lot where I came inside her and made her mine, after we dripped sweat and cum in the record store, we returned to find dinner ready, and Mike locked in the bedroom complaining about a headache. The rest of us ate and played card games and as the night wound down the kids peeled away from the table leaving Kat, Elle, and me to clean up. I left to do the dishes and Kat told Elle, "It's too bad the kids are up... if they go to bed, we could all go skinny-dipping." Elle later reported these probing words to me with an air of annoyance. Kat did love the idea of skinny-dipping, but what Elle still didn't know was that Kat had long fantasized about blending the families, both of us living with our children and our others. She had been priming the quartet with polyamorous visions from the *Ethical Slut*. Before dinner Kat half-joked about getting Mike and Elle drunk or drugged and naked in the same space. If the stars aligned, the pool could be that place. "They just need a little push," she reasoned. I told her that idea would never work, for as much as Mike didn't see her, he did observe when others did, and he definitely saw when she sought to be seen. In those moments, I could see how she would cringe when he'd signal "adjust your skirt" or "button up your blouse," or suggest with hand gestures to "cover up," or "change your dress, you can't walk around like that," and on occasion "put something over that," and "are you really wearing that to the beach." She hated it, but surprisingly she always acquiesced—I blamed the sick soup of a Minnesota mother turned over-watcher husband. Each time she pulled her pink hoodie over a low-slung top she'd reason "he is just in a mood" and "there is no use fighting now when I won't be here much longer." So, while blending families and skinny-dipping was an interesting idea, there was no way he'd willingly partake in my windblown cock touching the same water as her bikini-less form. And for all of his not thinking of her this way, despite Elle's natural beauty, her longer legs, long dark hair, almond eyes, and full breasts, if he actually did see Elle that way, his desire escaped even my keen eyes.

But still, had I known that skinny-dipping was on the table that night, I would have run out of the kitchen naked to encourage it. Instead, I drank too much beer, and to Kat's surprise (everyone's), I put myself to bed. Moments later Elle followed into our room. I stirred and she told me that everyone went to bed, too tired from the sun. She wanted me to fuck her, but I couldn't, my cock was limp. My mind was too full of Kat, our drive and Dale's parking lot. Elle threw her arm over my body and tugged at it, but my cock did not betray Kat that night. I waited for Elle's breathing to steady, and I went out to see if I could find Kat in the kitchen. We'd told each other we'd meet there at midnight.

The kitchen was empty, but the pool lights were on. I went to the far window to look out at the night sky, and I could see her swimming topless in the deep end. I planned to watch for a moment before I joined her, but then I saw that Mike was sitting in the jacuzzi staring hard at the house, not noticing her as she breached the water in the shallow end, not turning his head as she stood up, tits facing him then me as I hid in the shadows, stretching, lifting her arms above her head as if slow dancing. When he didn't move, she slid over the blue tile separating the pool from the jacuzzi and emerged with her bottoms in her hand. She set them next to her top at the edge of the jacuzzi. He seemed tense; they exchanged words for a moment and after the exchange, she waited, standing naked before him. I imagined she was giving him a passive opportunity to reach out, but he didn't.

He was still pouting, later I'd find out about what.

After a few unacknowledged beats passed, a ready, naked, and in theory, willing woman exhibiting body language suggestive of openness passed him slowly – arms, tits, then her naked ass over the tile, back into the pool. She returned to the shallows after one lap. She stretched and leaned and moved her hands above her head again in that slow dance. Later she told me she wasn't trying to be sexy, but she clearly was, I almost dove in to fuck her right there. She lightly moved her hands over her breasts. She checked, but he didn't look. His eyes were on the house. He said something to her through tense lips. He looked angry. Her mouth moved, her face said that she was confused. She looked hurt and upset. She left to swim another lap then into the jacuzzi to his left to lay her head on her folded arms that crossed on the concrete ledge. She settled in with her head tilted slightly to the side to take in the stars. She pensively looked out into infinity while her pussy was tickled by a lazy jacuzzi jet. As she pretended to be thoughtful, all lost in the Milky Way, I could see it unfolding. She was waiting to see if he'd take her right there, but again he didn't move. It was their standard nighttime manipulative sex ritual: as always, he was testing her. He wanted to know, after whatever they just argued about, would she come to him? He spoke, hands gestured a bit and she responded with a soft face. And then she did, she went to him. Her hand reached down to find his swimsuit still on. I saw her speak. She must have said that everyone was asleep, reasoning that the house had been silent for over an hour. With her words, with her soft face, he rose with his suit in hand and fucked her awkwardly from behind as she stared off blankly into the stars, his eyes fixed on the house, and mine fixed on betrayal. It was a mechanical three minutes, pure throwaway sex as far as I was concerned, but still my blood was boiling. When it was over, after she bent to pick up her dry bathing suit, after she left behind wet footprints, I took my limp cock back to the bed where Elle was sleeping, and I began writing my latest "I think we need to take a break" email.

***

We knew we were still sleeping with the others. We had an agreement, an understanding that eventually we'd have to perform those duties, but we told each other that we wouldn't seek them out. What's more, she told me that it didn't matter if she did seek it out.
"He's uninterested, he doesn't care to, he couldn't, he doesn't even like it."
She colored many scenes describing the lengths she could go and still be ignored: he'd be in bed watching a documentary and she could walk in dressed in lingerie with her vibrator in hand, pass his side of the bed to lay down on hers, and he'd leave her untouched and undisturbed so that she could make violent love to herself.
"Babe, I've got five minutes left here, you know how I love the *Taco Chronicles*."
And in five minutes she'd be done, toy washed, hands washed, toy back under her pillow, nightshirt over lingerie, phone in hand still tingling from the pressure on her clit as she texted me her latest fantasies. Consequently, I never imagined that she'd allow for this sort of jacuzzi betrayal. The contrived and obligatory sex

act of a certain type of woman, yes: The Amazon Prime spendthrifts, the porcelain dolls tied to car payments, those more concerned with dental insurance and 401k's than romance, the song birds and hunted doves who sing to pay rent for the right to be in a cage. But I never dreamt that while her pussy was still tingling under the dinner table from our record store date, she'd consent to taint our sacred act and in that same day let his cock touch what I had awakened. To watch him from behind the curtain like Polonius while he awkwardly stabs, and we both die a little: "Thou wretched, rash, intruding fool, farewell! I took thee for better: Take thy fortune." And really that was it, I took her for better and from behind my curtain I made angry soliloquies: "so, yes, take thy limp-dick fortune from the flaccid ring wearer, too tied up and dried up to fuck a pussy properly, take thy fortune oh mistress of the fake orgasm, the desert cough of the cumless fuck, say the words and shake your ass so that he knows when you can both stop pretending."

My Polonius heart bled just a little behind the curtain of shadow, behind the dark of night. I reasoned for her, as I often did, that this was unavoidable, that it didn't matter because he didn't believe in our sort of magic. Because he didn't, he couldn't see it when it was right there before him, he would never know how we transformed a space, how we made the world shrink away and fade into the enormity of the universe, how we transformed into priest and priestess of cock and cunt and danced all frenzied in bacchanalia, in trance, eyes locked as we recalled where we first met beyond the sky. Yes, he would never know these things, but she did. So, on this night, like those nights when he shamed her into covering up, she consented to her role, she consented to obligation. I completely understood, but I still needed to pout about it. I let my Victorian mind run into madness, "to put herself in that position after we shook the world with our sacred act, to cloud what we had become with obligation. It was blasphemy!"

I lay in bed, listening to Elle's deep breathing. I was broken. Furious and hurt. I couldn't sleep. So, I got up to wander the halls and just over the pounding of my racing heart, I could hear that she was puking. While she puked into the small hours of the morning, I wrote her a letter where I imagined myself as a romantic sort of Giving Tree. God, I hate that fucking story. It wasn't the warped story as much as the misunderstood message that self-important and idealistic mothers read into it. It was about selfishness, manipulation, and betrayal and a certain kind of abusive love that requires the giver to give so much that they are twisted and deformed into something horrifying, that changes them in ways that makes them small and hollow like the soul of the taker.

After Dale's, after we marked each other in that parking lot, and after seeing her in the jacuzzi with him, I began to feel like I was giving too much, that I was too readily providing the balm that allowed her to exist in her own private sun-beaten, drought-ridden Doll's House. I was too willing and eager to soothe her skin after she baked in the heat of his ever-looming wifely expectations. I was there on those too many nights when he left her to wither. I was there to wring the moisture from what few leaves I had left so that she might carry on; and when her mind was cracked and blistered and she was too frantic, I held her and we cried and we breathed, and we wet our hands and faces with each other's tears so that she might pretend a little longer. Here, however, in the wee hours of my turmoil, basking in the glow of her thrice fucked day, I began to think dark thoughts, to pull a little on the loose thread of our love.

I stirred to voices everywhere as I lay in bed trying to finish my latest epic "I need space" poem, *The Giving Tree, the Adulterer-Cuckolded* edition. Elle came in and said that everyone had been up for hours.

"What are you up to? You never sleep in." I didn't tell her, but I never went to sleep. When I finished pouting and my eyes stung too much from squinting at my phone, I dragged myself out of bed to find Elle in the kitchen talking to Kat and Mike. I said good morning as I moved toward Kat, toward the coffee, maybe to touch her elbow. She avoided my eyes. I thought for a minute that maybe she knew I was watching last night, but she couldn't have known what I saw. Whatever the case, something was off. I walked out to sip my coffee and to dip my legs in the waters where she fucked and soon, she waded into the pool next to me. Waist deep, she stood there awkwardly in silence.

"So... what's going on, what was that all about in the kitchen?" I asked.

"What? Nothing," she lied, eyes looking past the patio to the thick sliding door that led to the kitchen. "I just didn't sleep well."

"Oh," I said as a concerned person might.

"I got really sick and puked all night."

"Yikes, I definitely heard some puking going on."

"Was I that loud?"

"Yup."

We paused to check the shadows and then I tested.

"But I feel like there's something going on, you totally avoided me in the kitchen just then. You wouldn't even look at me," I said.

"Well, remember when Mike didn't come out last night," she said.

"Yeah."

"He was upset. He accused me of having an affair with you. He said I only smile when you're around, and I'm always running off with you." Eyes blank, watching the door to make sure everyone stayed in the kitchen.

"Damn. What'd you say?"

"I told him I wasn't. That we were just good friends."

"Has something changed between us? Are we just good friends now?"

"God no. I love you. We just have to be careful. He's watching us now."

"I understand, but it's hard to think nothing has changed after last night."

"What, no! Nothing has changed," she said, probably thinking that my comment was related to Mike's accusations.

"After last night, I can't help but feel like we aren't in the same place any more," I said, trying not to say the words.

"I told you, he cornered me about us. I couldn't tell him, not with all of us here, and then I got really sick."

"What made you sick," I asked curiously.

"I don't know, it happens sometimes."

"Do you think it was because the jacuzzi was too hot?" I

probed.

"What…?" she said, looking confused.

She stood facing me, perfectly still in the pool, her mouth hanging open to let the cicada speak when she should have. I can plug the memory of this face into so many of her Doll's House retellings. This face, this self-saving look of confusion and hurt, I learned of it as she poured her Doll's House secrets into my ear every time we discussed our situation. That face that birthed that look became famous as she unfolded the discussions she had with Mike over the years. This face in this pool, was the hanging face she had described giving to *him*. Almost without fail, each of our hotel rendezvous contained a moment where she'd play out this scene for me. She'd sit up in bed naked and mimic the look she gave him as she retold each of her Doll's House stories. This was the face she gave him each time he accused her of sleeping with me; the face she gave him after he confronted her upon reading her journal where she confessed that she had lost herself in marriage, that she was no one's songbird, that she tired of being trapped in his Doll's House; the face she gave him on his birthday, when after Elle and I left, he told her that he knew she'd be divorcing him within a year, and it was the face she gave him when he wanted her to be responsible for the decision about the baby. We'd lay in bed naked after fucking for hours and she'd tell me the sins of the over-watcher. Every confrontation went exactly the same. He'd accuse in his well-trained way, eyes down, legs crossed effeminately, hand on his knee, and he'd speak softly with qualifiers and backout clauses floating in his speech, but giving enough to her so that if there was a grain of truth she might waver and speak it. She never did.

Each time she gave me these secrets I'd ask, "What did you say?" The answer was the same every time.

"Nothing.

"I didn't say anything, I just stood there with my mouth open."

I could see it in its perfect simplicity as I played my own game with her on the edge of the pool—as I wandered closer to saying the words that I was trying to get her to say. Her mouth agape and eyes soft, this was her body language response to an emotional threat and as she honed this defense over the years, she realized that with it, she was in control. As she learned, her natural-unnatural pause showing hurt and confusion gave the Doll's House inquisitor the burden of filling in the meaning behind her expression. It was a beautiful and artful trick; she didn't have to tell the truth and didn't have to lie. The tactic worked well in her Doll's House dynamic because he didn't want to be wrong about the control he had in his house. He wanted her to be the image of the wife he had created, and so at home this less skillful, hubris driven "she'd never do that to me" inquisitor, whose mind projected the reality he wanted to see, would fill in the gaps for her. She didn't even need to speak.

… and begin…

Inquisitor: What's going on between you two? Are you having an affair?

Director: remember, the questions alone are a blow, they are powerful. They hurt. They hurt because they are the honest fucking truth, but he doesn't know that. But use that, use that truth, the truth that you are doing it, that you are in love with

249

someone else, true love even. Maybe even soulmates. Soulmates can't stop, right. Use that. You are going to leave him; you just need to figure out how and when. Use that reality to feel the pain the inquisitor will feel when he finds out this truth, use that emotion to direct how you respond. Let the question hit you and then do what comes naturally.

Ready? Reset everyone. Reset. Mike, Mike, hit that line one more time, can ya pal?

2, ... 3, action.

Over-watcher, gatekeeper, builder of houses and cages and cutting boards and spoons:

What's going on between you two? Are you having an affair?

You (Kat): the question hits with a force to the chest. Taken aback, a half-step back, shoulders roll forward, caving in to protect the heart from this attack, head down, but lifting to reveal soft eyes and an open mouth, the eyes begin to wet – not because you have been hurt by this truth, but because it is truth.

Director: Mike as rehearsed... on with the soliloquy.

The inquisitor: (Notes in pencil read, 'Reasoning for Kat') "Her face, this is a look of confusion and hurt. After those heavy and impossible accusations, she has no words for me, she is too hurt to speak. She would never... How could I have ever imagined this small delicate creature, this tiny bird of a woman, all full of lies and deceit.

Director: Shame, remember the shame. Feel it. Yes, yes, feel it hard for even asking your wife that question. Remember, in this non-response that she has honed and rehearsed and used to much success, the fool *will* feel shame for having pushed and questioned her thusly.

She and Mike had well-matched manipulation techniques at work in her Doll's House. Hers, the artful mouth-hanging defense, and his the manipulative empathetic ploy, where he didn't really want the truth, he had no interest in coaxing the sting of the whole truth out from behind her decaying gallbladder, he solely wanted her to feel what that face showed him, because for him, in appearing to feel shame, for asking the question, for doubting and then letting the too fantastic version of reality slide, for letting her off the hook; in exchange for that, she would cage herself for a time and she would go to him in the dark as she once did.

My tool, however, was persistence.

I could see the words hiding just behind the mouth she left hanging open and I pulled at them.

"You know, people often get sick if the jacuzzi is too hot, or if they stay in too long."

"What? What are you talking about?" she said, now looking annoyed.

Two, three, four… I count to eleven, letting the cicada fill in the quiet. Eleven is a long time for silence.

" ******* "

"I saw you in the jacuzzi last night."

"What do you mean?" She hesitated, still not quite putting it together. I could see her mouth hanging open, hoping that I'd fill in the blanks for her, hoping that I'd register her confusion and hurt at this line of questioning as something I should let go (just as he might), but there was no one to answer for her, even the cicada went silent for a moment. I heard the quiet of the desert and reflected, amazed at this scene, at the sheer intricacy and nuance of this dance; she refused to speak the truth even as I drove us straight for it.

"Jacuzzi? What are you talking about? We all went to bed after dinner."

"We did. But you didn't."

She still looked confused, so I gave the words to her hanging mouth.

"Come on, really...? OK. I couldn't sleep, I got up, went to the kitchen, saw the light in the pool, went to the back door hoping to find you, and saw you fuck him in the jacuzzi last night."

Her face went ghost white. Her legs almost buckled in the shallow end of the pool under the weight of the words.

"I, I, don't understand..." she stammered.

"After dinner Elle came in and woke me up wanting to have sex. I couldn't do it, believe me she tried, but I couldn't, not after our day together. So, I rolled over and pretended to sleep until midnight when you and I said we'd meet in the kitchen: clearly you thought I passed out for the night. I got up and saw you walking in the shallow-end topless. Just as I was going to join you, I saw you move next to him, so I waited... and then..."

She looked sick and just stared at me with her mouth open.

I said, "Look, I know things happen at home, we both know we sleep in the same bed with them, but here, only hours after we fucked twice, and after you cried in my car after telling me to cum inside you... after you begged me to make you mine. I just don't see how you got to a place where after all of that, fucking him in the jacuzzi felt like the right thing to do."

Just then we froze. Mike brought out her breakfast and set it on the edge of the pool. He told her to be sure to eat.

Egg, bacon, and avocado wrapped in a flour tortilla.

"I didn't want avocado," Kat complained.

"You look like you're going to be sick again," he said.

"I don't feel well. I can't eat this. You can have it," she said sliding the plate to me.

"Do you want something? Some medicine?"

"I'm fine, really. I just can't eat."

"All right, gotta go back in. Elle and I have food on the stove."

I picked it up again. "I understand we're still tied to our others, but after our day together, to cap it off by fucking him... I can't believe it."

She was on the verge of tears, saying, "I didn't know what to do. He was just so angry and sad. And I didn't want him to find out about us this weekend." Her words were eating me alive. I was gone, fading out, listening to the cicada drone as she damned her people-pleaser personality. "I didn't want to fight. Not last night. And I know that he and I are over, but I don't want him to be sad about it. I don't want to be the one to cause it. You know I've always been a people pleaser."

I was processing... affair, love, soulmates, us, earth shaking

253

sex that unifies the heavens, he accuses her as he has done a few times before and fucking him in the jacuzzi under our stars is passed off as a side-effect of being a people pleaser. And now I was wondering, what happened on all of those other "mouth hanging" nights of accusations, all of those other awkward nights that I helped to facilitate? How exactly did those nights of people pleasing go down?

Despite myself and my doubting internal dialogue, I said, "I get it. I do. But I'm hurt, and I can't help but think that you knew what would happen if you went skinny-dipping with him."

She pushed back. "I did it because it's fun and freeing. It had nothing to do with him. He was just there."

"That's kinda the point. You made that choice with him there. You had to know…" I replied, leaving room for her to fill in the words. She didn't. I paused for hanging mouths and for the cicada and I continued, "When you jump into a pool topless with a man, he will form ideas, and then when you take your bottoms off in front of him, those ideas are confirmed, and when you pull up next to him and use your hand to help him bridge the gap between his moody pouting and the naked woman tilting her ass next to him, there isn't much left to reason. You had to know where that would lead." I thought of my past email describing how the others could sense a change in us when we had altered each other, how they were drawn to it, how it made them want us in their limited way. And I thought about our rendezvous, the bathroom, Dale's. I knew that what we did at Dale's sent a mushroom cloud of joy over Palm Springs. She knew. She knows.

She told me it didn't mean anything, that it was quick.

254

I stabbed. "I know, I was standing right there."

She reminded me of all his secrets, the secrets she offered me under the sheets during our hotel stays, that he couldn't get off with her. That she was too wet for him.

"Too wet?" I chuckled like I did the first time I heard this. "Like I told you, there is no such thing and whatever, I don't care. I understand what we do at home. I understand what we have to do. We're both doing it. And really, I'm not upset about the sex, I'm upset about the timing. After our day together, after we connected like that, I don't understand how you not only allowed it to happen, but that you were the instigator. I still can't believe it. He left it to you to decide, he didn't go to you, and there were a hundred ways that your conversation about us could have gone, but you actively chose fucking him in exchange for his silence. And worse, I can see that with all of your evasive maneuvers this morning you were never going to tell me. I just don't know what to make of all this."

"It didn't mean a thing. I just felt like I didn't have any other choice. I was literally crying while he was inside me. Do you know how mortifying that is? I had to fake an orgasm so that he would stop. It was horrible. I never want to feel like that again. It literally made me sick. I puked all night because of it. Last night, I promised that I would never do that again. I will never have sex for obligation."

And I felt shame for pushing, for watching, for my persistence.

That night, back home in San Diego, while we lay in our separate beds, I sent her my *Giving Tree: Adulterer-Cuckolded* epic-poem email suggesting we end it there.

She responded with this, this beautiful and heartbreaking note on the subject of A *Night Under the Stars: Obligation and Jacuzzis.*

Obligated. Obliged. Bound. It was odd. The therapist was in tears. Shouldn't that be me? But I'm cold and lifeless when I say the words. Cold when I am performing the act. That is what it is. An act.

She wanted me to think of the trauma I was causing myself. The trauma I may not be able to reverse. Her voice trembled as she dabbed her eyes. I began to think. What other obligations am I performing in this house? This is not who I am. This is not who I pretend I am, which is the same as who I am, right?

I wanted to reach out to her. To tell her it was okay. It hasn't happened that often. Only a few times this last year. I could count them on one hand. Yes, sure, I felt Obligated, but I didn't feel much else. In fact, that was the only feeling he gave me: obligation. And that gave me nausea. And the nausea, I was getting used to that. How sad is that? At least it was fast. Barely felt a thing.

I may be more fucked up than I realized.

I'm not sure this is the boat you want to hitch a ride on to the end of the world.

I hope you do.

I would sink with you.

I love you.

And like that, we were healed.

I was such a goddamn sucker for her.

Queen or Kept Woman

It was like that for our first year, dinner table negotiations, cars and sex, clubs, holding hands at art shows, Palm Springs, and an abortion, and crying, a lot of crying, and laughing, and silly precious moments, and the beach, and full moons, and poems written in the dark next to our others, and photos, and videos, and emails full of love, lust, and desire, and hotel rooms and glorious acrobatic sex, and hopes, and plans. I was ready. She was planning. Early on, she set her first marker, to save twenty thousand dollars to ensure that she was financially independent. Check. Next, the holidays were approaching. Then, birthdays. Birthdays over, she said she was having the conversations with Mike, she told him she needed space. She went away to visit her mom and her sister, to bond with female energy, to align her thoughts on her doll's house existence, to complete her plan. She went, but her sister came down with a mystery illness which took all of her time and energy, she came back tired and distracted with the plan still needing work. I was frustrated. I needed to end it.

I told her; I have an extra ticket to Punk Rock Bowling at the end of September. I have a hotel room. Four nights in Las Vegas. Single king bed. And no matter how much I want you there. No matter how much you should be the one to use that ticket, to share that room with me… the building awareness that I will be alone is eating at me… where we are now, I don't see you using that ticket. I am beginning to realize that your tendency is to pull back, not to move forward. Evidence: you telling me that we need to wait, first after birthdays, then after Xmas, then after you have some savings. A decision keeps getting kicked down the road.

I can't live this life where someone else is stealing my nights by the fire with you and my nights in a tent with you, and my nights under the moon, my mornings in bed, my nights of passion. To be clear, I understand you are not currently having these nights of passion with M, but every night that passes is a missed night for us. So, each night our potential laughs, dances, punk rock shows are happening on the other side of the mirror in that other world… and because we whisper, write, text, cry that we are soulmates, because we are, I feel I am being robbed and treated unfairly. We are coming up on two years marking the most amazing relationship we've ever had, built on absolute openness, acceptance, empathy, and the knowledge that what we have doesn't happen that often. With all of this, no matter my desire to open up, to tell them… you want to hold the inevitable at bay to buy a few more hours with your daughters. I understand, but it is hard to watch your life unfold in that house, with me on the other side of the dinner table – your feet reaching out to me beneath. Every time we get close to making this real, you kick the can just a little further down the road because in the ultimate irony, the only person you can be open and honest with is me. You are afraid of telling your truth to your friends, family, and husband.

So, because existing here, hanging on to your texts, clandestine phone calls, and videos as if my life depends on them (because, currently, it does), I am drawing a line. I can be your platonic friend, your fuck toy, or your soulmate; they all have their limitations and only in soulmate do you get to have everything with me. Friends don't fuck. Fuck toys aren't in love, don't write poetry and stories, and soulmates should not exist largely through text messages and pre-dawn rendezvous in cars. They should not be panicking to delete text threads, or to hide emails, or to clear phone logs, or to delete hotel reservation confirmations. They should be tangled up in sheets, or legs wrapped on a sofa, or drifting at a punk rock show, making summer travel plans together, holding on to each other's words, savoring life. So, from this point forward, I want you to know, if Elle asks, I will not lie. Tell me I am no longer yours and we can break cleanly or tell me I am your soulmate and let's get on with it.

She praised me for being strong and setting boundaries. She loved me. She was crying as she told me that she just needed a little more time. The girls. Olive. Through wet eyes she asked if she could still text me that she loved me, if she could still send teary photos, write me love letters. She promised that she was working on a plan. It would happen. She told me that it was in the works, but it was coming along slowly, clearly slower than I wanted. She asked if we could meet one last time at a hotel, just to have time alone, so that we didn't have to worry about someone walking in on us. I consented. I always consented. So, she booked a hotel room "to talk or whatever." It was the Seven Seas Inn. We were on the ground floor on the back side hidden behind ferns, palms, and birds of paradise. On that day, for the first time in a long time, the rain fell hard in San Diego. I was still emo from our looming "ending," and I was pouting hard. I decided that this time, I wouldn't talk. After all, I already said what I had to say. I knocked. Walked in thinking, "I am here to listen."

I closed the door and turned to find Kat looking up at me like a wounded doe. She didn't speak. We just stood there at the door holding each other. We kissed passionately like we'd find the answer in the back of each other's throats. She pulled away to find my eyes, to promise me that she'd find a way to tell him. She said, "We are meant to be" as she took off my shirt. "Just a little more time" as she kissed my chest. The words began to trail off – softer and softer, "You just need to trust me. Trust us." She held my gaze as she knelt before me and unzipped my pants. "God, I love you," as she licked my cock. I was silent. I let the rain speak for me. I held off orgasm by losing myself to the sound of the rain and the irony of her lower back tattoo. It kept flashing into view and disappearing as she repositioned her ass. Fading black script, Arabic for "queen," but I remember how she mentioned that years after she got it, she discovered that it had a secondary meaning, "kept woman." The emotion, the rain, the hotel room, the cock in her mouth, the tattoo, its dual meaning screaming its warning and it was the one thing that kept me from blowing my load right then. I was writing a goddamn thesis on this tattoo with Kat kneeling before me. It was a reminder of the duality of her life, a symbol for the choice she would have to make: to live as Queen, or kept woman. Fuck.

We moved to the bed, and she climbed on top of me. All I could think of was that fucking tattoo and her promises, and she was lost, biting her lip as she pulled at her nipples, she settled deep onto my cock, tears began to form as her torso twisted – she was crying and smiling down at me, sweat and tears matted her hair to her face. The rain pounded out the soundtrack to her convulsions and I knew the truth. She couldn't fake this, the queen would leave the cage. And when enough silence passed, I spoke.

"How do we untangle this?"

"If it was just him, it'd be over now. I need time to figure out what to do with the girls. I will be divorced soon. That is a fact. I'm sorry about Palm Springs. I really am." And to show that she was with me, she offered me his secrets again.

"I just want you to know that it has been a long time. *A long time*. I can't even tell you the last time he came inside me. I don't even think he can. He has a problem orgasming. He just can't." She repeated their age-old sex issue: "When we did have sex, he'd blame me and say that I was too wet." She continued: "And because of that, when we do have sex, I'd fake an orgasm so that he'd know when to pull out and call it a night."

"Does he cum on you?"

"God no."

"Then what does he do?"

"That's just it, I have no idea. We are so messed up."

Sooner in the Next Life

The next morning, we met at Sunset Cliffs to talk. We walked the hills and held hands until we came to the edge of the cliffs that looked out over the crescent moon-shaped shores to the south. She pressed in against my back, my left hand behind, tied to her right, her left hand on my shoulder where she nuzzled her head. We stood frozen, spellbound by the pulsing sea. Paralyzed, we watched the waves crash in our Dale's parking lot pose. Right there, in that moment, we promised to enact our plan to be together and to live out the rest of this life in full honesty and authenticity. I said, "I will hold on" and I added, "But when this life is over, we will find each other sooner in our next."

***

She and I were more like maenad than anything else. Lost Soul Tribe desert wandering maenad, frenzied and drunk on the milk and honey of poetic ideals; the moon when it breaks just over the horizon, but not just the moon, the reflected moon in the sea, a deep lake, a shimmering wet and filthy gutter, the pool of a Palm Springs rental, its crystal rings like the bright rings in our eyes and all its many crescent forms; and the sea for its depths and its breadth and how it builds and destroys and never stops and how it is tied to the moon and the wind and the sun and how it never ceases to be what it is, for the unknowing and the everything of the sea; and love, the pure unasked and reciprocated vision that let us see each other as we were, for the romance of seeing beyond the filth of the day, to find the center of the other and acknowledge, and validate, and love it, love them for it, and to let all of the small fade away in the presence of this beautiful center; and for *true love* which was the song we told each other at the Seven Seas Inn as the rain beat down on the fat green leaves of the birds of paradise just outside our cracked door. We became rejuvenated with the rain, all lost in the sheets, and when we walked the beach that next morning and talked of how this life wasn't enough, of needing more time together, and we whispered songs of our inevitability, knowing that this, what we had become, was truly unquestionable, that we would have found each other somehow, some way in this life, no matter our circumstances. This life's impression would be so deep and burned into our essence that in the next life we'd follow the clues to find each other sooner. For almost two years we grew into this: we observed, we laughed, we loved, we fucked, we negotiated our time with our others, and negotiated our time in-between them, and then we negotiated not just our future, but our forever future together, even our afterlife, beyond the afterlife. Our first year was marked with trials and testing and as we passed each test, each day we deepened our connection. We waded through all of our dinner table negotiations (that's what they were, right?), the cross-paired fantasies, the rhythm of her Doll's House, the danger of every rental in Palm Springs and the abortion and each time we came out glowing and inseparable. The second year we shifted to find that beyond the trials we had fallen even deeper, deeper than we imagined possible, finding that we'd truly been fused together. In this second year, we'd given into each other fully and found that we couldn't unwind without tearing ourselves apart. So, we performed our rituals daily and stoked our poetic ideals, whipping each other into a bacchanalian state of pure intoxicated ecstasy, so that we might survive the wait. We dressed ourselves in fox skins to buy time and to tell our lies, to hide behind the eyes of another beast. We dressed in rabbit skins to run together in the desert and to hide beneath the cool sand for a while to watch our hearts beat and when we couldn't take it any longer, we dressed in wolf skins to fuck, to paw and tear and snarl and bite at each other like the beasts we were.

As we fell deeper into each other, it became too much to bear. I was tired of weaving stories to tell my family. Tired of buying time for her girls, tired of feeling her pull as we sat across from each other at our weekend dinner parties; we cross-paired four, our body language, words, eyes all in love with someone else. Tired of lying in bed absent, quiet. Tired of lying next to someone who let me go long ago, wanting to know what it would be like to wake up next to someone who hadn't. Tired of watching his eyes watch mine at the dinner table, tired of seeing his hand slide across her back as he walked through the room; that should have been my hand. All of those small moments that we were losing out on every day: to roll over and throw my arm over her, to move with her in the morning, to bump into her in the kitchen and kiss the back of her neck in passing, to lay on the couch and fall asleep, to watch a movie together with legs tangled, to have dinner and know that we would go to bed together, to find the moon's rings in her eyes as she moved on top of me for the hundredth time, to start it all over again in the morning.

So, when Mike proposed we all go to Hawaii together, I said that I didn't think I could find the time (I could have). I didn't want to play this game anymore. I couldn't. I did care for both Mike and Elle. I never forgot them, but Kat and I had said our words, words that one cannot take back, and I didn't want to lie to them anymore. From the beginning, I told her that I didn't want to do this. The week after we saw The Quakes at the Soda Bar, we met on the patio of the Ould Sod to deal with what we had done that first night. We were there to check in, to say that this was a mistake, and hope that the other would say that it wasn't. We arrived at the same time. I ordered a Guinness, her a Smithwick's. The bartender was an old Irish man, balding, blue eyed, with a slight accent. The sort where I knew he had been in San Diego much longer than he'd been in Ireland. He counted out my change and said "Cheers." We sat on the back patio, both of us nervous and unsure. Her asthma betrayed her. I could see her slow breathing accelerating as we talked. She was anxious and excited. As time passed with each sip of beer we moved from "What the fuck have we done" to acknowledging how deep our friendship was, to negotiating how to be this open and free with each other going forward. I loved our group: Kat, Mike, and Elle. I didn't want to fuck up what we had, and I definitely didn't want to hurt anyone. Prior to falling in love with Kat, I felt like I was really good friends with Mike, but I also knew we hit our ceiling long ago. The depth of our friendship halted at the walls he threw up so that no one got too close; Elle taught me to watch for this trick. As our connection grew over the years, his sympathies

265

shifted to Elle, the pleasant and the equally distant. These unconscious allegiances set the shape of our friendship in stone. He and I talked bourbon, beer, and politics (if he brought it up), but that was it. If Mike were a character in a play, if we were searching for his motivations, this is where we'd find him.

Mike, the primary breadwinner, woodworker, husband, father of two young girls.

He is handsome, tall, dark haired with soft brown eyes; emotionally distant with a set of perfect teeth that he prefers to keep hidden.

A classic type dropped out of a European noir film.

Generally, he prefers to keep to himself and would rather stay home; moreover, he prefers that Kat stay home as well. Mike sees his primary role as father to the girls and anchor for the mercurial Kat. His essence is to dampen her lusty ways, to shape her misguided will, to redirect her errant thoughts. Father, mother, teacher, watcher, over-watcher; he is all.

Considering all of this, we were as close as two men could get. He loved Elle and our kids, and I loved him and his. However, I wanted to be seen, truly seen, by someone, and Kat wasn't just anyone. We were the best of friends who had reached down and found the small hidden part of ourselves that resembled who and how we longed to be; the part that we allowed others to chastise and demonize as we navigated our early life. We went on so long living this way, still trying to be faithful to who we believed we were, but seeing no evidence, no sign of hope, no hint that this dream was anything but what others suggested: pure selfishness. We grew and the world taught us how to love as it wanted us to love, and so we did what people do when they find "good enough;" we became faithless and buried our true selves. We had convinced ourselves that everyone was right about us after all, and then everything inside us (everything but our dreams and the poetry we read), even our waking mind, was pushed down to quell the discontent in favor of this other lesser model. We reasoned that it was only lesser when compared to an unattainable dream. What we had with our others was amazing, enviable even; therefore, we should be satisfied. Only, we weren't.

Not until we found each other.

So, at the Ould Sod, we sipped our beers and felt how light we had made each other with just a kiss, with just the possibility to finally validate what we had almost forgotten in ourselves. As we finished our beers, we tried to say, "never again," but we couldn't. We talked of how much we had to lose, how young her girls were, how we did not want to be unfaithful, how we loved our others. And with my last sip I told her that her family meant a lot to me, and that my friendship with her was so valuable that I'd prefer we didn't go forward with *this* if our friendship was in danger, and we stood in the empty back patio of that Irish bar and kissed a long, deep, and soft kiss until she had to leave to pick her girls up at the Y. As we parted, I felt a wave of guilt, not for the kiss, but for the lies I was about to tell.

It was too hard to be in the same space with everyone for more than a couple of hours. Kat and I always found each other sitting too close, staring too long, smiling too much, or getting dangerously sexual while the others were just outside the door. Mike and Elle would sit around the fire on the patio. Kat in the kitchen. Me, restless. I'd pop in the house for a beer. She'd smile.

"Hi." I'd touch her elbow and she'd look out the window before she kissed me. I'd pull away and check the door, and we'd kiss again. Her hand would fiund my cock getting hard and in an instant, it would be in her mouth for as long as we both dared. Three or four hours together in the same room and we couldn't keep it together; we would certainly be discovered in Hawaii. What's more, I told her just a month ago, this was our last summer of lies. I wanted to set things right and we were too close to moving on cleanly for me to go to Hawaii and fuck things up.

She told me she wasn't going, she said that Elle should go, but worst case, his mom would go to help him with the girls. Mike had already bought the tickets.

A week before Hawaii, Elle and I went over for dinner and she asked, "So, when do you guys leave?" and I saw Kat's face fall. Just then she realized that she hadn't told me yet. Mike's mom wasn't going, and Elle certainly wasn't, but she was. Elle asked, "Do you need us to watch the house?" Kat asked me anxiously, "Do you think you could water my garden?" I held it together. "Sure," I said, faking a smile. "Let me show you what to do," and she gestured toward the door.

I closed the door behind us after following her out. "So, this is how you tell me you're going to Hawaii?"

"I'm so sorry. I meant to tell you, but everything happened so fast that it slipped my mind. But honestly, it was made very clear to me that I would only be there to watch the girls."

I noticed her wording, "It was made very clear to me." That was her exact wording. That had an odd ring for someone who was supposed to be setting the boundaries on her failing marriage. I pointed it out and she clarified, "It isn't a romantic getaway. Honestly. It's for the girls. I wanted to go for them. It will be our last time all together like this."

"Sure. Whatever. This is just a shitty way to find out. Were you even going to tell me tonight? Probably not, because what if I were upset? I'd be sitting at the dinner table all emo and the others would have no idea what was going on. There is no way you were going to tell me, so what... I'd find out when you landed? Seriously, you could have told me. It's weird that you left it to Elle. Really weird."

"It was all so last minute. I didn't even think... I promise, I am going to talk to him about leaving him when we get back from Hawaii. I'm making a plan. The girls will be in school in August. All the newness will distract them from me moving out. I'm going to figure it out. I promise."

"That's great, but don't forget, we're all going to Palm Springs when you get back. We've waited this long, let's save it for the week after. Now show me how to water these plants."

We had an unspoken agreement: I would take care of the plants and she would take care of me. I promised not to water the leaves of the tomato plants and she promised that she was just filling the role of babysitter.

That night, she applied the hiding-in-plain-sight method, announcing at the dinner table that she'd like me to FaceTime while watering her plants, to ensure that I didn't murder everything.

On the second day of their trip, I biked by the house to tend the garden. I sent Kat a text and she immediately FaceTime. The screen was all smiles and teeth and red nose. She was on an outing with the girls. Out for ice cream and adventures. No sign of Mike. I didn't ask. She didn't mention him. We were both pretending he wasn't somewhere on that island. She turned the camera and I saw her white sun hat and the girls' legs swinging under a table in the background. She saw dry tomato leaves and deep smile lines and poofy hair.

I tried not to be jealous, I tried not to think of what she and I would be doing if we were there together and I had done a pretty good job of that until later that night, when Mike sent us a photo of her leaning over the balcony in her crop top terry-cloth PJs. She leaned over the rail, her braless tits hanging in the dark spaces of the open underneath catching the Kona winds; the winds were my hands tracing the lines of her body, over her legs, over her belly, moving beneath the loose fabric, up to touch her small mounds, extending to the edge of the hardening pink. She side messaged me to tell me that the winds set her nipples off, and she imagined fucking me right there on the balcony in the dark. If I knew her, when Mike left the balcony to check on the girls, her hands became mine for a moment and they caressed and twisted her left tit.

The next day the price for a photo of a watered squash was high. She was dressed in bed with a beer after a long day at the beach: black tank top, beige skirt, her favorite orange panties beneath. She spread her legs, lifted her skirt, and pressed the glass of beer where she wanted me to kiss. Her thighs were tingling, and her pussy was wet and pulsing and from total visceral-recall, she could see my face buried there from just days before. The memory was so intense, heightened with that glass pressed into her panties, that she had to excuse herself for a moment in the bathroom. She didn't have much time, she had already showered and changed for the night. She closed the door and pulled up her skirt, braced herself with her left hand on the edge of the sink as she did with the mirror in Mary's house, and her right hand dove beneath the orange lace to become my mouth parting the petals, finding the wet, finding herself in the mirror just before she dropped her head to cum, no longer worrying if the white noise of the fan covered the quiet moans that came with the convulsions. She held her fingers inside for just a moment to feel the involuntary pulsing squeeze. She sent me a photo of her glazed first and middle fingers in the form of a peace sign, showing how the cum webbed between them, to show me how I affected her even twenty-five-hundred miles away.

"Everything OK," he'd ask.

"Yeah, just reapplying lotion," she said. "I got so burned."

The week transpired thusly, ending with the selfie she sent me from the airplane sitting next to a smiling Olive. "Coming home to you. I need to feel your weight on my body."

The next day I saw her in Palm Springs.

L'appel Du Vide

She was there. He was there. Our kids. Elle. All of us smiling and hugging in our rental positioned just on the fringe of the Movie Colony, just on the edge of the high desert. I thought of how we made this pilgrimage again, of how this house of the Temple of the Lost Soul Tribe, the Palm Springs Chapter, embodied the lack. How we had truly become this place. How even its topography was speaking to us. How it sat on the north end of this desert like a low-rising vulva above those other hard-sun-fucked gaping and gaped twin whole desert towns. How this desert city had leached into everything, only existing to give shape and depth to the cunt of a sea to the south, this blue-haired bone-hard perch of land that housed bleached white smiles beneath sagging bags of skin, dragging on in the blistering heat to wring what was left of life from the host, to provide the ash for the temple that we might spread the black and the gray of the too late deceased about the palms and dates to fortify our smoothies and shakes.

It was a goddamn aged whore of a desert town, too much rouge, eye liner, mascara, cologne, so much cologne needed to hide the stink of death. We were becoming the cunt of the sea, all musk and reek and void and lack; and fat watches, when on the precipice of death, our life-anxiety told us to watch time closely.

Every second counted as we pondered the cages we chose to keep; too much perfume, somehow too much fur, no shoes, and not enough teeth and two pursing lips touching two yellow fingertips and the pink tinged edges of cigarette butts, and thin, black-dyed moustaches and yellow teeth just above a gray soul-patch on a quivering chin. This town was pure performance art. No one here was who they really were, no one who they wanted to be. The lack was palpable. Everyone here wanted to be what they once were, what they never were, what they could have been. It was never about who you were, but who you could have been, who one thought they should have become. It was pure fantasy, it was self as Frank, Dean, Cary Grant, Elizabeth Taylor, Marilyn Monroe, Dorothy Lamour. Pure lust in a skinny black tie, a sarong, a pencil skirt, a braless halter top, at the dinner theatre, the dance of the seven veils, a Tom Collins, and a champagne cocktail. Every bit of it undulated for want of something fresh. It literally ached for want of something, anything, for something wet, something new, something other than pure heat and black asphalt mirages, for want of connection, for want of the gods to reach down from the sky to massage the mound above the void, to press into the mound, to lay their weight upon it, to pummel it with the wet of rain.

We were those who imagined ourselves as others. We made this semi-annual trip, this pilgrimage to wade in the pool with drink in hand and Sonic Youth in our ears, to be baptized anew in this fresh-from-the-source lack that crawled out of this cunt valley to sting us in the chest and the throat like a hum of bees riding on a knot of snakes. Our lack, our bleeding hearts, our stung and bruised necks, this house, this town, this fucking

273

valley, this wet, but always too hot, never satisfying pool clung to our skin and tongues and smelled of incense, of chlorine, of latex, and pussy. And when the wind changed when the sun wasn't quite up, the black asphalt pissed its stored heat back into the sky, it pulled in the air from that dead sea to bathe us in the light sulfur sting of spent semen and shit as we started our day. It washed over us, and we smiled, and we waited for cover, waited for an opportunity out of sight from our others so that we might shake the dew into our waiting mouths, so that we might live as we wished we could just for a few moments. We were too much. Too on the precipice. I felt balanced on the roof-top edge of the San Jacinto Cliffs, leaning over too far to challenge the breeze, to dare it to let me go, wanting it to let me go, wanting nothing more than to fall. I was hard, full cock and balls, into the Call of the Void, prepared to fall with her. I could hear it beg me to yield. I could feel her hand on my back, breath on my ear, slight pressure from her hand and her words, but I didn't need any encouragement. I was ready. Everything in ceaseless unison; the pulsing Vulva Temple of Lack, the dead cunt sea, her words on the wind, the vermin in my liver, heart, and chest with their cicada-like persistence, all whispering, "one more step."

This is Dangerous

Kat and I were the first to the pool. As we waded deeper so that we might touch, the families followed us to abuse the sacred space. Feeling overrun, I exited to take refuge in the jacuzzi, set some thirty feet behind the pool. It seemed the designer of this house considered the distance she and I would need for cover. I slouched into the water. I pretended to be content. I pretended to be pensive. She got out of the pool and asked if anyone would like a beer. Mike was in the pool playing with the kids. She handed him a beer, and then walked over and climbed in the jacuzzi to hand me mine. It was five p.m., full daylight. I was perched in the back, facing the pool, legs beneath the bubbles extended to the opposite side. She was there opposite me, also facing the pool, positioned over my leg and she ground her pussy on my shin. My foot hung on tight to the opposite ledge so that she got the resistance she needed. She pressed into my leg as she did the arm of her mother's couch when she first learned how to masturbate. She reached back with her hand, her gaze never wavering from the pool, Mike and kids playing some thirty feet away. She reached back, knowing what she would find. She arched her back and slid her round ass over my lap; she pulled her bikini bottoms to the side to take me in. I leaned back, to the back edge of the jacuzzi, and she leaned forward.

For those others who might not be, who are not, as well versed in the art of surreptitious love making, it might be hard to imagine how others fuck while looking so far apart, but it was all in the magic of the jacuzzi; the bubbles concealed everything. Beneath the fury of the undulating water, she leaned forward and sat her ass all the way back to settle at the base of my cock. I was full in her wetter than water pussy, her head was steady watching her kids play with her husband while her ass thumped into my hip, driving deeper. We banged on like this until Elle, from the kitchen through the large floor to ceiling windows, noticed that Mike was in need of another beer. As the sliding glass-door opened, we parted like tadpoles who sensed a foot on the shore, momentarily dispersed and appropriately disinterested in each other. Elle checked in. "We're good." Two beers. Still full. Now warm. And as Elle popped back into the house, Kat smiled and turned her back to the pool. She sat up on the top step of the jacuzzi, pulled her bikini to the side, and dove in; I watched her fuck herself right there with her husband and daughters filling in the backdrop.

Where Only We Go

As the day slipped into dusk, I started dinner. Kat disappeared down a dark hallway to the sound of our Tom Petty mix: 'Time to Move On' faded into 'Wildflowers'—yes, this song *again*. Oddly, fittingly, ironically, horribly, 'Wildflowers', I tried to forget that song was woven into their wedding: "It was ours now," she said. I am not being clever with these song drops; she and I dedicated a lot of time to producing the soundtrack to our departure and it played all around us everywhere we went. So, yes, Tom Petty and the fittingly disturbing wedding song 'Wildflowers' and the bodies of our others beyond the glass, everyone else outside as if in some other world that couldn't touch the lovers in the kitchen.

What does a lost, desert wandering, depraved chef make while high on beer and jacuzzi fuck? Ribs, homemade BBQ sauce, roasted potatoes and corn. She reappeared and slid into the kitchen.

"Thank you," she said with her back to me while cutting the green off strawberries.

"For?" I asked, genuinely lost in preparing dinner. She looked to the sliding glass door.

"You, your cock, seeing me. I love how we fuck. It's incredible."

"It is." I smiled while stirring the sauce.

"Do you like this skirt?" Her back was still to me, but she angled her ass just a bit.

"I do, I recognize it from your Hawaii photos. I really feel the skirt and I are connected," I said, laughing.

"It's good for drying out. No panties." She winked and went back to the cutting board. I suddenly realized that we were in the middle of one of our fantasies. This house with its glass walls protecting us on the inside with its glare; air-conditioning, Tom Petty, us two cooking together in the kitchen; our others on the other side of the glass might as well have been in another world. Vinyl pool floaties, squirt guns, the brutal sun, Mike, Elle, and the kids.

She sang as she quartered the strawberries, moving her ass like she did when we were backed against a barstool. She leaned over the kitchen bar to reach for a small white bowl as I approached from the side. She had a mischievous smile which she drew out as she took her suggestive strawberry-communion. I had written this exact scene; exchange the strawberries for sourdough and that which lies beyond the glass for the Scottish Highlands, and we were literally living out our dream. The world outside was gone so I reached down to the back of her thigh to find the edge of her skirt. I let my hand peek at what lay beneath as I stood by her side. The water for the corn was starting to boil. I let it. Kat swaybacked into my hand and it was like wading into a Georgia summer. I could sense her need to move, so I held my hand perfectly still under that orange skirt. She danced her 'You Wreck Me' dance to provide the motion she needed; the water was still boiling and she was arching back and contracting. The world was gone. The Highlands. The pool. The world beyond the glass. The room beyond the kitchen island. She didn't notice the blow-up ball from the pool striking the window, she wasn't there, or anywhere, any longer. I lifted the skirt and moved behind her. The music stopped. The water wasn't boiling. It wasn't one hundred and five degrees outside. The edges of the world had folded in, faded with vignette, everything slid from penumbra into black, completely erased. I joined her where only we went.

When I came back, the filter opened: the pan was red from boiling out all of its water, Lupen Crook was singing 'If You Love Me Come the Morning,' the one hundred-and-five-degree sun beat in through the window, squirt guns dripped their discharge down the glass as I dripped down her leg. Kat lowered her skirt, placed a bowl of strawberries next to some goat's cheese and sliced sourdough.

She walked to the glass door and called out, "Girls, I have your snack."

A Trusting Heart

The weekend pressed on this way. That scene, it was the essence, literally the essence of our life those last two years. Everyone was there. Everyone, always somewhere else nearby. Wherever they wanted to be. Just never with us and here was the end of year two; we were light years beyond filling the gaps in this pitying of paired loveless-marriages, we had made a whole new life out of celebrating each other. Our hands were everywhere, our eyes stole glances at each other and looked for space to touch each other. The next night, my kids were on their devices, Elle fell asleep, and Mike went to read to his girls. In all of this absence, she stayed in the pool to skinny dip. I was drinking a beer quietly in the jacuzzi and climbed out to have a closer look. I was unsure if she was waiting for him, but when I found her, she said she was waiting for me. He never came. She swam up to me on the edge of the pool and I pulled at her nipples. I needed to check to see if we were safe; I told her I'd be back. I went in to check the house and waited quietly. I thought I heard Mike stirring, so I waited longer, too long. She got out of the pool and walked to the kitchen as I slipped out a side door, returning to the jacuzzi. In the dark, I saw a phone light pop on in the kitchen; she texted me to come find her. She wanted me to take her again over the kitchen island. Just as I was about to join her, I saw the light go on in their bedroom. Mike had noticed that she was missing. He followed our scent. I could see him approaching her in the dark of the kitchen. I could tell that she thought those footsteps were mine. I could see her face flush under the light of her phone. I knew that her pussy was waiting, but there he was. She fumbled for words. Defeated, I watched her follow him into their room.

On this night, our last night in Palm Springs, earlier at dinner Mike saw something that broke everything open. We sat, Elle and Mike on one side, Kat and me on the other. This night was like all the rest. The conversation flowed easily, too easily, and we drank and laughed, and she touched me beneath the table, and I didn't pull away. It was all the same as it had always been. However, now Mike had two years of building concern and a full-length window behind which she and I sat. The glass became a mirror reflecting how we touched beneath that table. The touching of feet was an innocent game we played every night we sat together. She'd reach out because she couldn't take the distance, or because she'd see me drift all moody and emo at our distance, or even just because she was moved by a song. She'd place her foot on top of mine to calm me, when the words from the stereo became too real, if the conversation drifted too close to our reality, or if his hand above the table would linger too long at her back. Tonight, however, she was high from floating with me in the kitchen and our feet lingered too long and the window reflected too much.

He saw it all happening. The floating. The smiles. The eyes. The subtle, the innocent laughs and silly play; not enough to accuse again, until the inexcusable, and unforgivable. He saw our touches reflected in the window and he waited. Normally, each night he'd pass out reading to the girls, but tonight, he waited. He waited and followed the scent and found her wet and ready to be fucked again in the kitchen.

"Aren't you coming to bed?" I'm sure he asked.

Red and flustered. "Uh, yeah, just got out of the pool," she must have said. I saw him walk to the glass to search for me in the backyard. I was well hidden. Eyes floating like a crocodile in the distant jacuzzi.

This time it was his turn to evoke the ritual of the hanging mouth. So, as she stripped down to change into her nightshirt, to slide out of her wet panties, he pressed.

"What were you two doing tonight?" "What?"

"Is there something going on with you two that I need to know about?"

"What? Who are you talking about?"

You *taught me, always ask three times. You must have taught him the same trick.*

"Did I see you two playing footsies under the table?"

He never saw her bent before my cock in the doll's house kitchen (as we did), he didn't find us both coming out of their bathroom on the 4th of July, he didn't follow us to Mary's to see what the neighbors saw through the window, nor did he find us in the car(s), the pubs, the hotels; he saw our feet touch under the fucking table.

Her mouth dropped. Again, not from shock. She knew what she was doing, what she did. She upheld her half of the bargain; her mouth continued to hang in all of its perfection. It waited for Mike to complete his Doll's House charade and fill in the lies for her. And he did. He'd play the game that would have her stay silent, that would have her hold onto the truth that he never really wanted to hear in exchange for the guilt that made her go to him in the night. He was clever. He would pout and lower his eyes and sting her with words that came with keys for cages, and he would know it worked when she came to him in the night.

That next morning, she told me everything. I heard the shame in her voice for all of our lies and I saw the hurt in her eyes for living a false life with one who still loved her. She whispered his well-crafted and rehearsed lines: "I am not trusting you with my eyes, but I am trusting you with my heart." Powerful, stinging, and evocative, it pulled at all of her strings. It was questioning and giving, knowing and pointed. They said, "I know what I saw, but I can't believe what it must mean." He wanted her to deny it, but all she could do was stare in shock with her open mouth and let him fill in her words and her meaning.

She knew we were nothing but liars. This inauthentic life went against everything she believed, everything she practiced everywhere else but with him. He was not suited to her emotions, fits of rage, fits of wonder and wander. Long before I came along, she was afraid to tell him that beneath all of the too much, there was even more that she had been hiding. He had already shown his displeasure at the version of Kat she dared to share with him; he'd never suffer Kat in her true form. This dichotomy ate at her soul. After all, she spent her days on Zoom calls training professionals to be their true authentic self, she spent hours with colleagues and students reflecting on the power of authenticity and truth, she prepared lessons for students on the subject, brought those lessons to her own children, and she knew that there was nothing more authentic than how she and I were together, and yet she chose this double life.

She lied to him, her children, and herself at home pretending to be who her husband thought she was. Worse, she told me the truth about everything, him, us, her; the truth of how we were undeniable, destined to be, written in the stars, two halves made whole when we were together, true loves and soulmates, how she couldn't live without me, how we would never part: she poured sweet honey into my ear when she needed me. Those words made me love crazy and blind. Incapable of reason. She was all I could see. She used the words to stall and buy time with those she lied to at home. What was the harm in that small lie? She saw the purchase of time as a technicality, a mere bump in the road to a long life of freedom and happiness with me. Surely, I would forgive the silence she gave Mike to allow her to buy just a little more time in her Doll's House; and I did. And I did. And tick, tick, tick, tick. So, I didn't blink when I heard the words and learned that night's truth.

"I am not trusting you with my eyes."

"I am trusting you with my heart."

Hanging mouths must pay for their silence.

She came to him in the night.

Those words got to her, and they did what they were supposed to do. She quietly went to him, remembering that just minutes before I was pulling at her tits by the edge of the pool. She recalled her soliloquy on sex for obligation, and how it affected us both so deeply. Last, she remembered the rules from her high school in Minnesota: "blow-jobs don't count."

In the morning, it seemed that the entire house was wiped clean of the previous night's events. The magic of desert dreams softened everything. Even our lies were wrapped with the magic of the desert, for when the truth was witnessed under that table, the truth became the lie, and the lie became the truth. Here in Palm Springs, even the truth wanted to be something else. "No, no, there wasn't anything going on," her hanging mouth confessed. "We are just good friends. Inappropriate, yes, but we were just being silly. I'm sorry, I was a little stoned and drunk. I'm sorry. I'll pull back," she lied. The rest of the day was uneventful. The desert stole all of his desire to imagine what that seemingly innocent, but inappropriate, gesture meant. He couldn't imagine it was anything but a prelude to a friendship beginning to get a little too close. He'd never believe that it was the echo of years of deep and deeper deepening connection.

The kiss of her mouth on his cock finished quickly with her hand was all the evidence he needed that the world was right. That night, the dark was on her side. He never saw her eyes wet from fulfilling his Doll's House obligation, those eyes that stared into the dark as her hand cranked below his waist, those eyes that closed to find the void as her mouth slid over his cock, those eyes that couldn't find oblivion. Had he seen those eyes, he might have let her go right then; had he heard her obligation soliloquy, he would have been ashamed for holding on. Had he known that those eyes were made wet each night at our distance as they read my poetry, that they closed to find me in her dreams; he would have relinquished. But she kept all of this from him to stall and soften the blow.

She and I waded into the pool and spoke in hushed tones of appropriate awe befitting two lovers about to drop an atomic bomb on their families. She retold the events of the night, and I could see the truth hanging above her like a noose. I said, "This is it, the last day, tomorrow is the day of no more lies. Everything will be okay. This is what we were planning to do. We were going to launch this plan when we got back to San Diego anyway. Now there is no turning back." She and I were of the science of deceit, each relationship its own experiment; me to her, her to him, her to Elle, and so on. We had pulled apart every molecule of every moment and reduced it to the smallest unit in which it was still recognized as itself. She and I were bound up in the molecular structure of lack and we planned to divide it even further, down to the atom. We'd fire the culmination of us together into the center to end our lack, to split the neuron-lie that would flatten everything – the Doll's House, my family, her family, everything in dust under a mushroom cloud sent to rain down genesis over this dry unforgiving desert city. We weren't doing this to destroy, but to start over. To set them free from the burden of us, to set us free from these constraints. To blow it all up so that we might begin again.

We escaped for a while on a trip into town. We sat together in my car discussing our move forward, what our lives would look like after we told the others. I could tell that she was nervous. I was being pulled apart by the butterflies in my stomach. She told me that she wanted freedom, but she warned me that I better not abandon her. She laughed as she said that I better not cheat on her. We both laughed. She knew I wouldn't. She told me that we were forever. We were in the car "looking for parking" as our others walked downtown Palm Springs in pursuit of date smoothies. I tried to calm her worry. I said, I see you in your entirety and I love every bit of it. And this is how you see me, right? I will never waver. I am not a cheater- her eyebrow lifted. I know, I know! We don't count. I want a life-partner. And to have one who can see me, who I see and love to my core, is a gift. I am a person who loves deeply, and this is what I will do for you. I will see you. I will love you deeply. Every song is you. Every movie. There are so many things I want to share with you. I believe in soulmates. You are mine and I am yours. I have cheated with you. We have cheated because it is hard to trust the soul when this world teaches us not to, and it is easy to settle and harder to walk away when it is "safe" and "good enough." But, long ago, we had already walked away in spirit.

While we waited, I read her a piece I had written that morning: In this world it is hard to be authentic and true. Together we are authentic versions of ourselves, we are fire, desire, a rogue wave of energy who wants to bask in the lust for life, who wants to wring everything out of life, who wants to fuck and be fucked, be held and hold, and take care and be taken care of, and have small sweet moments, quiet moments where there is no space between us if that is what we want (often it will be), and have everything mean something because it does. It means to celebrate life, to mark life with celebrations, to let these things, this way of being, be the thing that ties a couple together, not safety, or good enough, or obligation. This, us, is our true form in unity with another who actually encourages the growth of our true nature. It is the ultimate authentic existence based on mutual respect, based on the mutual desire to see and be seen unfiltered and uncensored, to be taken seriously and not be shunned or shamed. To be allowed to live. To be encouraged to live by someone who wants to see what the other looks like in full bloom (because potted plants never reach their true potential).

I said, we are too important to each other to miss this opportunity. Cheating on you would be a crime against my soul. We both have a lot on the line, and at the end of the day, everything that I've written here is too much to lose. You are too much to lose. I would never jeopardize this. I love you to my bones. We will be OK, I promise.

Just then a set of date shakes rounded the corner. Kat squeezed my hand, let go, and settled deeper in the seat. She gazed out the window overlooking the palm trees until she was handed a plastic cup with a red straw. We split it.

Bloodletting & Bleeding Out

Eighteen months post-abortion, a year and a half of blissful connection, some five hundred and sixty days of artful meetings to quench our thirst, birthdays and hotel rooms and holidays and mornings in the back seat of my car, evenings in her car, and weekends at the doll's house. The tormenting mornings waking up with our others to be consoled by the words we sent through the ether in the black of night to let the other know that we were still there, that we felt each other in our dreams, that we couldn't stand the distance any longer, that together we gave that miserable ether language its meaning. The painful nights lying still in bed with our others, knowing that *we* created something entirely new and undiscovered, and we were wasting it away. Eighteen months of probing the furthest edges of love and trust, of forgetting that we ever felt lack at all, eighteen months of making a plan to be together to live our most authentic lives, to create a space for us that would be free of lack. This is the untangling, the bloodletting. This is where lives are torn apart. Betrayers revealed. Lovers uncovered. Compassion abandoned. Empathy impossible. Everything resembling humanity cast aside by all but Elle. On the day of no more lies, there was angling and bargaining, half-truths, fraction-truths, and lies, so many goddamned lies and simultaneously, too much truth. So much truth that it burned like salt in wounds and sweat in eyes, rubbed red and raw by probing fingers and fuck it all if that didn't make it worse. And the lies, even worse, the truth, for it tore flesh and shattered glass, and faith

Did you still have faith? Did you not learn from Book One?

This untangling, it shattered diamonds and things harder, much harder, much, much harder to find, much harder to keep.

The lies and the truth shattered trust.

The words, all of our lies, too big for this earth, burst out into the sky and seeded the nimbus that hung over our houses and finally, finally the sky gave in and loosed its hard wet. In a flurry, it pissed down fat drops of hot knives and stones and the acrid rain of betrayal stung my flesh awake as it soaked my skin with the lies that I had accumulated over the last two years. I marveled at how even the heavens weren't immune to our lack; even the rain I begged for was poisoned. And these poison words fell hard against cold frozen faces and the pain made us new again. We were born-again adulterers and destroyers set to carry out the lost soul tribe reaping cycle. The words hit faces with deep dark lines shaped in strange masks, with shadows under furrowed brows shaking with ticks and twitches, with hard, hard angry eyes that warned to stay away. The cold words cut, bit, and tore. Oh, fuck, how they cut. How they cut.

And trust. Trust between us, them, them and us. Trust and irony, how it all dug and twisted rusty knives with bent blades into soft ripe intestine. Lives were rubbed raw, so deep it took a moment for the body to bleed, but once it did, it wouldn't stop. The type where at times, depending on the size and location of these wounds, they could be managed: inside the forearm, the shin, the knee, any of these are manageable even in the midst of the thumping dull pain that never quits and seems to pain us more than the sharp pain of the initial wound. The type where it is possible to reason that the pain is temporary and it is possible to find a way to function even with the wound constantly reminding you that it is there. This, however, … this deluge of lies and half-truths was different. In our untangling we ensured ourselves a full-body wound, we flayed ourselves and then our others and then our children. And some of us weren't used to be cut open like that. To feel the bite of the wind against exposed flesh and nerve. To feel one's clothes matted to raw sinew and bone. To have to tear those clothes off the body to assess the wound. Worse, to have to clean the wound in hopes of surviving at all. Every movement aches and stings so badly that the gut wants to vomit.

The end of our affair, the moving on from our others, the plan enacted to find each other on the other side, in our poetry over the years, we had given it various names. Kat and I named it the Day of No More Lies, the Untangling, the Unwinding, and the Bloodletting, but those names weren't enough to describe what it meant to look a wife or a husband in the eye and say the words we had to say; it was much more. It was an unwinding of those sewn together so tightly for so long that as the years passed the flesh grew and blended over its stitches. This was the pulling of a thread tied to terminus at our core, a black hole in the truest sense, not a nothing, but a seed of desire and lack at the center with such immense weight and gravity that nothing could escape. It wound the thread of plans, lies, and half-truths into this void of lack spinning out of control with its own multiplying enormity. To be undone was to undo everything; so, no, not a day of no more lies, not an untangling, an unwinding, nor a bloodletting. It was bleeding out.

The Day of No More Lies,

A Day of Never

Sunday afternoon. We all hugged goodbye in the foyer of our Palm Springs rental and gave promises to see each other soon. On the drive home, with Elle and Mike driving each family, Kat and I sent a flurry of texts checking in with each other. Halfway home she began to angle, preparing to soften the blow for him, but we swore to stick to the plan.

Me: Remember, I am telling Elle after dinner.

K: I'm so nervous. My stomach is in knots. I might puke.

Me: I know baby. We've got this. Me and you.

K: I know baby. True love always wins.

Me: Feel free to tell him whenever he brings up the foot thing again, and he will, probably after the girls are put to bed. No?

K: I'll text you as soon as something happens. Let me know if you tell Elle first.

Me: Deal.

There was no going back.

***

Sunday. 1:28 p.m.

K: I'm not sure what to say if he asks about us. I'd rather he not know that it's been two years. I don't want to give details. But maybe it will be good for my soul to be completely honest.

One forty-five p.m.

No details if possible.

I am a nervous wreck.

I love you.

He knows.

He is upset.

I can't answer when we fucked. I keep avoiding it.

He is ranting about disrespect right now.

I don't know what to do.

We are in love and it wasn't a fling, there isn't any going back. It was two years. This is the story of us falling in love.

2:44 p.m.

Fuck.

I can't do that to him right now.

We have done this to both of them. We can't drag this on with half-truths. We didn't stop, because we are in love. And we aren't stopping. That has to be clear. Like we said in the car, we will not abandon each other

4:03 p.m.

We will not!

I'm having conversations with him and crying.

I tried to keep it focused on me and my needs.

Your needs? Tell me you are not pulling back. Your hesitation is not reassuring.

I'm not.

I am keeping it focused on me though, because I think that is only fair to him.

He shouldn't have to hear all of the details. This isn't about that.

He is going crazy.

5:08 p.m.

Elle knows. I kept it focused on me as long as I could, but she asked a lot of questions. Two years is too long. She asked three times. She asked if I love you. I said yes. She asked if you love me. I said yes.

She didn't seem phased at all. She is taking this better than I am. She said that you and I are good together.

Oh man. This is beyond

How are you?

I love you.

Teary, but OK.

I am not doing well.

I don't know what my next move is.

I don't know what to do next.

As you guessed, I don't have a solid exit plan.

The plan is me and you.

We will figure everything else out later.

Yes. But I mean right in this moment.

A plan that doesn't involve telling the girls.

Finding a place.

Getting my own dental insurance.

You can stay at your sister's.

You don't need to tell the girls much. I'd start with 'I'm taking a vacation.'

Dental insurance. You are kidding, right?

6:19 p.m.

No. These are things I need to think of.

What's going on over there?

We aren't fighting or arguing. We're just talking about you and me.

So, how dead am I?

He doesn't want to see you.

Not what I was asking, but understandable.

He is asking if I'd work this out with him.

I said no.

This is really fucking hard.

I can't bring myself to answer anything other than we fucked.

I can't.

I love you.

I am doing what I said we'd do. I am telling the truth. She just asked if we were together prior to the abortion. I said yes, but that I didn't think it was mine.

Jesus.

Does he think it was all me?

I told him it was me.

He blames himself.

How's it going over there?

Not good. *She* seems fine. I am a wreck. I'm just feeling the weight of everything.

Do you still love me?

Yes, I do love you.

I have to try to get some sleep.

Goodnight love.

Xoxo

We gave ourselves Monday to get things settled with our others. But, when she woke, everyone, she, Mike, and both the kids were sick.

11:50 a.m.

We all have fevers.

The girls are wheezy, coughing, and sneezing.

Yikes. Sick? I'm sorry baby. I hope everyone is OK.

Dang, that is some bad timing. I love you.

We can do this.

We can do this together.

4:04 p.m.

I know. Together.

I am just confused and overwhelmed.

I need to sort through myself.

Overwhelmed I understand. Confused, I don't. We know who we are to each other. That can't be undone.

6:15 p.m.

It can't.

I'm sitting with the truth.

I am doing what I think I need to do at the moment.

Which is to be here for the girls.

They are sick.

They need me.

I need to talk with Mike.

Did you tell him everything?

6:22 p.m.

Elle knows it all.

6:23 p.m.

My insecurity in this moment tells me you are qualifying

things.

8:28 p.m.

When I hear "You are sitting with the truth?" I hear, you are feeling guilty, but he doesn't know everything. It seems like you didn't tell him about soulmates and true love and stars and growing old with me. That feels like it is important.

8:37 p.m.

He knows a lot.

Forgetting you?

Far from it.

OK. Trusting. Closer, not further away?

10:44 p.m.

Closer. Always closer.

I love you.

OK, tomorrow?

Of course. We need to figure this out.

11:57 p.m.

The kids are so sick.

They both have really bad fevers.

I am putting them to bed.

Fair warning for tomorrow.

I have a fever too.

1:13 a.m.

I love you.

I love you.

8:40 a.m.

Presidio Park at the top.

8:43 a.m.

I love you

I love you.

*Photo

*Photo

We met at the top of Presidio Park on Cosoy Way. I was wrestling with the irony of this location to decide how to unwind our families: I remembered playing Kubb here on her eldest daughter's birthday a few years ago.

Kat parked at the bottom of the hill and began the long walk to my concrete picnic table.

I sat in agony during this painfully long melancholy procession and studied her gait.

It was thirty seconds stretched over an eternity.

Kat wore torn jeans and her sandals with the blue buckle, the ones I used to tease her about.

Two old men were playing frisbee. The one closest to me would curse loudly as he threw the disc. "Fuck yeah!" When he'd sling it, he'd glance sideways to see if I was watching with his 'look what I can do' eyes. I kept perfectly still so as not to encourage him.

She wore a loose purple T-shirt I'd never seen before. It looked like it had been rolled up in the back of her bureau since college.

Her hair was pulled back into a messy ponytail.

There was another man following a toddler through the grass. The boy must have been about four. He wore purple Crocs. The father wore headphones and kept his eyes down as he passed. He wanted to see me maybe even less than I wanted to see him.

She did not wear her glasses.

The boy was happy to see that the slope of the park allowed the sprinkler water to pool at the park benches. He was busy jumping from puddle to puddle.

I wondered what was playing in those headphones.

I could see it in her walk. She was broken. As she approached, I could feel the cold change in her heart telling me to keep my distance.

I stood as she approached the bench. I went to hug her and kiss her cheek, but she pulled away. I realized that not wearing her glasses was a tactical ploy. She had planned to reduce me to a mere blur on the other side of the table. She couldn't see the lines in my face that had once inspired her poetry. She couldn't see the eyes that hovered above her so often with pure passion and fire. She couldn't see my surprise, my hurt, the questions on my brow. She didn't speak for a moment; her face was frozen like her heart. So, this time, I gave her the words she couldn't say. "So, this is it, huh?" She turned her head, looking off into the blur of the east to coldly say what she had surely rehearsed in her car: "I have to be there for my kids." Silence. And more silence. I felt ill. I felt my stomach revolting. "They were sick all night. I was up with them wondering who would take care of them if I wasn't there. You know how he and his family are with Olive. He said he wants to try to keep the family together and I'm afraid of what would happen to Olive if I weren't there."

I began to ramble.

"I can't believe this. You told me that even if he wanted to, you wouldn't, you said you would never. We talked about this, I said he'd fight for you and you told me that there was no way you'd settle, no way you'd go back to him, no way you'd live in

299

that doll's house."

I tried to breath. She avoided my eyes.

We sat in silence for a moment and when I caught my breath I rambled again.

"Just yesterday, you told me we were true loves, and that true love always wins. What happened to the day of no more lies? I told Elle everything. I told my kids. You knew I was telling her everything, just like I told you on Sunday. And now, after I burn myself, you back out because he's willing to work on it?"

She was still looking away.

"How is it even possible that he'd take you back after you told him what we were, what we've done, the plans we had? What exactly did you tell him about us?"

"I told him that you see me."

I sat waiting for more, but that was it: "He sees me."

"He probably thinks that it was your idea to come clean. Did you let him believe that? He probably has no idea that you would have just kept this going in perpetuity." *Silence.* "He sees me? Seriously? Are you kidding me? That's it? That's all you said? No wonder he thinks you can work it out. Fuck, I gave you those words." I said, "if you just tell him that I 'see you,' he will say 'tell me what to do and I'll see you too.' So, you gambled with my line and you were surprised that it worked? Is that it? And you were surprised that he was willing to work it out even though I told you he would. Fuck, I told you that this would happen and you swore you wouldn't fall for it. Damn, do you even know what you've done? You've given yourself up entirely to become a nanny in a doll's house. This is the exact opposite of what you wanted for yourself and your girls. This is abortion manipulations all over again. You do the 'act,' and he gets to hold it over you. I can't believe this. If you wanted to back out, all you had to do was stick to the lie you already told him in Palm Springs and then tell me that we were through. Fuck, I tried to break it off with you just last month, but you begged me not to. Goddamn, I was willing to let you go. We could have at least been friends. But instead, because it was convenient for you, you betrayed everything you've ever said to me about authenticity." I was rambling, "No one is taking someone back if they said, 'it is over, I am in love with someone else. Not just in love. He is my true love. We are soul mates. We have plans to grow old together.' There really isn't anything to work on when that is the truth. But you saw an opening and took it no matter who you burned. Fuck, that is some grade A fucking Irony. I mean, I guess I shouldn't be surprised." *Silence*.

Her eyes were lost on the horizon.

I couldn't stop.

"Let me see if I understand this. You didn't want to hurt his feelings, so you didn't tell him the truth, so with this not-so-bad-version of fucking me, he begged you to try again, and you were surprised that he begged, and you began to reason me away, right?"

I was not sure she was listening any more, but I was sure that I couldn't stop myself.

"So, you left out that we were true loves, that you can't be happy with him. You left out that you have been planning to divorce him since before I came along, but you were waiting for the right time. You left out your happiness and what we are to each other entirely."

Pause. Breathe.

She was still staring out at the eastern sky.

I told myself to stop talking. It didn't matter. She was gone.

"I just can't believe that you angled your way back into that shitty relationship. This is classic behavior of the abused. I can't believe this."

She definitely wasn't listening any longer.

I was catching my breath. I sat quietly for a few beats, trying to gather my thoughts.

I was calmer, but I had more to say.

"You won't even look at me."

It finally hit me. It didn't matter. I realized that she'd let go before she set her parking brake.

She tried to look in my direction.

"What did we do all of this for? And after you begged me not to abandon you... not to cheat on you."

No glasses. She couldn't see me anymore. She was looking through me.

My eyes were stinging. Burning desert hot.

"You know what this means, right?"

I was choking on the words, throat full of Jesus Christ thorns.

"I'm never going to be able to see you again."

"Never."

Feeling my mouth fill with hot sand.

My eyes followed my tears to find the concrete table; I mumbled, "Never," the word trailing off half-finished. I was remembering our first meeting at Ould Sod when I said that I didn't want to do THIS if it meant that we might not be friends someday.

"Never."

The hum of bees was filling my head

This was too much to lose.

"Never."

Never: It's the nothing that is left after the bleeding out.

I was full of California, full of empty, full of lack.

I was the lost soul tribe

How She Chose to Keep Her Cage

We sat lost in silence, momentarily prolonging this "just before Never." My fingers dragged at the pool of tears I spilled on the table as the knot of snakes turned in my gut. Everything silent, all but those goddamned bees. They were busy stitching together all of our exchanges from the last twenty-four hours, looking for clues. They found them in her Monday texts and her Presidio words. When he asked the question and her hanging mouth was betrayed by the tears at the realization that she and I couldn't go back, she must have thought that I already told Elle. Those tears told him too much of our truth. He didn't need more words to fill in the void. He knew that Kat had been unfaithful. When it hit, he began to howl and wail like an animal caught in a trap. It brought their girls running as if they heard the ice cream truck pulling into the living room. They heard their father's proto-human cries and at the base of their brains where all of our animals are kept, they knew what those howls meant. They told the children that their world was ending and now the children were crying because their parents were crying. They'd never seen this before. They'd never even seen their parents argue. They didn't care that she had been bridled in this Doll's House, they didn't care about her freedom, her dreams and wishes, her future, they didn't care that there wasn't enough passion in her life. None of that mattered to them. When Kat saw their faces hurt by her lies, none of it mattered any more. In that moment, in the midst of this untangling, it became about survival.

As the bees pulled all of her texts and emails together, I could see the scene play out before my open eyes. I could hear every discussion in his Doll's House happening last night in a slow-motion dream. They were crying because *she and he* were crying and I heard the first six notes tumble out of the piano as Nick Cave drifted into "The Weeping Song."

The children crawled up her arm and asked,

"Mommy, why is Daddy crying?"

"Because Mommy hurt Daddy," she said.

"Why would Mommy hurt Daddy?" they wept.

"Because Mommy isn't a good person," she cried.

"But why aren't you a good person, Mommy?"

"Because I did bad things to Daddy," she wept.

"What bad things, Mommy?" And they all wailed together.

"I told so many lies," she howled. With this song, she had forgotten everything that wasn't about survival. She had forgotten her four-year-itch, the evidence that her marriage wasn't enough to fill her lack; she had forgotten being unseen, unwanted, controlled, abandoned during her abortion, manipulated often, stifled daily, left to twist alone, life force unmatched, unobserved. She had forgotten the nausea, the obligation, forgotten her true love, that true love existed, forgotten her soulmate. What are souls anyway? Souls. The *lack*. She forgot the lack. She had forgotten it all, because the angling she used to keep him close worked too well, even she couldn't believe it. So, when her children's words ground her to bits and there was nothing left of her, life was no longer about joy and experience, no longer about her needs, her life. In that moment, she had lost her imagination. Keeping the Doll's House in order was all that was left. That version of Kat alive, on fire, lusting for life and authenticity was sentenced to a life in the attic of her mind.

I was settling in to the silence. I was getting used to the snakes wrenching my gut; I was learning to love the song the bees sang me. As I thumbed the wet, I made on the concrete, I began to think of all the poetry we had written each other using ships as imagery. I fell in love with a line she wrote me concerning sea-going vessels and wild unruly seas and how they can snap the mast and crack the hull. How we'd endure no matter what. After all, was I not the storm, was I not the diluvian dreamer? It was the last line of a beautiful and meandering and rambling piece, the sort she and I were prone to writing. Five stupid words that sting my eyes as I type, for what they meant then, and their ironic meaning now: '*I would sink with you.*' I chuckled a painful and ironic sort of sigh thinking something about ships, ports, and storms and him. And then the bees became unsettled. I was scrambling, I wanted to reverse this unwinding, I wanted to stuff it all back up into the body, all of the exploded springs back into this broken heart.

I remembered that I had written her an email.

I told myself to stop, but I couldn't. I had one last email. Never is such a long time.

I meant to send it the day before. I wondered if it would have changed anything if I had.

I wanted to walk away. I knew she had let go, but I couldn't.

I still believed in the words we wrote each other even if she didn't any longer, so I said, "I wrote you something. I want to read it to you." Her face twisted as the snakes too found her belly. I read:

I know you know these things, but they are important to say because it isn't often that a spirit like yours is acknowledged or nurtured. In a world like this, that can leave a lot of room for soul-crushing doubt when there shouldn't be any, I want you to know how much I love you. I love you in ways that I don't fully understand, that I am just coming to understand. You have taught me so much. Our bond has created a reality that people dream about, that they write stories about. We are both Edna from The Awakening and like her, this world still isn't ready for us. Because this is so, we have the same options: wade into the sea, suffer in silence enduring the consistent gray, or run away. To compound the difficulty of our decision, we are surrounded by people who doubt and say that we want too much, all because they have never experienced and don't believe in true love. And why should they, it is laughable. But here we are, and it is a miracle of miracles that we found each other. For years, our lives quietly wove around each other, keeping us just out of reach, and when we finally found each other, even we didn't believe what we were seeing. I didn't believe it. I didn't want to. It would be easier if it weren't so. But we were put here, we put ourselves here, we sent out our signal unconsciously - our life force cannot be contained - we drew each other in. This is a miracle, it is magic, it is true love and the reason we couldn't stop, the reason I won't stop, is because we are special. You are my bones and blood, my ocean, my moon. I can still feel you standing behind me at Dale's record store, I can still see you in Mary's mirror.

Everywhere. The dot in your eye, the scar on your hand, the huge freckle on the left side of your pussy, the cartilage on the tip of your nose, your smile lines, the touch of your skin, the taste of your neck, the look in your eyes when you are above me, the way you love, the way you want to be loved, the way I love you, your dreams, visions, fantasies.

We have reached a tipping point. Do we go back to our cages, go to the sea, run away, or do we fully embrace what we have been making, this something new that only we have discovered? I know this is hard. Our families have been affected, but if you asked anyone, would you suffer fulfilling your roles, or like us, would you pursue true happiness and a new way of being while being the best versions of yourselves? No one would hesitate, nor should we.

So, here I am. Not blinking, saying that this is our time, this second phase will be tough, but I know the power of true love. And I believe, as you've said a dozen times, that true love wins. Let's say yes to this harvest moon.

I love you, Kat.

She seemingly ignored my words and stared out to the east again where later that night the actual harvest moon would rise. I reached out to hold her hand. She pulled away. Still looking east, she said, "I will never forget you. I'll never forget what you've taught me. Please understand, I have to try for the girls."

I was not graceful. I said again, "That's it? Two years of us saying that we are inevitable, true loves, soulmates, and in a matter of hours we went from starting our lives together to you thanking me for teaching you how to be your authentic self with *him*? That is so fucked up."

"No. That isn't it at all. It's for my girls. I promise. I am just not a good person. I have done a lot of bad things. You deserve better. I need to work on myself. I need to be a good mother." I could see the storm building inside her as she began to spiral. Her childhood was clawing at the base of her skull, she had internalized all those shitty nights of worry looking out her second-story bedroom window in Minnesota wondering when her mom was going to come home. She never registered that she was chasing her mother's ghost, projecting her own abandonment on her daughters where it never belonged. She was afraid that in the act of leaving she'd become her mother when she never was, nor would be (I guess... never would have been). She couldn't shake that her daughters might even for a moment feel as she felt when her mother hurt her. "They will never have to wonder when I am coming home," she must have told herself last night when she sat up with her sick children. She implied what she had never consciously said aloud: she'd never forgiven her mother for leaving her quaking at that window; she hated her for emceeing that too loud voice in her head that shouted down all of her beauty. Kat staying was an unconscious, and misplaced, protest against her mother that defied the logic of the situation. The similarities were none and logic was scarce.

Mother's ghost or no, all Kat knew was that now, having felt the full crushing weight of her lies on the faces of her children, she would indeed be willing to exchange her happiness (and mine) for never having to be the source of pain for her daughters, no matter how temporary their pain may have been. Kat's mother wound deep dark strong roots into her daughter. It didn't matter

309

how many nights she, or we, had reasoned the pain away, it was happening now, and she wasn't used to be torn open like this.

I tried. I used the language of our abortion discussions. "Listen to yourself, you're punishing yourself for what we've done! If you did all of this to better yourself, for true love, then you aren't a horrible person, you're brave. You don't have to punish yourself for that."

She pushed back against this idea, she said that she wasn't brave, that she was a coward. She paused and she said, "Maybe I am punishing myself. I don't know. I have to work through this with him; I can't abandon my girls."

"Abandon?" I repeated. "We've been through this. Kids that young survive divorce relatively easily. You know that. And you wouldn't be abandoning them. You'd be saving yourself, so that you could be the best version of yourself for them." She had written me those very words on so many nights. Now those words seemed foreign to Kat.

"This is unbelievable. Just two days ago in the Palm Springs kitchen, for the hundredth time, you told me that we'd always be together because true love always wins. Are we not soulmates? Is this not true love? Tell me that this was all a lie. Tell me what we had was a lie. Tell me that you don't love me, tell me that we're not soulmates, so that I can understand this, so that I can let you go." Her eyes trembled and her mouth hung open. I silently acknowledged the meaning she wanted me to understand. I saw it all in her eyes. It *was* all true, every word: her eyes welled and shook in silence, and said "it is true love, we are soulmates."

She lowered her head and sobbed.

Though I Loved Her

I kept searching for something that made sense to me because this ending just didn't. I had tried to end it three months before, but she called me back. If she wanted to stay with him, one last lie and we could have ended it cleanly without burning everyone, we could have still been friends, she could have stayed friends with Elle, but she called me back. Every fucking time. She drew me back: she sent me poetry, and stories, and photos, and videos, and rented countless hotel rooms. She begged me to come back every time I set boundaries. And I did. Every time I said, "I will hang on for us." And now this? I never spoke one lie during our affair, not one half-truth, not to Elle, Mike, or her. Had any one asked, I would have told them. I would have told them everything. Sitting there at that cold concrete picnic table at Presidio Park, I now knew too late that I had been manipulated by an anxiety driven opportunist with abandonment issues.

She broke our lingering silence, and now ten painful minutes in, she finally looked me in the eye and whispered, "For my girls." I could see her eyes welling and shaking. They were distant and pleading eyes that for the first time during this discussion lent the meaning she desired. But in this asking, this asking for me to let her go for the children, it didn't feel rehearsed. It broke me. I was frozen, punched in the gut. "Let me hold you one last time. One last kiss," I asked. She didn't speak, though she moved toward me. In this moment, we were not honest in our motives; this embrace was not a letting go. It was to seal our bond. I felt her breath rattle wild. It slowed as she nestled into the pit of my arm and inhaled deeply. This inhale, this was how we started and ended every hotel stay: we closed our eyes and inhaled the other to imprint our essence so that we could find it when the consistent gray of our other marriages crushed around us too tightly.

We stood there breathing too long. Too hard. Too deep. Too much.

Though I loved her, I was letting go, although I didn't know if I could. I'd try to let go for her, I would; though I didn't know how, though I didn't think I really could. I was letting her go (Here. Now.), trying; I knew that I'd chase her in my poetry, in the eyes of anyone I met, that I'd chase her in my dreams; although I loved Milla, Olive, Lilly, Alex, Mike, and Elle... Kat... *Kat*... I knew I couldn't let go...

As I began to turn and walk away, I saw a glimpse of the real Kat. She was now wholly the person she was trying desperately to hide from me. If she were the mountain I told her I saw in our first few months of our affair, she was now a landslide collapsing into herself. Literally about to crumble under her own weight and slide into oblivion. Her chin shook and her eyes rattled as she dragged herself to her car.

I wanted to go to her, but I was lost. I turned and walked to the top of the hill to sit amongst the needles beneath a pine tree.

Kat sat in her car at the base of the hill. She was watching me. When she caught my eye, she turned to sob into the steering wheel and it set me ablaze all over again. I was on fire. I looked away and from the corner of my eye, I saw her drive away.

"Goodbye, baby."

Blood Oath

In a flurry of absurdity, I went home to Elle. We were standing in the kitchen.

"How are you? How was your day?" she asked quietly and sweetly in a manner unbefitting the news I shared last night. I went to speak, but I was all tears. I was sobbing in hard spasms that rose with the convulsions in my gut. I stood there and sobbed into her shoulder. I managed to speak the words, "She broke it off with me."

Elle was kind, strong, and understanding. She whispered, "Who knows, you two might work it out. She is just confused right now. I can see how you two got together." I cried and sobbed that we didn't just break up. "For him to take her back…," I said. "I have to be erased. She loves me and if she sees me…" There was no chance, no crack in the door, Kat was busy fulfilling the role of confessed but repentant adulteress. She was hiding all evidence of my existence precisely so that she wouldn't accidentally see me. She was busy deleting emails, texts, photos, throwing away the dildo, tossing out my T-shirt she slept in, tossing out all the clothes that reminded her of me (definitely that green dress from the Long Beach Marriot where we first fucked), putting away all the books and records that spoke our truth, promising never to reach out to me, promising to report any contact I might attempt;

in short, as her mother and mother-husband taught her, she was to blame, and like the dream Ocean who wanted to be free, but was overcome by lack, Kat was overcome by soul- crushing guilt. She had conceded, deciding to settle into a lesser version of herself. Kat had decided she would be a good enough wife going forward. She would willingly follow all doll's house rules in exchange for a good enough life.

Elle hugged me and asked if I wanted to try to work it out with her. I was all tears and sobs, "I ... I, no. I can't." I couldn't. What did we have to work out? We hadn't been a couple for years. I sobbed, "I can't. I am too fucked up right now. I can't just flip a switch and pretend that I didn't love her. This is so ridiculous, just last night we were calling each other true loves and soulmates. I just can't." Elle didn't speak, she just stood there quietly in our kitchen holding me while I sobbed into her shoulder ~ while I wallowed in the filth of my own despair.

***

It has been three months, and I was right, I couldn't let go. I am still in her (his) kitchen, any (all) of our hotel rooms, at the Casbah, the Ould Sod. I am truly living behind the veil, the one where we once thrived. I am occupying all of these false spaces writing this fucking filth, literally sitting in our booth at the Aero Club typing these words, drinking our whisky. I didn't intend for everyone in my life to know what Kat and I were and are no longer, but in a series of unfortunate events and confidant betrayals, they all seem to know, and most of them also know Kat. I know too that as a result she has hidden herself away in

314

those ivory-stucco towers of her doll's house. She only exists at work and at home. She no longer has any sort of freedom. She tells herself that she has what she deserves; 'more than she deserves,' to relay the quote precisely.

Her reach extends as far as her half-truths can carry her in the small circle of friends she has, of whom I was not acquainted. Mike and Kat, they are trying, but they have started this new life with more lies and more secrets. They aren't telling any one. They don't want people thinking what they'd think of her if they knew she had a hand in creating this monstrosity: if it was two years spent as fuck toys, she was a whore; if it was two years spent making plans to live the truest most authentic life with her soulmate and in the last moment just before freedom, she threw it away and chose to keep her cage for "security," because he was willing to forgive her, she would be not only an whore, but the worst kind of self-serving coward: an opportunist. For those friends and family that knew our secret, they chose the former, for those that didn't, they pretended that I didn't exist.

It may take her a while to rattle out of the pain of all of this, but when she does, she will see what she has done in the name of security. It will come to her. Eventually, she will realize that she has poisoned her new beginning with half-truths and her artfully clever confessions that bordered on lies. She will see his machinations. She will see hers. She will feel the pull of her four-year itch, hear the words she imagines her grandmother would speak: run, find the moon, find him. She will have to hold her tongue. She will have to think of him, and me, before she speaks at parties. She will have to hold it all in, never be able to speak of true love or soulmates in his presence again (or any one's

315

presence for that matter). She will have to tell half-truths to her friends. They could never know that she, beholder and administrator of all things authentic and true, gave up on true love, that she sold out because she didn't think that her children could survive divorce when all modern evidence suggested otherwise. Worse, she will have to lie to her girls. I think of how she bought herself the time she always wanted, but marked her children's lives with this new specter of deceit and surrender. I think of how phobias are learned from parents, and so too is surrender to Good Enough. I think of how one day when she is lost in thought folding laundry on his bed, she might catch a mirrored glimpse of the painting, the *Woman in Black*. I wonder if she will make the connection that she has fully become the painting that she consented to hide away for him in the upstairs master bathroom, like some whore in the attic. Her bright red heart beating smaller and smaller for no one. She will be tolerated there, up the stairs at the end of the hall, beyond that last door: close it, lock it, turn on the fan, turn on the hot water; this is where you get to be your true self. Like this, out of sight. Over time, like her feelings on that painting's final resting spot, she will come to be satisfied with this result. She might even begin to believe that she chose it. What else is there to do but internalize the lie or psychologically split? "Where else could it have gone," she might wonder. Is she asking about the painting or herself? Even she doesn't know any longer.

She would have to hold all of this in to buy more time in her Doll's House, never telling anyone but her secret online journal what she told me in her silent response to my questions- that she knew we were made for each other, that we were indeed true loves, that we were soulmates, that she screamed I was her bones and her marrow, her blood, that I was the other half of the star dust that made her whole, that I was her only, that she ended it, that she made a mistake. That she gave it all away to keep her cage.

It no longer mattered who we were, or who she was. It was done, but who was I now? Who was I now that it was done? Who was I after giving all of myself to someone so freely only to lose them? Who was I after trusting …? Trusting? It wasn't even trust, it was far beyond that, it was a blood oath sealed by the blood that boiled when we touched, the blood of our marrow, the blood that wrote our poetry, the blood on my cock that stained those hotel room sheets, the blood of someone's fetus for whom we both cried. Who was I now that Kat had broken this blood oath without the ceremony, the compassion, and the empathy that I had once believed were innate to her character, that our time and connection deserved? Who was I now that I had wet Elle's sleeve with my disbelief and dejection at my loss for another woman? Who was I now that I had spoken these truths to my children? Who was I now, after telling them that I was opting out of all of this comfortable certainty and love at home because I found that true love actually did exist? Who was I…?… who would touch the hem of her dress, who would bite at the nape of her neck, who would write the poetry of true love, who would lift and twirl her into bed with laughs and giggles, who would drive the words into her heart, who would weep at what they'd become, who would walk away alone, who had given it all away for a chance to be with her.

Retro Vertigo

You shouldn't read this section. I haven't done a good job of presenting myself well, of staying neutral. Was I ever neutral? This is how one writes full of lack – full of bile and poison and bites and stings. Full of the hollow falsity of California. It is the worst of me. And I fucking hate it. I should be better than this.

I am not.

Dear Reader, you deserve to see me this way, after all, you've stayed with me this long.

I want to put fist to face. Whose? I don't care. Mine. His. I just want blood. Someone's. Any one's. Mine. Mine? Mine isn't worth that much right now, but I am willing to give it for the cause. I am willing to give it for the pain I feel. Oh, sacred temple of Lack, oh Lost Soul Tribe, the transformation is complete, I am the dry well at the world's end and I am full of the bleached bones and gray ash of the dead cunt of the sea; full of the hum of bees, the song of the cicada, and a knot of snakes. I am a crooked tree bent like her crooked words, hunched, ugly, and deformed, so dry, ready to ignite, willing to level a forest, a town, wanting to set a doll's house ablaze. I am the Jesus Christ thorns, hard spined to tear flesh, looking for a false savior to crown; made for pain, engineered for destruction, I am the desert coyote whose entrails litter the tile floor of a Palm Spring rental with shit lies. I am the ship on the bottom of the sea. Broken and alone, for no one sank with me despite the words sent nightly through the ether, written on napkins while our knees touched under tables, traced into my spine in hotel rooms, breathed into my cock by that face made for lollipops. I want to hurt someone like I've been hurt – can someone be hurt like I've been hurt? I fucking hate Mike. I can't help it. Even if I believe all her stories of marginal abuse, he has done nothing to me. He is but a mild manipulator, a rightfully jealous husband converted into a receptacle of strobe-light visions of Kat shaking into oblivion over my eyes; an unwitting receptable of my cum; a void for her anxiety; and, a cage for her worry. But don't fret sir, you will get what you want; her mother has taught her well. She will blame herself and lock herself up. Stay the course, sir. The smooth middle awaits.

I'm on fire. My hurt is ripping through the forest of my mind. Everything is smoke and ash and I can't breathe. I am swimming in visions of Bambi and Thumper running from me to an orchestrated cacophony of strings. My nerves are exploding with pain. I see red. Isn't that the color of hurt? Behind all of this, behind the hurt, I can see the truth. This petty anger, it isn't really for Mike. There is sadness and pity when I think of him: sadness for what I took from us, pity for where his mind must go at night. The hatred I felt was mine. It was all for me. It was for walking up to the precipice with Kat and letting her eyes, her words, her heart, and her mind (I haven't said it enough, or maybe at all, I love *how* she thinks [fuck, I loved her]) … it was for walking up to the edge of the void and letting her urge me on when I was poised to walk away. It was for telling her that I would jump first, for trusting that everything that made up who we were meant that she would follow. It was for being fooled.

I do not envy him. I do not pity her. Mike will never be able to trust. Kat will never be trusted. In their reconciliation, I know he means nothing to her. If there was ever a line she repeated most, it was "he meant nothing." He was a placeholder until she saved enough money and built up enough courage. But clearly, I am not a good judge of character. Perhaps now she will be able to manufacture something with him and live a long happy life; however, I imagine that will be hard for her. I do know her better than anyone; she can't suffer store-bought anything, even less, store-bought love, romance, and sex. We, she and I, will forever haunt her relationship with him. At best, he will be a competent father and over-watcher. Father. Nothing more. She is mother. Sometimes sex-role fulfiller and imposter. Mostly roommate. But don't worry dear reader, FAMILY IS MARKED SAFE! No one will be abandoned! The threat, the thief, the taker, the monster has been walled up, forgotten, never existed. Unimagined. Close your eyes and it will go away.

So, here I am looking back with this new forced perspective, from this retro-vertigo high-anxiety reality feeling entirely used. The audience in the theatre of my mind is laughing at the fool. My eyes only see thorns, bites, stings, pain, and hurt. My world has been colored with this filter, so it isn't odd that while bathing in the warm venom of lack and humiliation, I read Nin's story *Two Sisters* and found it to be oddly prophetic. It is a small and obscure story, so twisted it couldn't be anything but fiction, but here it is, I've lived it in modern day. If ever there was a Donald and Dorothy, it is Kat and me. This connection may have been imagined, maybe even forced, but venom was racing through my veins; I saw the betrayal everywhere.

Donald was a minor player in this tale, but he and I occupied similar roles. He loved Dorothy, but she married someone else, proving that they were never who Donald thought they were. Dorothy had traded their passionate nights together for a dispassionate coupling with her husband Robert. Brokenhearted Donald gave up pursuing love entirely and found new predilections in the form of loveless multi-partnered sex games. Later, in a chance meeting with Dorothy, with these new eyes, he was able to see who she really was – an animal that wanted to be fucked, that wanted to be recognized and satisfied as animal. Dorothy was intrigued by the news of Donald's games and although "happily married," she wanted to play. So, happy to consent, Donald and a gentleman accomplice fucked her wildly like beasts, spurring Dorothy on to orgasm over and over. When Dorothy finished, just as when Kat finished with me, she walked straight home to be found by her husband primed, wet, and radiating on the sofa. And he, although sexually powerless, was keen to her animal scent: he moved to advance with his awkward hands, to take her in his limited way.

In this unlikely fictional tale of crooked kink from another century, Robert was reflected in Mike's reality. He who would follow her scent of fuck and Costco condoms to find her primed, pre-orgasmed, and glowing, already open and dripping with my warmth, was the modern Robert. Kat became Dorothy, Dorothy became Kat lying on the sofa glowing from ecstasy, allowing her husband to perform his stilted marriage pact, allowing him to fuck her dripping hole to the *memory of our frenzy,* of her orgasms, of my cum lingering unwashed in her slit. My froth providing lubrication for his cock, all the while knowing that in this second fucking, orgasm was a gift he couldn't offer. We don't know if Dorothy too faked her orgasm, signaling the end of this obligation for her husband, but the similarities were remarkable. How did Nin foresee our folly?

I am Donald-post-modern. I have been transported to the twenty-first century as a mere animal fuck toy, a filler of moments and memories, a balm for a falsity, a salve for "good enough," an ointment to heal the wound of the unwinding, the last drop of water in a desert of lack, of post-diluvian emptiness in this Southern Californian well of want, a provider of fantastic imagery, a personal log of erotica and pornography that she can use as inspiration, that she can call upon to peak beyond the easy middle of the Ibsen-made and Kat approved "good enough" as she gets fucked to boredom in her Doll's House. I can't help but wonder how many times did he take her as I leaked out onto his cock? I can't help but wonder going forward, what memories will she access to hurl herself over the edge of climax?

I think of how she has been marked, how she has chosen her fate to reflect that mark, how she has chosen to align with the alternative meaning for the script on her spine. She is Queen no longer. The tattoo now reads 'kept.' Kept woman, whose back is bent from the weight of lack within her cell, whose mouth is magically tied shut against the words of our poetry by the sacred rune scribed into her spine. She who should have been queen. She who would have had something so magical that others would believe it myth. She who recoiled in fear at the unknowns our love had made. She who handed her crown to her husband in exchange for the security of a cage.

I drift into thought, wondering if I'll ever see her again. I think, at best, I'll be like her tattoo, always there, but hidden out of sight. Whatever the case, I know that my ghost will be there in the voices that call when the day is quiet, when it slips into the twilight spaces where the last rays peer over the crest of the ocean to transform every space into something magical; where Iggy's words mean something real; where our words mean something real; where it is Henry and Anaïs, not Henry and June; this is where half-truths and half-lies are forbidden; where duty and roles do not win out over true love; where we say yes to the family ghosts that show us the way.

In her long-faded bruises, in her bones, in her blood, her marrow, her fantasies, in her dreams, I will be there.

Book V

This is How Endings Are

One Last Harvest Moon

On those September nights when the harvest moon is about to bloom, we Southern Californians are taunted by Arizona's monsoon season. The warm air over the Gulf of Mexico is pulled in over the western desert cities and the air grows so thick that our clothes cling to our bodies, so thick it coats the mouth, nose, and lungs. For San Diego, the monsoon is torturous, always bringing inescapable heat and humidity and sticky sleepless nights. It rarely brings rain. When it does venture within reach, the lightning storms often set our dry brush, palm trees, and houses on fire.

I see giant swirling shapes thrusting violently into the sky, just on the edge of the horizon moving west. The clouds pulse and tease with their pregnant bellies: the thick warm air, full and moist, reminds me of her bulging dripping slit, waiting to be fingered by the gods to drop the rain. On the horizon I can see arched black feathers pulled from beneath the clouds trailing as they slide west with the winds. The feathers in the sky mean rain for the desert mountains somewhere out there, promising deluge and orgies of flash floods to rape those far away cunt valleys.

The fickle monsoon that rarely wets our sidewalks, rarely travels far enough west to paint our sun-cracked asphalt, and rarely wets the herbs, squash, and tomatoes in her garden; for the first time, in too long, is sliding overhead. Today, we have become someone else's horizon.

Not two miles from that potted garden surrounding that Spanish-style Doll's House where I am no longer welcome, I stand on Park Boulevard looking out into the sky for the lightning, wanting to feel the thunder, wanting to feel the sky shake over me and wet me with its tears as she once did. I stand there recalling her story, how she learned to fuck herself during those Minnesota storms, her legs spread to her mirror and the open window, recalling how she imagined me as that storm, a storm so passionate that it rinsed the grime of life out of the skies, peeled the filth of the day off the walls, the dirty fruit out of the trees, that it washed our pedestrian shit off the sidewalks and reset the world. I am staring into the sky waiting for the lightning, ready to count for thunder, hoping for rain, for change. A woman in yoga pants and a Bowie shirt stops just on the corner of Robinson and Park, just in front of my floor-level apartment. I am pulled away for a moment by the conversation on her phone. I can feel her like the electricity in the air. She is upset, nodding, making quiet grunts. She ends the call and pushes her glasses up into her hair. She mashes the heels of her hands into her eyes. She is sobbing. I've never seen this woman before, but I want nothing more than to hug her, to tell her it'll be OK even though I am not sure I'll allow myself to survive this day. I am powerless, I can't approach her. I'm waiting for a signal from her. I freeze. I am a coward through and through. I hate myself down to my bones and marrow, for I am the filth that needs to be washed clean. I hate myself for not moving toward her, I hate the world for making me think I can't comfort her, and I hate myself all the more because I've never seen her before, but I need her, I needed to see someone like me: low and raw and torn and bleeding... wishing for things to be other than they are. She sees me and I turn back to the black. I see a man in a white T-shirt, jeans, and a flat-brimmed black hat, a couple walking their dog, a man under a blue tarp in front of the Barber and Shave. I can feel their lack. Their eyes follow mine and they join me waiting for lightning and the fires, all the while hoping for rain. I know they can feel me. I tell them without words, "It will be OK." I feel the moon; she is there but unseen. "To call her forth, to beg for change, I sent the prayers, the eucalyptus, the cedar, the oak, and the pine. I sent them into the sky, I begged for a cleansing storm." We can all feel it upon us, the warm night air, the thick but gentle breeze, the black swirling clouds now directly above, over, and beyond us, over the sea. My arms tingle. The lightning *is* coming. Just then, it rips across the sky and the crosswalk counts down for us: "22, 21, 20, 19 ..." And the sky shakes like it is breaking in half.

Again. "11, 10, 9 ..." And the ground shakes and drops begin to fall, reminding me of her hotel eyes. "Closer, not further away." I let out a sad laugh.

Again "... 3, 2, 1" and it shakes. "Always closer, not further away." I can see her in the pool mouthing these words to me. "Fuck."

I close my crying eyes.

I open my arms.

I open my mouth and wait for communion.

For a moment I feel it. I feel everything. The wind on my ear, the sorrow of the woman on the corner, the electricity teasing the hair on my arms, the hunger of the man under the tarp, all of the lack, all of the eyes of the people upon me as I walk under the black sky to meet the rain in the middle of the street, my arms outstretched like the dying crooked trees of this wretched desert city. A smile, a sick twisted smile born of the part I played in this tragic comedy flashes across my face and I stand there to take it all in, to wait for it to fill me up, to take my lack.

I am the patient one, the hollow one, the one who dreams too much, who lives in dreams, the broken scarecrow Jesus standing in the middle of the street, daring city buses, daring the lightning, daring the universe. "You can't take anything from me because I've given it all away." And my need lasts longer than the rain. The cloud-covered moon, its invisible rings, the invisible gods, have given me just enough to survive a little while longer with this lack. And just like that, no longer closer, but further away.

I know she heard the thunder and thought of me. That will have to be enough.

Shakespeare is for Lovers

After the storm, after the never, after the after, after closer became further away, after her bruises had long faded, after the buses conspired not to take me away forever, after the lightning fired all around me but shrank away from my cold swelling eyes and never hit home, I thought of her. I thought of how in these last days I was wrapped up in Shakespearean tragedy. Southern California was my Denmark. The ghost of a king-father exchanged for a sister ghost and the ghost grandmother of the burlesque, haunting and shrieking their warnings from the battlement, setting the tone for this theatre. The inbreeding of this court found fetid ground at the dinner table with a Doll's House manipulator armed with soft brown eyes, an asexual wife armed with mortar and brick and apathy, an opportunistic whore-mother whose weapon was half-truths and a hanging mouth full of clever silence, and a man predisposed to deceit, dreams, and melancholia, mourning not a dead father, but a dead marriage, and the loss of what only the day before *this ending* my lover and I were calling true love. How could we four write anything but the darkest of comedies? How could this be anything other than tragic?

Before Act Five, Scene Two, before we were all laid out on the floor with regret and confusion and before this slow-drip death left us with the ending we felt we deserved, before all of our plans were twisted and the poison we set out for others found its way into the wrong cups, before I was cut deep with the sword she had poisoned, before she handed that blade to her husband, before I too took up my own poison-tipped blade and swung it wildly, no longer caring where it landed; in this ending I saw Kat in the throes of Ophelia. Holding her herbs, bent over the madness of love, twisted by duty, torn by guilt at the idea of splitting time with her girls. She was all too aware of how it would look to those people that made up the small voices in her head, her head where she spent most of her waking life. And when those voices were too much, as they often were, she would venture into her garden where the sun would bleach those voices away like the fish bones on that desert sea shore. In her garden, this woman-made anomaly sitting full in the sun of the Southern California desert, she tricks the drought and the sun and the lack like she has tricked her heart. Even in *this* she buys more time in the lack by trading the dead earth around her Doll's House for something false but passable, for something manufactured, but good enough. Good enough but all the more inauthentic. Even here she settles for good enough, shoveling and raking through her store-bought and packaged mulch, spraying her plants with the imported wet that they crave twice a day, trying to forget some rhyme about how potted plants never reach their true potential, trying not to make the connection between those potted plants, and pets and doves and skylarks and song birds and giving trees; and hard perfect porcelain dolls, and stuffing and rags with thread for smiles, and wires for binding and white shining walls for cages and a Spanish-style doll's house for a wife-mother queen.

She stands full in the desert sun, trying to keep the lack of the lost soul tribe at bay: white hat, green gloves, rusted trowel, ready to dirty her knees for potted fruits.

She is of the earth and she sings …

Rosemary, for remembrance,

I see you here in the moon, and the sea, and the headlands.

Tomatoes for True Love

Eat now my dear, for they fade too fast …

Radish for Guilt, for Obligation, for my Nausea and my precious Roles.

Pray you, fulfill, and abide.

Squash are for Soulmates

To be split and hollowed out here,

Perchance found earlier in the next life …

Beets are for blood

For mine on the sheets and on your cock

And how I taste the earth in you

Basil for its double meaning

I love you, and hate you…

This is *our* herb, I'll grind it with pignoli, garlic, oil and salt to take you in my mouth once more.

Marigold

Have you seen them potted beneath my window?

If you please…

… they are here to call your soul to visit in the dead of night.

Am I not Psyche? I swear not to spill the oil this time.

And if you promise to come, I'll hold you where it's safe, where no one else will find you, tight in my dreams.

Thyme. Thyme is for courage,

I would give you some, but all was left in the sun and

forgotten, dried up from lack and want of rain…
    Rue is for me,
    For my tattoo.
    After all, aren't I the queen?
    I was once, with you…
    But now it reads 'the Kept One,' for I am.
    See? … just here, sealed by the mark on my skin.
    Rue is for me, and this herb I'll keep next to my bed.
    Columbine for you, the too open, too willing, the faithful and the faithfully faithless, the lost, the lover, the fool, the poet, the twister of words, the bright star, the brightest star, the star-dust deceiver, but over and above all, the most deceived.
    …the most deceived…

***

Later that night, stripped down and baked from the sun, she will settle into her bath. She will lay back to wet her hair, to wait for the water to wash away her true-love conversion therapy. Her hand will find her breast and she will remember times of other hands, hands in waistbands, under bras, over lingerie, in cars, in clubs, in cheap hotels, and hands that could have been: hands on Paris balconies, or in some small moss-covered cottage in Scotland. Her chin will shake while fighting back tears, crying for these incessant memories and wasted fantasies, wanting of reprieve, asking, "How long will all of these things that I hide away keep flooding in like some river of Denmark," and then, face red from tears, like a thief she will quietly crawl into bed to read by his side, remembering how in days past she wrote, "I would sink with you."

The Truth is in There Somewhere

This is how endings are. They shape and define things. They set meaning in place. This ending reshaped everything I experienced over these last two years. Despite my feelings that all of it, our words, our hands, our depths, were all real, they are lost to the stars and the moon and the sun. This broken ending of scorched earth is the truth now. Nothing here will ever be the same. We were just players in this Southern Californian forever drama, the lack-drought, fire-death cycle, to be shattered anew over and over again whenever we close our eyes. Always and forever, our past is colored with the gray ash of this ending.

My hands shake from lack of sleep. I see moving shadows slipping into this world. I see through the veil that splits time. I can see the cracks in the multiverse and there I can find the parallel universe where her kids didn't get sick that night, where she isn't scared of becoming her mother, where she isn't afraid of inflicting her mother's hurt on her own children, where she doesn't buy time with half-truths to soften the blow for her manipulator, where she doesn't choose to keep her cage, where we don't wait until the next life. I see the shadows cross my field of vision, shaking me back to reality. At night in my waking dreams, I can see everyone sitting with me in the desert: Kat, Mike, Elle, Kat's grandmother, Maya, the kids. No one speaks, but I know the words behind their eyes. In this reality, no one is satisfied, but isn't that the nature of this desert? It is there to teach us how to survive with lack and I am still learning. No, that isn't quite right. I won't learn, I refuse. I am screaming, kicking, banging, puking, revolting against the pricks, full on rejecting that life has to be this way. I am trying hard to let go of the 'why' that drives this new lack simmering inside the base of my gut. I am trying to let go of my need to know why she kept pulling me back if she thought there was a chance, she'd have to let me go. I don't think she knew, not until that night of pain (why am I defending her?). That's when I felt the change in the air. She knows I can feel her across space and time. She knew I could see through her angling texts that night and her lying texts that following morning. She knew I could feel her heart breaking as she typed them. She knew I could feel her chest exploding as she hit 'send.' And she knew I was dying as I received them. I felt the moment that she ran out of imagination. Who has time for imagination and authenticity when a fevered husband is howling and children are wailing and the matted bloody cloak of lies you have sewn to your skin, that became your skin, is torn from your body?

All she felt was hurt burning through her exposed nerves.

Hers. Theirs. The children. The house. All bleeding out. It all closed in on her. She will remember these last days like a movie, like something that occurred to someone else: the spinning, the vertigo, the voices, the shaking, the cold, that moment, the moment that for the first time ever she tried to be honest with him, when he asked, "did you fuck him," and she cried before the words crawled out of her mouth and when she could speak it was only part of the truth. And she will take her last secret to the grave: how she allowed him to believe that guilt (not my deadline) motivated her to come clean. It was all so perfect. This was how half-truths and silence became forgiveness.

She couldn't say the words. She was swept away with the strobe light reality of pain and hurt in motion. She remembers him sitting on the bench. Then standing. Ranting about disrespect. Crying. Children. Children crying. Gesturing to the children. Sobbing now. She thinks he might puke. He can't speak. The words are stuck. Trying to speak between sobs. And all she can do is watch. Her hand is on her leg and it is shaking. No. The leg is shaking. The hand is trying to stop it. She just wanted the pain to stop. She wasn't used to be torn open like that. Even worse for Kat, she wasn't used to be the source of her children's pain. Our plan, the plan we had been building up to for two years, the plan that we agreed to execute in our last weekend at Palm Springs, the plan we confirmed as we texted each other that Sunday afternoon, required imagination. And imagination is a luxury. It is a luxury one cannot afford when one is on fire.

Really, what it comes down to is imagination. To live the authentic life that Kat and I had designed together while I ran down her leg on a hotel bed, while I wore the perfume of her pussy on my face as we laughed and drank and rolled in those beds, imagination was required. It was the foundation of everything we were built upon; take it away and "good enough" begins to sound good enough. To have true love in this world, one must have imagination

In all of this, wondering how this became our ending, weren't we both dreamers? Weren't we hopeless romantics?

Weren't we? I thought I knew her. I did, but then I am reminded of something I heard a long time ago: when people tell you who they are, listen closely because their words will not be lies. All animal, howling over these keys, I scoured the emails and texts that she had sent me throughout our affair and this is who she said she was:

I am a good teacher
I am good at my job
I am a horrid mother
I am a bad person
I don't deserve anything
I don't deserve any one
I don't deserve you
I am a coward
I am a bad wife
I should never have married.
I am not made for marriage
I am not the person he thinks I am
I am not the person I have been these last few years in this house
I am a bad friend
I am a cheater
I am a whore
I am a liar
I am an acquired taste
I am not sexy
I am an exhibitionist
I should be punished
I am not worth it

I am fucked up
I am a fraud
I know that I will be divorced within five years
I am definitely not worth it
I am a thief
I am yours
I am your true love
I am your soulmate
I am closer
Always closer

This. This is the truth. And in spite of all of this beautiful vulnerable filth, maybe because of it, I still love her, every bit of her. I love her for all of this and more. And because I love her, I hope that she survives the lies upon which her new life has been built, I hope that she finds joy, or at least a *good enough* good enough. As for me, I have to get on with letting go. These words... my hope is that they will help me let go. We were indeed too much, even more together. We touched every room, we touched everything, everywhere. There is nowhere to hide. When I see the moon tonight, I know that she too will look for the moon. At this very moment, I am at the beach thinking, writing, sitting on the mound at Tourmaline, just past where we stood as we kissed, and I watch the waves knowing that one day she will sit here and watch these same waves thinking these same thoughts. We marked every spot we touched. There isn't anywhere in this town that is safe for me, for her, for either of us.

A New Desert Dream

In the end, after I pressed my spoon of words into the back of my throat, I did find pearls amongst the pain, but they have done little for me. Those pearls might actually hurt more than the lies. I fucking hate this – all of these words. I want to burn these pages that I have printed and proofed. I want to hide everything I've done. I want to hide away and forget everything I've lost. I want to press delete and imagine that I haven't wasted these last few months in a futile attempt to make peace with whatever I was, or whatever I have become. I want to run from what I have made. But I won't. I can't. It is all I have left of her and it was beautiful after all. Even after all of the ugly that it made, it was still beautiful. Fuck, I miss us. I miss her.

Funny, as I contemplate deleting these very words, I sit and wonder at the book she and I would have written; I think it would have been like us. It would have been unique, wild, and unpredictable. I think of how it would have been full of the beautiful and the dangerous. It would have been beautiful. It would have been full of the too much that we were, full of whatever would have been left behind after our joint cleansing storm. We had mana, we opened the veil and on the other side we found who we felt we were supposed to be, who we couldn't be with our others. Who we never were with any one else. Who no one else allowed us to be. We were cherry cola, the smokiest whisky, the bluest cheese, a slow Sunday morning with coffee and a torn and twisted bed full of long stretches and hands and yawns and slow Sunday sex, and more coffee and more hands and more fucking, and Rick and Ilsa in Paris, and the fattest harvest moon hanging just over the hill with the Joshua trees, and the winding Islay roads, and lace, and belt loops, and napes and ear lobes, and begged-for-bruises, and promises of hotel balconies, and the most beautiful, ridiculous poetry. Pure deep connection and lust and painfully open trust that comes from letting go of ownership of each other, but wanting to be with each other all the more for the letting go. It would have been beautiful.

***

Considering the ending I was given, after the spoon revealed the pearls, and after I bled out as I pressed the stake of words into my chest, I could see it all spread out before me ... goddamn, we never held back. In every moment but our last, we stared full and hard into each other's eyes and truly let go. In each other we found the depths of the Marianas and we were Leviathan, we were new and undiscovered and therefore a threat; a threat to the world, a potential virus of joy, too dangerous for this life. More than that, we were the seraphim *and* the brightest star, we were the highest order of being and yet we were blasphemous. Our very existence exuded pure angelic ecstasy and challenged the social order. For two years we cast everything else aside to make our own kingdom, to rule not on earth, but beneath the soil: as above, so below; where it is warm and wet and full of life, full of all the tiny things that give life meaning, so that everything we touched was touched with this joy. We made our world in every fucking room we occupied. We weren't only inevitable, we were unavoidable. Our aura spread with jet-steam winds littering the desert with our impossibility. It ruined love for others. It ruined love for us.

We pulled and pushed each other as if in a dance. We balanced on the edge of this small world while staring into each other's wet shaking eyes as Ur-lovers crying and chanting at the constellations, fucking under the sacred moon and its luminous rings. We were inextricably connected; when she touched the sand of the beach, I felt each grain; when I touched the waves of the ocean, the cool of its waters moved her; when she felt the cold wind beneath the wild moon, I felt it and shuddered with her. I am in her blood, and she is in mine. Even with this very wrong ending, we are forever linked, forever haunted, both forever changed. Ours isn't a wound for healing, it is for scabs on the brain to pick at in the dark while we lay next to someone else; it is for scars that will last a lifetime because our joint experience has left us with a new sort of lack - it would be too much to leave this wound alone.

It is because we know what life wants from us, but what we... I... it is only 'I" now; there is no *we* any longer – reset – because *I* know what life wants, but what *I* don't want to give away, I won't. I won't let the hungry ghosts of this California desert...

I won't let the lack wring the dreamer out of me.

This is for the wounds that cut deeper at the memories and for the stories tied to our songs of experience, bound up in our

Siamese-California-desert-dream; for the scars made by tearing us apart, for the ghost life we still lead at night when we visit each other's dreams. The soul cannot be bound and will not be chased by Psyche's oil. For the wounds that cut deeper still in the waking day when we remember the chance, we had... the chance we let slip away. For the ghost of the book we would have written together and all of our unwritten poetry. For the ever-wound in the center of my chest for losing my best friend, for knowing what I have become to her, so that she can make it through each day. I am threat, I am enemy, I *am* mistake. I am something to ask forgiveness for. I am inspiration for penance. I *am* Leviathan, I am erased, hidden away in her mind. And yet, all of this, these words that even still sting my eyes like the burning desert winds – it is for the healing they bring, for the gift of sight, for helping me see my true self on the other side of catastrophe. It is for allowing me to know that these depths, the depths of being that I imagined long before Kat, were actually possible, and for the gift of showing me that even after being burned and broken down into the finest gray ash, after being reduced to the smallest filthy molecule that makes up who I am, and finding that even after everything, after being torn open to the world, left to bleed out for all to see, I am still a romantic, I am still a dreamer. It is for the gift of knowing that even after all of this, even after losing everything, I would still bet it all on a chance to touch the divine.